Before the war, Belle Ainsworth led a life of pleasure and privilege in the Deep South. Five years after losing her fiancé at the Battle of Gettysburg, she is still alone, with no prospects for marriage among the remaining men of her acquaintance. But out west, there are possibilities. And when Belle answers an ad for a mail-order bride and boards a train to San Francisco to meet wealthy restaurateur Robert Romano, it's with the hope of at last making her dreams of family come true.

When the train is robbed, Yancy McLeish, a disillusioned Union Army hero, rescues Belle from her attackers—and lays claim to her heart. But Belle has pledged her troth to Romano and intends to honor that commitment. It's a decision she soon regrets, for her groom-to-be is nothing like his letters. As she plots a course to escape Romano, Belle prays that road can lead her back to the safety of Yancy's arms, where she believes she was always destined to be . . .

Visit us at www.kensingtonbooks.com

Books by Shirley Kennedy

Women of the West Series
Wagon Train Cinderella
Wagon Train Sisters
Gold Rush Bride

In Old California Series
River Queen Rose
Bay City Belle

Published by Kensington Publishing Corporation

Bay City Belle

In Old California Series

Shirley Kennedy

LYRICAL PRESS
Kensington Publishing Corp.
www.kensingtonbooks.com

First Electronic Edition: July 2018
eISBN-13: 978-1-5161-0439-0
eISBN-10: 1-5161-0439-0

First Print Edition: July 2018
ISBN-13: 978-1-5161-0442-0
ISBN-10: 1-5161-0442-0

Printed in the United States of America

FOREWORD

As the reader will no doubt discern, Meiggs Wharf, which plays a prominent part of the story, later became San Francisco's famous Fisherman's Wharf. It was built by Henry Meiggs, a man some called a Victorian hustler. At one point in his career, he paid off his money lenders with bad checks and had to flee to Valparaiso, Chile, where he couldn't be extradited. The story has a happy ending, though. He made a small fortune building railroads in South America, returned to San Francisco, and paid back every cent he owed his creditors. Meiggs Wharf stretched an amazingly long two thousand feet into the bay, some two hundred feet longer than it does today.

Chapter 1

Savannah, Georgia, 1870

Miss Annabelle Ainsworth, known as Belle, never missed the semi-weekly meeting of the Georgia Ladies of the Confederacy. At today's meeting, held in the parlor of the Elihu Barnes residence, visits to veterans' hospitals were arranged and the annual report from the Committee Dedicated to the Beautification of the Graves of the Glorious Dead was heard and approved. Soon both old and new business had been efficiently dispatched. As they always did, the members conducted themselves with profound dedication. The war had ended over five years ago, yet the consequences of that terrible conflict lived in the hearts and minds of everyone present. As far as the ladies were concerned, General Lee's surrender at the Appomattox Court House happened yesterday.

Refreshments and social chitchat followed. Ordinarily Belle enjoyed this part best, but at the moment, her mind kept wandering. If there was anything more boring than listening to the endless prattle of Miss full-of-herself Allegra Barnes, she didn't know what it was. Not that she'd let it show. She sat, teacup in hand, face carefully arranged in an expression of attentiveness, as if she couldn't hear enough of Allegra's account of her struggles with her latest achievement in the art of embroidery.

"So I decided to go with the dollhouse cross-stitch," Allegra rambled on. She paused and got a curious grin on her face. "But enough of all that. Ladies, I have something exciting to tell you."

"What?" came a chorus of curious female voices, including Belle's and that of her sister, Victoria, who sat beside her.

"I'm going to get married."

Everyone gasped. Belle set her cup down with a clatter and exchanged stunned glances with Victoria. In the old days before the war, such an announcement wouldn't have come as such a shock, but now? Who on earth was Allegra going to marry? More to the point, who was left to marry? The war had cut a deadly swath through the male population of Georgia. The battles at Gettysburg, Bull Run, Wilson's Creek, and more had taken countless Confederate lives. If a bullet hadn't felled their brave soldiers, then dysentery, typhoid, and God-knew-what diseases did. And even if they'd lived... Belle felt a twinge of sorrow, as she always did when she thought of Bridger, her brother. He'd survived the war but would never be the same. Come to think of it, neither would she. At the age of twenty-five, she should have been comfortably married by now, with at least a child or two, but she'd lost Jeremy, her fiancé, at Gettysburg. In fact, most of the beaux who'd courted her were gone now, so here she was, single, childless, living with Victoria and her husband. Not that she led a useless life—far from it. Her busy sister depended upon her to help care for her three children who all adored their aunt Belle. In turn, she loved them so dearly she hardly missed having children of her own, or so she told herself.

Victoria was the first to respond to Allegra's stunning marriage announcement. "That's wonderful news. Is it someone we know?"

"Not exactly."

"But of course he's a Southerner."

"Not exactly." Allegra got that smug, superior look on her face that annoyed Belle to no end. "Don't worry, dear, he's not a Yankee."

"Then who?" came the chorus. "Tell us! We're dying to know."

"His name is Edward Smith, and he's a respectable merchant in the city of San Francisco." Amidst a sudden, shocked silence, Allegra continued, "We've corresponded. He's asked me to marry him, and I sent a letter this morning telling him I accept."

Like everyone else in the room, Belle could hardly believe what she was hearing. "You mean you're marrying a man you haven't even met?"

"Why not?" With a defiant gleam in her eye, Allegra reached for a newspaper that lay on the table next to her. "Have you not heard of the *Matrimonial News*? It's printed every week in Kansas City, a most respectable publication. Here's the ad I answered." She opened the paper and began to read. "'A respectable gentleman of thirty years old, six feet tall, 170 pounds, doing a good business in the city of San Francisco, desires the acquaintance of a young, intelligent, and refined lady, of a loving disposition from eighteen to twenty-eight, one who could make his home a paradise.'" Allegra laid the paper in her lap and flopped out her hands. "How could I resist? I wrote back. He responded and wants me to come. He's sending me a train ticket, and that's all I'm waiting for. When it arrives, I'm off to San Francisco."

Mrs. Beauregard Bedford Stuart cleared her throat. All eyes turned to the group's highly respected president, a formidable figure with her silver-grey hair worn in a stern knot, and her starkly plain, black bombazine dress. She gazed at Allegra with a mixture of alarm and incredulity. "Are you actually going to become one of those mail-order brides?"

Allegra tossed her head. "Indeed I am, Mrs. Stuart. You can say what you want about staying loyal to the South, and I would if I could, but I can't. My beloved Frederick was killed at Bull Run, so where does that leave me?" Her gaze swept the room. "I'm as loyal to our glorious dead as you are, but that won't warm my bed at night, now will it?" She sat back in her chair, pleased her indelicate remark had caused a few nervous twitters. "Look at me. Twenty-five years old, young and pretty if I do say so. But who's to care if I'm pretty or not? Our men are gone. What am I supposed to do? Drink tea and decorate graves until I'm fat and wrinkled and wither away?"

"But, my dear..." Seldom at a loss for words, Mrs. Stuart seemed unable to speak, as if she'd choked on something.

Victoria spoke up. "But Allegra, think of the chance you're taking. What if you travel clear across the country only to find this Edward Smith isn't who he says he is?"

"Then I'd come home." Allegra turned her attention to Belle. "Your sister is married and has her children, so how could she possibly understand? But you know what I'm talking about, being as we're the same age and both of us still unattached. You're such a pretty girl. Like me, if it weren't for the war, we'd both be married by now, with children of our own." She picked up the *Matrimonial News* and opened it again. "Listen to this, Belle. 'Established restaurant owner of good character, thirty-three years old, six feet tall, 170 pounds, brown eyes, seeks to correspond with respectable young lady of pleasing appearance, preferably of full form. If interested, write to Robert Romano,' and it gives the address." She raised her eyes. "You fit his requirements perfectly. Just think, we could be neighbors in San Francisco. Wouldn't that be lovely?"

Belle could think of nothing more unappealing than living next door to shallow, arrogant Allegra Barnes. But she would conceal her aversion to such a prospect and be polite, like she always was. "I'm flattered you'd ask, Allegra, but I'm happy as I am, thank you. Marriage isn't everything.

I like my life as it is, and who knows? Perhaps someday the right man will come along."

Allegra met Belle's remarks with an annoying burst of laughter. "Highly unlikely, and you know it."

Yes, she did know. Only too well did she know, especially when she lay awake in the middle of the night, her heart aching because she must face the unbearable truth that she would never be married, never have children of her own. Not for the world would she reveal her true feelings, though. She shrugged with feigned indifference. "Whether the so-called 'right man' shows up or not, I'm perfectly content with my life."

Allegra folded the *Matrimonial News* and dropped it back on the table. "I suppose you think I'm crazy, but I'm not. Give it some thought. You might change your mind."

"Thank you, Allegra. I'm always open to new ideas." Nothing like a polite lie to avoid any further discussion.

* * * *

As Weldon, their stableman, drove them home, Victoria couldn't stop talking about Allegra Barnes. "That poor man in San Francisco doesn't know what he's let himself in for."

Belle nodded in agreement. "If he expects she'll make his home a paradise, he's in for a rude awakening."

"How nervy of her to imply you'd be interested in that ridiculous ad. If she thinks you'd actually leave your beautiful home for a man you've never met, she's lost her mind."

Belle took a moment to answer. "Actually I don't think Allegra has lost her mind. It's that awful war that's turned our lives upside down and twisted our thinking."

Victoria returned a disdainful sniff. "The war has nothing to do with it. Allegra's always been a meddler."

Belle didn't bother to argue. Victoria would never understand. She was one of the lucky ones. Before the war started, she married Harlan Beeman, a well-to-do young trader. When the time came, like every other able-bodied man from the South, he joined the Confederate Army. Through what the family considered a small miracle, he'd returned home unscathed. Now, although his business had greatly suffered, he provided a good home not only for his wife and three children, but for Belle and their brother, Bridger, as well.

Belle threw her sister a rueful smile. "You wouldn't understand. Despite what you might think, Allegra's only doing what she's driven to do. It's human nature for a woman to want to be married and have children."

"So what am I not understanding? What about you? Do you mean you're not happy living with us? I thought—"

"Of course I'm happy. What would I have done without you?" Belle meant what she said. Before the war, the Ainsworth family lived a comfortable life among the genteel citizenry of Savannah. Her father had made his fortune on the Savannah Cotton Exchange. Her mother reigned as one of Savannah's leading social figures. Their four children grew up in a city considered one of the most serene and picturesque in the country, known for its grand oaks festooned with Spanish moss, elegant architecture, fountains, and green squares. But their paradise didn't last. By the time the war ended, the Ainsworth family had been decimated. Belle's father, who'd been made a colonel, died at Antietam. Her oldest brother, Gregory, died a hero's death at Chickamauga. Bridger, next to the oldest, survived but at a terrible cost. Their beloved mother died of typhoid before the war was over.

When Weldon pulled the buggy to a stop in front of the Ainsworth mansion on the outskirts of the city, the Beemans' three children tumbled out the door to greet them. "Aunt Belle! Aunt Belle!" Tommy, who was ten, Ellen, five, and Amy, three, rushed to their aunt and threw their arms around her.

Ellen asked, "Did you bring us presents?"

Belle bent to untangle all the little arms. "Not today, sweetheart, but maybe next time."

As they went inside, the children crowding around her, she noticed a peculiar expression on her sister's face but didn't think to ask why.

* * * *

"Bridger? Are you awake?" Belle knocked on her brother's bedroom door. He hadn't come down to dinner tonight, and she wanted to know why. "Bridger? Answer me!"

"Come in if you must."

Her brother's sullen voice came as no surprise. More than ever these days, he kept to his room, isolating himself from his family and the few friends he had left. Almost total darkness met her when she opened the door. "Good heavens, Bridge, let's get some light in here."

He lay on his bed and watched while she took a match and lit the paraffin lamp on his dresser. "If you've come to scold me for not coming down to dinner, you can go away."

"I didn't come to scold you about anything." Belle sank into a chair beside her brother's bed. The sight of him filled her with sadness, even though she should be used to the way he looked now with his pale, thin face, emaciated body, his left sleeve folded and pinned because his arm wasn't there anymore. "We missed you at dinner."

"Of course you did. I'm such charming company these days." With his one arm, he pushed himself into a sitting position, his face twisting with pain.

"Is it worse today?' She wasn't asking about the arm. He could have easily survived that and gone on with his life, but at Bentonville, during the last days of the war, he'd been wounded in the stomach. Miraculously he'd survived, but at what cost? The mini-ball that tore through his intestines had caused irreparable damage. Her heart wrenched whenever she remembered Bridger before the war: handsome, strong, confident with a touch of arrogance, a devilish gleam in his eye as he flirted with the young belles who adored him. But now? Everyone knew, Bridger most of all, he wouldn't be around much longer.

"The pain's the same. Let's not talk about it. Tell me about the latest meeting of your Georgia Ladies of the Confederacy." A shadow of the old Bridger appeared in the playful grin he gave her. "I can hardly wait to hear."

She welcomed the opportunity to make him laugh. "Well! You would never in a million years guess what that awful Allegra Barnes is up to now...."

She related the events of the afternoon, including, with a trace of laughter in her voice, Allegra Barnes's shocking announcement that she was going to get married, and her hilarious reading of the ad from the *Matrimonial News*. When she finished, she sat back and grinned. "Did you ever hear of anything so ridiculous? And what's funniest of all, she read another ad aimed at me. She thinks I should be a mail-order bride same as she."

Bridger didn't laugh as she expected. For a time, he remained silent, as if mulling over what to say. "I think you should answer that ad."

"What! You can't be serious."

"I am serious." He paused as if mulling some more. "You've got so many days on this earth. No one's more aware of that than I, especially now when I don't have much time left." She opened her mouth to protest, but he raised his hand. "Don't bother. I face the facts and I'm fine with it. I worry about you, though."

"But why? I'm doing fine. I lead a full life and am perfectly happy."

"Are you?" A corner of his mouth pulled into a slight smile. "All during the war, when I was slogging through the mud in Tennessee, and God knows where else, thoughts of home were all that kept me going. In my head I carried a special memory of you. We were at a ball, the last one I ever attended if I remember right. You had ribbons and roses in your hair, and you were wearing that purple dress, the one with the puffy sleeves and big skirt." He grinned. "You looked like you were floating in the thing, like a big, upside-down tulip."

She smiled, remembering. "The purple velvet. I wore it only the once at the Debutante Cotillion, right before Fort Sumter happened and the war started."

"You looked beautiful that night, and that's the image I carried. At every ball, do you remember how the boys were after you? Charlie Sawyer, Tom Peterson, both Ackerman brothers. You had your pick."

Her smile faded. "There're gone now, all of them."

"That's my point, Belle. That damnable war wrecked your life as well as mine. Now here you sit, trying to convince yourself you're blissfully happy when you're not, and don't tell me otherwise."

She opened her mouth to protest but changed her mind. His words had struck deep in that secret part of herself where she hid her unceasing despair. In silence, she looked toward the ceiling, then finally back at her brother. "You know me too well, Bridge. I try not to think of the old days. What a silly, shallow little fool I was, nothing more on my mind than the next ball and who would fill my dance card. I simply assumed I'd marry and live happily ever after."

"I think we all did. But why look back? All we really have is not yesterday, not tomorrow, but now."

"I've adjusted. I thank God for my family. Harlan, Victoria, the children"—she placed an affectionate hand on his one arm—"even you, you grumpy old rascal. But that's not... That doesn't... What's hardest for me now are those awful moments when I realize I will go through my life without someone special to love, without someone special who loves me. I'll never have children of my own. I'll never..." The words stuck in her throat. If she didn't watch out, she'd start to cry, and she wouldn't have that. Her problems were nothing compared to those of her doomed brother. She forced a laugh. "Look at me, feeling sorry for myself. Don't worry, I'm happy. I feel needed. What would the children do without their auntie Belle?"

"They'd survive." Bridger gazed into her eyes with a blazing intensity that surprised her. "To stay in the South is to rot away. There's a man for you somewhere, but not here. You need the guts to go find him."

Poor Bridger. He sincerely meant what he said but had no idea how totally impractical, how absolutely absurd he was sounding. "I'll think about what you said. Meantime, will you promise you'll come down for breakfast in the morning?"

"You can change the subject all you want, little sister, but if you want a life of your own, I suggest you answer that ad."

* * * *

The next morning, Belle joined Harlan, Victoria, and the children for breakfast in the dining room. Bridger hadn't appeared, which, she reflected, was just as well. Ordinarily Harlan, with his balding head and slight paunch, presented the perfect picture of a levelheaded businessman, but today he was on one of his rants. "Damn Yankees!" he raged between bites of his omelet.

"What have they done now?" Belle asked calmly. They'd been through this before.

"Kept us under their thumb is what they've done. Thanks to the carpetbaggers, our taxes get higher and the price of cotton sinks ever lower. After five years, we're still under military rule. My God, haven't we suffered enough?"

"Don't remind us," Victoria said. "Those terrible days are best forgotten."

Belle heartily agreed. Living through the war was bad enough, but at the end, when General Sherman's troops took Savannah, the nightmare began. At least the Union soldiers didn't burn the city, like they'd done in Atlanta, but they wreaked their devastation just the same. They destroyed the railroads, digging up the rails, heating them over fires, wrapping them around tree trunks and telephone poles. "Sherman's Neckties" they were laughingly called. The soldiers broke into homes and businesses and stole what they pleased. Worst of all, they blockaded the port and seized all the livestock and food from the local farms, leaving the population to starve. To this day, Belle could hardly look at a Union soldier without remembering those terrible days when they had nothing to eat. When Victoria's children were crying, weak from hunger. When she feared they'd all starve to death, and they about did. "It's hard to forget those days, Victoria. Whenever I see a blue uniform, the old fury rises inside me and I can hardly be polite."

"I will hate the Yankees until the day I die," Victoria exclaimed. "And General Sherman the most." She picked up a bread basket. "More biscuits, Harlan? At least we're not starving anymore."

Her husband's agreeable grunt told them his rant was over. Actually Belle could hardly blame him. He'd been rich before the war. Now, like nearly all Savannah's merchants, he'd lost his fortune and was just squeezing by, constantly beset by rules, regulations, and new taxes decreed by the Northern-influenced state legislature.

Tommy spoke up. "Aunt Belle, are you taking us out today?"

"Indeed I am." Belle looked at her sister. "I hope it's all right. I promised I'd take the children to the riverfront. You know how Tommy likes to see the ships. Maybe there'll be one coming in."

Victoria smiled. "Of course. They do love to be with you, Belle. What would I do without you?"

How good to be wanted, and needed. Bridger meant well, but he failed to understand how thoroughly she'd adjusted to her new role in life. "It's my pleasure, Victoria. You know how much I love the children, and you, too."

The children finished their breakfast and were eager to leave. Belle shepherded them from the dining room, had them wash up, and was leading them to the stable when Amy, the little one, declared, "I forgot my doll. I left it in the dining room."

Amy was hardly ever without her favorite doll. Belle turned back toward the house. "I'll get it, sweetheart. You children go ahead. Tell Weldon to hitch up the buggy."

Back in the house, Belle headed toward the dining room. She was almost there when she heard voices. Harlan and Victoria must be still there, no doubt lingering over another cup of coffee. She was about to enter when she was struck by the peculiar tone of Victoria's voice, a stressed, near-desperate sound she'd never heard before. Belle never snooped, but something made her stop outside the door and listen.

"...it's hopeless, Harlan. She's stolen my children away from me. They'll probably start calling her 'Mother' soon, and I'll be left completely in the cold, just someone who happens to live in the same house."

"That's nonsense." Harlan was using his most soothing voice. "*You* are their mother, Victoria. No one can ever take your place."

"Ha! The other day when Amy cut her finger, who did she go running to? It wasn't me, it was her wonderful aunt Belle, and that's because my children love her the best now."

"Then why don't you talk to her? Seems to me that would be the most sensible solution. Just tell her to back off, don't give the children so much attention."

"I could never do that. Belle's been wonderful to the children, and to us, too. I would never dream of hurting her feelings."

"Then I don't know what to tell you."

"What can you say? There's no solution. Belle will be with us for the rest of her life, and I'll just have to live with the pain of knowing my children love her more than they love me. Oh, look, Amy forgot her doll. I'll try to catch them before they leave."

The scrape of chair legs told Belle she'd soon be discovered. She darted away, barely making it to the stable before Victoria arrived, doll in hand. "I found Amy's doll." She smiled at Belle. "So sweet of you to do this. What would I do without you?"

Belle accepted the doll. She forced a smile, not easy considering her insides had turned numb and a dry sob burned in her throat. "Always my pleasure, Victoria. I feel the same. What would I do without *you*?"

Chapter 2

Yancy McLeish lived deep in the woods. If he had his choice, he would never get farther than a mile or two from the log cabin that nestled amidst tall firs, pines, and cedars, overlooking the blue waters of Moose Lake. What with hunting, fishing, and trading with the local Indians, he could pretty much never leave, but he liked his coffee in the morning, a habit he'd picked up in the army. He liked sugar to sweeten it with, plus a few odd items he couldn't grow, shoot, or hook on a line, so much as he hated to, there were times when he had to make the five-mile trek to town.

And besides that, he had to pick up his mail. As he rode into Jackman, towing his pack mule behind him, he didn't look forward to his visit to the Jackman General Store and, in particular, Mrs. Louella Pierce, store clerk, postmistress, and persistent busybody. He'd be polite, like he always was, but had to brace himself for that moment when he walked into the store and she'd loudly declare, "There he is! One of our brave boys in blue! You've got mail, Captain McLeish."

For one thing, the mail she sounded so excited about never amounted to much, nothing more than an occasional letter from one of his old army buddies who knew where he was, or maybe a catalog or two. For another, he wasn't "Captain" anymore, nor was he wearing blue. After his discharge from the Union Army, he couldn't get out of his uniform fast enough, couldn't burn it fast enough. And brave? Anyone who managed to live through the hell of those so-called "heroic battles" didn't give a damn about brave. They were grateful they'd survived the slaughter and happy to still be alive.

Yancy reached the store, tied his horse to a hitching post, took a deep breath, and walked inside.

"Ah, there's Captain McLeish! Our brave boy in blue."

Good God. "Hello, Mrs. Pierce. Just came to stock up on a few things. Pick up my mail."

The round little woman with sharp blue eyes looked like she was chomping at the bit to tell him something. "I've been waiting for you to come in. Wait till you see." She trotted to the mail counter at the back of the store, ducked behind it, and came up with a letter. "Look! It arrived a week ago. I thought you'd never come in. Mercy me, it's clear from San Francisco."

His heart jumped, but he didn't let it show. "Is that so?" He gave a mildly interested shrug and reached for the letter. Without giving it a second glance, he stuck it in the buckskin pouch hanging from his belt. "Thanks, Mrs. Pierce. I'll read it when I get home. I'll be needing some supplies. Coffee to begin with..."

He wasn't being spiteful and took no pleasure from the look of disappointment on the postmistress's face. How could he explain he did everything alone now and wasn't about to share his personal life with anybody? He'd learned a lot of things from the war, but the main thing he'd learned was if he didn't let himself get involved with anyone, then he wouldn't get hurt. Besides, he liked the solitude and no one giving him advice, telling him what to do.

When he left, he slipped out quietly, grateful Mrs. Pierce was busy helping another customer. He packed up the mule and had mounted his horse when she followed him out, bursting through the door and down the steps like her life depended on it. "Wait up, Captain. I wanted to talk to you. Did you know we have dances at the church every Saturday night?"

"No, I didn't know that."

"Well, you really should come sometime. We've got girls galore who'd love to meet a handsome hero like you."

He wasn't a hero, and handsome? She had to be joking. Years ago, Mother used to embarrass him when she bragged about how tall, lean, and good looking he was, how all the girls were attracted to him. Four hard years in the army took care of that. Now he was more like tall and gaunt, and when he looked in a mirror, two war-weary eyes that had seen too much looked back at him. "I'm not much for dancing, Mrs. Pierce."

She beamed, all rosy cheeked and friendly. "Well, you keep us in mind now. If ever you want to meet a pretty girl, you know where to look."

"I'll do that." He touched two fingers to the brim of his hat and rode away, leading the loaded pack mule behind him.

Only one person in the world could be writing him from San Francisco. He figured to wait till he got home to open the letter but hadn't got a mile out of town before curiosity got the better of him. He reined in his horse, pulled the letter from the pouch, and examined it closely, front and back. Postmarked San Francisco. George Washington stamp in the corner. Fancy that. His brother had seen fit to spend three whole cents on him, and he couldn't imagine why. He unfolded the letter. Of a heavy, quality parchment, it had a fancy gilt letterhead at the top. Good for old Ronald. He'd always wanted to be the biggest toad in the pond, and now it looked like he was.

Bank of the Golden Gate
From the Desk of the President
My Dear Brother,
Ever since you were discharged, I've been trying to find you. With the help of an agent from the Pinkerton Detective Agency, I finally tracked you down. I must confess, I was astounded when I learned of your present whereabouts. I'm aware of the many travails you went through during your time in the Union Army, but for the life of me I cannot imagine why you've taken to the woods. According to the agent, you're living entirely alone with nothing but Indians and bears for company.

Did you know Mother has come to live with me? Lately she's been ailing and longs to see you. She thinks, as do I, it's high time you came out of the wilderness. My bank continues to prosper. Why not come to San Francisco and work for me? I have made a fortune and so could you.
Yours truly,
Your brother, Ronald J McLeish

At the sight of that signature, Yancy burst into laughter. *I know who you are, Ronald.* Just like him, though, a stickler for proper protocol, proper behavior, proper everything. When they were growing up, Ronnie was the good little boy, a parents' joy, so well behaved he'd never been spanked. Whereas Yancy could still feel the sting of the birch rod on his backside, delivered by his fuming father. *Why can't you be more like your brother?*

Yancy tucked the letter back in the pouch, flicked the reins, and touched his heels to the horse's flanks. Father was gone now, but maybe, if he was looking down from heaven, he'd be thinking his unruly younger son turned out better than he figured. At least when the war started, he hadn't hightailed it to California like Ronald did. At least he stood and fought for what he believed in. For four endless, agonizing years he'd stood and fought. Come to think of it, maybe Ronald was the smart one after all, getting himself rich in the Golden State while his brother dodged mini-balls, ate unspeakable grub, held dying comrades in his arms.

He hoped Mother was all right. She deserved the best, and if Ronald could give it to her, then fine. In fact, he wished his brother all the luck in the world. He wouldn't be going to California, though. Not now, not ever. All he wanted was to live by himself in the wilderness, away from the world and all its suffering, until he died.

* * * *

Looking back, Belle couldn't remember much about the excursion to the riverfront. She knew she'd done her best to act normal for the children's sake but had gone around in kind of a daze, all numb inside, so shocked at Victoria's words she could barely function. When they returned home, she pleaded a headache and retired to her room. That way, she wouldn't have to go through a charade at dinner, pretending to be her usual cheerful self while hiding her anguish. Instead, she would visit Bridger. Only he could understand the terrible hurt that kept welling within her.

He frowned when he saw her. "You look awful. What happened?"

"Oh, Bridge..." She sank to the chair by his bed and related how she'd accidentally overheard Victoria and her devastating words. "Of course, I had no idea she felt that way. If I had known..." She swallowed the sob that rose in her throat and threw up her hands in despair. "I'm so hurt. She should have told me. What am I going to do?"

Bridger handed her a handkerchief. "First off, you can blow your nose."

With the trace of a smile, she did as she was told. "Then what do I do?"

"What do you think?"

"Nothing, I suppose. Victoria needn't know I overheard. I'll go on as before, only I won't be so involved with the children. But I love them so much...." For a moment, she squeezed her eyes shut, on the verge of tears again. "I wish Mother were here."

"Well, she's not. If you want the truth, you're better off without her."

She stared at him amazed. "How could you say such a thing?"

"Don't get me wrong." He shoved himself up on the pillow, wincing as he did so. "She was a wonderful mother, best in the world, and I miss her more than you'll ever know. But she ran your life, Belle. You never had to think for yourself. Mother had a rule for everything. All you had to do was follow along and you were fine."

"Well, she's gone now, and I'm thinking for myself."

"No, you're not. You're still the little girl who follows Mama's rules. Sorry. You should see the look on your face. It's true, though. You still follow what she taught you. Be polite. Don't hurt anyone's feelings. Keep your opinions to yourself because you don't want to offend anybody." He tilted his head back and gave her a piercing gaze. "And always be aware of what other people think because that's how you should live your life—according to what other people think about you."

She stared at him wide eyed. "I'm absolutely mortified. Is that your opinion of me?"

"Yes. But you should also keep in mind that you're my wonderful little sister, and I love you more than words can say. It's just… I worry about you. You're withering away here. You need a life of your own, but you're too afraid ever to break away."

"You mean I should be like Allegra? Answer that stupid ad?"

"That's exactly what I mean."

"I can't."

"Why not?"

"Because I've never been alone. The very thought of traveling across the country by myself is terrifying. I couldn't do it."

"Understandable. Far as I know, you've never been any place by yourself."

"I suppose I haven't. When I grew up, Nanny never let me out of her sight, rest her soul. Now I've got Weldon to drive me around. I couldn't hitch up a horse if my life depended on it."

"Spoiled rotten."

"You're right, I am."

"But not entirely. When I look beyond all those ruffles and bows, I see a woman who's made of sterner stuff."

"Really?"

"Yes, really. When the Yankees were here, and we were starving, you got out and hustled and found us something to eat."

Her spirits rose. Nothing meant more to her than her cynical brother's rare praise. "So you honestly think I could travel clear across the country by myself?"

"Why not? You know I've got money saved up. I'll give you the return fare, so if you don't like whoever you finally choose, then you can just come home."

She couldn't think what to answer, had to take a moment to absorb his startling offer. Up to now, Allegra—the *Matrimonial News*—the ad—had been nothing more than a trivial topic of conversation that provided a laugh or two. But now? "That's awfully kind of you, Bridge. Honestly, I don't think I'm up to actually doing it, but I'll give it some thought."

"Which means you won't. Come on. You won't be committing yourself if you at least write to the man."

Victoria's words kept echoing in her head: *She's stolen my children away from me.* "I love my sister. Nothing she could say or do would ever change that."

"Of course."

"But then I keep thinking, how can I stay, knowing how she really feels?"

"Look at it this way. What have you got to lose?"

"Nothing, I suppose." Up to that moment, she hadn't given a thought to actually becoming a mail-order bride. It had seemed such a totally outlandish idea. What would the Georgia Ladies of the Confederacy say? She could only imagine the scorn and ridicule they'd heap upon her head if she did such a thing. On the other hand...

She hated to admit it, but Allegra was right. *You can talk all you want about loyalty to our glorious dead, but that won't warm my bed at night.*

And it wouldn't warm hers, either. "I'd need a copy of the *Matrimonial News.*"

"You can't ask Allegra?"

"Are you joking? Certainly not."

"Not a problem. I'll ask Weldon to get you a copy."

"That doesn't mean I'm going to do it."

Bridger grinned. "Of course not."

* * * *

Yancy peered into the near-empty bag of flour and frowned. Time for another trip to town, a prospect he disliked more than ever. Not only had Mrs. Pierce stepped up her relentless crusade to entice him to one of her church dances, the last time he went, another letter from Ronald awaited him. Mother wasn't well, he wrote yet again. Really? Knowing his brother's tendency to exaggerate, he didn't believe it. Last time he saw her she was fine.

He'd go to town tomorrow. Today he'd go fishing, maybe catch a salmon from the lake or a brook trout from the stream that ran close by. How was the weather? He looked out the window and blinked with surprise. Here came two men, one behind the other, making their way up the wooded slope to the cabin. He recognized the man in the lead—Waneek, a Mohawk Indian who sometimes worked as a guide. Who was that behind him? Someone clumsy and awkward. Couldn't be an Indian. He went outside and watched as the two figures drew closer. *Oh, my God.*

Red faced and winded, the president of the Bank of the Golden Gate came struggling up the hillside behind Waneek. Yancy could hardly believe his eyes, not until the two arrived, and his brother, Ronald, gasping for breath, grabbed his arms and hung on, as if he might collapse at any moment.

"Yancy! My God, you were hard to find. I hope you've got some brandy in there. It's the least I deserve after all you've put me through."

During the next few hours, Yancy had to curb his curiosity. After Ronald paid Waneek and sent him on his way, he declared he must lie down and take a nap after his ordeal. He didn't wake up till evening, declaring himself ravenously hungry. Happy to oblige, Yancy cooked up a meal of salmon, rice, and corn. Not until they sat down to eat at the table in front of the large stone fireplace, did they have a conversation. Ronald looked well rested now. He took a bite of salmon and breathed a sigh of contentment. "I swear, that's the best salmon I ever had. Must be pretty fresh."

"Fresh enough. I caught it while you were taking your nap." Yancy took a close look at his brother. "I can't believe you came clear across the continent just to see me."

"I did," Ronald answered between bites of his salmon. "Don't you know about the transcontinental railroad? These are modern times, Yancy. You've got to keep up. There's a train now. It's not like I came across the plains in a covered wagon."

No, he hadn't heard about the transcontinental railroad but didn't care to say so. "Do you know it's been ten years since we've seen each other?"

"I remember that last time well. It was the day you joined the Union Army, and I took off for California when I should have..." Ronald's eyebrows raised inquiringly. "Do you hold it against me that I didn't join? After what you went through, I wouldn't blame you."

"Who am I to judge? You did what you had to do."

Looking relieved, Ronald spoke again. With a wry smile, he inquired, "Haven't changed a bit, have I?"

"You've packed on a few pounds." And that wasn't the half of it. Ronald was ten years older than he was, but people used to say they looked alike. Ever since they parted all those years ago, Yancy pictured his older brother as the tall, slender young man with the full head of hair he used to know. But he wasn't the same, not anymore. Besides the big gut and double chin he'd acquired, his hair had thinned. Only a few strands made a fruitless effort to cover a good-sized bald spot. He didn't look healthy, either. No man of only forty-two years should have been panting and struggling for breath like Ronald did when he came up the hill. "How have you been? Be honest. Have you been taking care of yourself?"

Ronald met his questions with a burst of jovial laughter. "Fine. Feeling tip-top. You'd put on a little weight too if you lived in San Francisco. Best seafood in the world. I dine at the finest restaurants now, the Cliff House, the Tadich Grill, where all the millionaires go." He fondly patted the considerable girth of his stomach. "One of these days I'll get around to cutting back, but meantime I intend to enjoy myself. By the way, I'm married now."

Yancy took note of the lack of enthusiasm in his brother's voice. "That so? Tell me about her."

"Well, let's see now. Her name was Bernice Bolingbrook before I married her. Does the name sound familiar? If it doesn't, it should. She's the daughter of Edwin J. Bolingbrook, the railroad tycoon. Meeting her was the luckiest break I ever had. If it hadn't been for her father, I could never have started my own bank."

"That's all well and good, but what is she like?"

"Uh...she's on the flighty side. Pretty, though. Nice figure."

Uh-oh. Ronald's lukewarm description told him a lot. "Any children?"

His brother's eyes lit with love and pride. "I have a little girl. Name's Elizabeth, only we call her Beth for short. She's five now. Pretty as a picture. My son, Richard, is eight and smart as a whip. We play chess together, and he's beginning to beat me." He chuckled. "Not that I mind. My children are the best thing that ever happened to me."

"Glad to hear that." Up to now, Yancy had tip-toed around the big question. He'd delayed it long enough. "So tell me, how is Mother doing?"

"That's why I'm here." Ronald put down his fork, reached for his glass of brandy, and downed a generous slug. "Mother is dying."

He'd suspected what Ronald was going to say, but even so, the words hit like a wallop to his stomach. For a moment, he bent his head, pulling some much-needed air into his lungs. "What's wrong with her?"

"She's been sickly for quite a while. Then recently the doctor found a tumor in her stomach. It's getting worse, Yancy. She's in a lot of pain now. The doctor's giving her large doses of laudanum. She talks about you all the time." Ronald got an accusatory look in his eye. "Didn't you get my letters?"

"I got them. Just didn't think it could be anything serious."

"Her only wish is she wants to see you before she goes. You always were her favorite, even though I was the good one and you were nothing but trouble. Am I asking too much?" Tears welled in Ronald's eyes, a sight Yancy had never seen before. "We couldn't have asked for a better mother, so here I am, come clear across the country to tell you so."

"You don't have to tell me, I know." He rose from his chair, walked to the window, and looked to where the fading rays of the sun cast long shadows over the lake's still waters. Some deer stood at the water's edge. Only three, but sometimes there were more. They'd come for their evening drink like they did every night. Yancy never tired of watching them, one of the many pleasures of living in the wilderness. He closed his eyes and saw his mother's face before him. "I remember all those times she stood up for me against Father, even when I least deserved it. She never gave up on me, though. When I was in the army, she used to send me things she'd made herself. I've still got the gloves she knit, and the..."

Damn, he was as bad as Ronald, getting all choked up.

He returned to the table and sat. "You've got to understand, I wouldn't stay."

"Anything you want. Of course, if you change your mind, you have a job waiting in my bank."

"My home is here. I want nothing to do with San Francisco. I'd say my goodbyes to Mother and then return."

"Absolutely." Ronald's face wreathed in a smile. "You might find our trip more enjoyable than you expect." He patted his breast pocket. "We'll be traveling in style, my dear brother. In here I've got two tickets on the Union Pacific train to California."

Chapter 3

June 7, 1870
Dear Mr. Romano,
I am writing in answer to your advertisement in the Matrimonial News. I am an unattached female, twenty-five years old, of good character. Dark brown hair, with a slender figure. I enjoy fun and social gatherings and am told I have a pleasing disposition. I am 5 feet 6 inches tall and weigh 123 pounds. I play piano and enjoy reading. I am in every way qualified to appreciate and care for a partner in marriage and a good home.
If you care to respond, please tell me more about yourself and your restaurant.
Sincerely yours,
Miss Belle Ainsworth, Savannah, Georgia

July 13ᵗʰ, 1870
Dear Miss Ainsworth,
I am in receipt of your letter of June 7ᵗʰ and can't tell you how pleased I am that you chose to respond to my advertisement in the Matrimonial News. Of the several replies I received, yours is by far the one that impressed me, so I hasten to tell you more about myself, as requested. I'm originally from Virginia where I graduated from William & Mary College with a degree in law. Being of an adventurous nature, before the Civil War started, I headed west and landed in San Francisco where I soon found a position in the fishing industry. It's a long story, but by way of hard work and frugal living, I saved enough

*money to open my own restaurant, Romano's Fish Grotto, which
overlooks San Francisco Bay. Luckily it has been a success and I've
been prospering ever since.*

*These past few years, I've been so busy with the restaurant, I've
neglected that part of my life that yearns for love, companionship, a
home, and family. I'm looking for a wife who will give me those things
and in return I promise security, protection in a genteel environment,
a good life, and my everlasting love. When I saw your letter, I thought,
she's the one. Am I wrong? I hope to hear from you soon.*

Sincerely,
Robert Romano

Sitting by Bridger's bed, Belle waited until he'd read the newly arrived
letter from San Francisco. When he finished and handed it back, he emitted
a low whistle. "Looks like you've found a good one."

She was hoping her brother would approve, and it appeared he did.
"He sounds sincere, don't you think? And I get the impression he's hard
working and a man of good character. I even like his name. Robert Romano.
Simple but strong. Plain but honest."

"He can't be all bad if he graduated from William & Mary. A lot of
my friends did, if you recall."

"Not only that, he's from Virginia, so that makes him a Southerner. I
gather he headed west before the war started."

Bridger grinned. "That settles it. God forbid you should marry a Yankee."

"That would never happen. I hate them all and always will. So you
think I should write to Robert Romano again?"

"That's your decision, but I certainly wouldn't stand in your way."

* * * *

Aug. 10, 1870
Dear Miss Ainsworth,
*After receiving your latest letter, I am emboldened to offer you
my hand in marriage. Although I'm not a rich man, as previously
mentioned, my restaurant is doing well. My home is not overly large,
but situated in a stylish neighborhood, with spacious rooms, a garden
both in front and back, and a fine view of the bay. Lest you feel any
trepidation, I assure you we will be married the day you arrive or*

next day at the latest, if you prefer. Enclosed is a small stipend for
your travel expenses, plus a ticket for your transportation.
    It is with a heart full of love and anticipation that I await your answer.
Sincerely,
Robert Romano

When Belle finished reading the letter to Bridger, he gave her a long, searching look. "So you've got your proposal. Time for a decision, don't you think?"

Belle walked to the window of Bridger's second-floor room, pulled back the lace curtain, and peered at the sun-drenched rose garden below. It was another hot afternoon in Savannah, too hot, really, yet she didn't mind the heat. She was used to it—felt comfortable with it because this was home. How could she leave? Maybe her life wasn't perfect, but now that the war was over, she led a life free of worry, secure in the knowledge she could live here until she died. She turned back to Bridger. "I don't think I can do it."

She expected a scornful answer, but instead, Bridger's eyes filled with sympathy. "It's a big step, Sis, and maybe too much for you. You haven't told anyone except me, so if you decide not to go, nobody's the wiser." He smiled, as if an afterthought had struck him. "Except that poor sod in San Francisco, but he'll survive. He can always place another ad in the *Matrimonial News*."

Robert Romano. Thirty-three, six feet tall, 170 pounds, brown eyes. Some other woman would have him now, along with the prosperous restaurant, the house in the stylish neighborhood, with gardens both front and back, and a view of the bay.

No! I don't want her to have him. "On second thought, Bridger..."

"Yes?" The way he was looking at her, like he'd known all along.

"I've changed my mind. I'm going."

"You're sure?"

"Sure."

"What does that ticket say?"

She pulled the ticket from the envelope and examined it closely. "How exciting. I hadn't noticed but this ticket is for the transcontinental railroad. I'll be traveling on the Union Pacific train to California."

Chapter 4

Omaha, Nebraska

The hackney let Belle off directly in front of the Union Pacific train depot. It wasn't much to look at, just a large, barnlike wooden building with a cupola roof and two pairs of train tracks running past the back side. Clutching her handbag and small valise, she watched as the hackney driver unloaded her trunk, and a porter piled it atop a cart full of luggage. She entered the building and stood in line at the ticket window. When her turn came, she presented her ticket to the clerk, who examined it, stamped it with a flourish, and gave her a boarding pass. "The train from Chicago is on time today, miss. We leave at 10:45."

Belle thanked him. Breathing a huge sigh of relief, she seated herself on one of the long wooden benches in the waiting room. Almost halfway there already! So far, everything had gone even better than she'd hoped for, partly thanks to—she laughed to herself—of all people, Allegra Barnes.

True to her word, Allegra had left for San Francisco shortly after her shocking announcement. According to her letters, her "respectable gentleman" had turned out to be even richer, more handsome, more wonderful than she'd expected. Blissfully happy, treated like a queen, she now lived a life of ease and luxury in her absolutely gorgeous home in the beautiful city of San Francisco. Knowing Allegra, Belle didn't doubt she was exaggerating, but her exuberant letters so impressed the Georgia Ladies of the Confederacy that when Belle announced she, too, intended to become a mail-order bride, some of the ladies wished her well. Not everyone supported her decision, but she didn't receive the derision and horrified disapproval she'd expected.

Shocked at first, Victoria begged her not to go countless times. Finally, seeing her sister's firm resolve, she gave her reluctant approval, never guessing her overheard words of complaint had played a large part in Belle's decision. Saying her final goodbyes to Tom, Ellen, and Amy was more painful than she even thought it would be. "Of course I'll be seeing you again," she told them. But would she? A trip clear across the country seemed like going to the ends of the earth from which there would be no return.

"You haven't seen the last of us," Bridger reassured her when she went to his room to say her final goodbye. "You're not going to the moon."

She managed a smile and didn't tell him that more than anything, she worried about his health and how much longer he'd be around. What if this was their last goodbye and she'd never see him again? "I do worry about you, even though you say you're doing fine."

"Don't be silly. I'll be around for a while."

She wanted to believe him, but when she bent to kiss him for the final time, a tear broke through and slid down her cheek. "Oh, Bridger…" She could not go on.

He placed a hand on her arm and gave a gentle squeeze. "It's all right, Sis. I've led a good life. I'll die happy, knowing you're happy, so tell Robert Romano he'd better be good to you, and if he's not, I'm coming back to haunt him."

Now, sitting in the noisy, hot depot thinking of her brother, she could cry again, but she wouldn't because he wouldn't want her to. He'd be pleased that so far everything had gone so well. The journey from Savannah hadn't been too terrible, just tiresome, what with having to take two different trains before she even got to Omaha. She'd arrived the night before and stayed in a hotel where she'd been given a lovely room with a soft bed. She had to pay extra for a hot bath, but it was well worth the money. This morning she faced the train ride fresh, rested, and stylishly dressed in her new brown wool suit with the draped overskirt, white blouse and gloves, ostrich-plumed hat placed firmly atop her upswept hair. Hard to imagine that in less than five days she'd be in California. Why had she been so fearful of traveling alone? Now the train ride didn't seem daunting at all. The rest of the way, she'd be traveling on the same train. Only the names of the railroad company would change: the Union Pacific Line to Ogden, Utah; the Central Pacific Line to Sacramento; the Western Pacific Line to the Oakland Pier where a quick ferryboat ride would carry her across

San Francisco Bay to her journey's end and the future husband who'd be eagerly awaiting her. What could be easier?

The train from Chicago arrived on time. Belle climbed aboard the third car from the engine and searched for a vacant seat. Not many were available. The first one she passed was next to a woman with a crying baby on her lap. *No, thank you.* The next available seat was beside an older lady, somewhere in her seventies, she'd guess, bone thin, with a face full of wrinkles, dressed quite elegantly in a dark wool suit and a small black hat decorated with black beads and a black feather plume. She was busy with some sort of crocheting. Belle bent over the seat and inquired, "Excuse me, is this seat taken?"

The lady's gaze swept over her. She dropped her crocheting to her lap. Her mouth pursed, as if she'd just sucked a lemon. "No, it is not."

"Then would you mind if I sat down?"

"Suit yourself."

Not exactly a warm invitation. Belle glanced up the aisle, but all other seats seemed to be occupied. So she would indeed suit herself and sit down, despite the lady's unfriendly reply. She settled herself and placed her valise under the seat. Would the lady remain silent? Would they ride clear to California without an exchange of words? Surely not, and she would try again. She placed a smile on her face and turned toward her seatmate. "Hello, I'm Belle Ainsworth from Savannah, Georgia. This is my first time on the transcontinental railroad, and I'm so excited."

She sat back and waited. Mrs. Sour Face would be compelled to reply or be guilty of committing a horrendous breach of etiquette.

The lady turned her head slowly, with obvious reluctance. "I'm Mrs. Edith Hollister from San Francisco. This is my third time on the transcontinental railroad, and I'm not excited at all."

"Oh. I see. Well…" Belle floundered around for words.

"You can speak if you like," declared Mrs. Hollister. "But I'm not one for idle chitchat. So you're from the South?"

"Yes, Savannah, Georgia." *Like I said.*

"Then you should know I dislike talking about the Civil War. That's all you Southerners talk about, even though the whole affair is long since over and done with. I find the entire subject quite boring."

Boring? Father, Gregory, Bridger, Jeremy, all the others. "Never fear, I wouldn't dream of discussing the Civil War with you." She refrained from adding, *or anything else for that matter,* but made no effort to conceal the annoyance in her voice.

Mrs. Hollister drew back, as if surprised at Belle's touchy reply. "No need to get huffy. I apologize. I had no wish to offend you."

"Quite all right." It wasn't all right, and neither was the woman's phony apology, but Belle said no more, and soon, with a long, piercing blow of a whistle and a near-deafening huffing and chuffing, the train got under way. She wished she was sitting by the window so she could get a better view. She wanted to see out, though, and was forced to peer across her aloof seatmate in order to see anything. There wasn't much. After the train left the outskirts of Omaha, aside from a few farms, her view consisted of sand and tumbleweeds.

"Not much to see out there, is there?" Mrs. Hollister asked.

Fancy that. Her unpleasant seatmate had spoken in a sociable fashion. Belle's inclination was to ignore her, but they'd be riding together a long way, and better to at least be on a speaking basis. "No, there isn't much to see, but I'm fascinated anyway. They say the building of the transcontinental railway was a great feat of engineering."

Mrs. Hollister wrinkled her nose and shook her head. "I really can't see what's so difficult about laying a train track. If you ask me, they could have laid the entire thing where the ground was flat, but no, they're bent on terrifying the poor passengers. We go through tunnels you think will never end, and bridges? Wait till we get to Evans Pass. That's in Wyoming. There's a trestle high over Dale Creek where you look hundreds of feet straight down. I give my heart to God every time we cross it."

Belle had studied enough geography to know two rather large mountain chains made finding a flat route to California impossible. She would refrain from saying so, though. "What's our next stop?"

"I've no idea, but it'll be soon. The train must stop every hundred miles or so to take on water. Something about steam for the boiler. So very tedious. I should think there'd be a better way, but of course no one's asking what I think."

To Belle's relief, they started chatting in a civilized manner, although she didn't appreciate her companion's negative views on everything from the railroad company's choice of routes to the crying baby up the aisle, who, according to Mrs. Hollister, shouldn't have been allowed on the train until it was twelve years old. Once she got going, there was no stopping her. Apparently she'd decided Belle was not only worth talking to but should be made aware of her high status in life. In great detail she described her fancy home in San Francisco—a mansion, she called it, "High on Nob Hill where the robber barons live." She lamented the fact that the train had yet to provide a separate car for first-class passengers, "Where I wouldn't have to associate with riffraff and low-class persons." But at least the Union Pacific Railroad had finally seen fit to add a dining car, far superior to when the train had to stop at a series of dreadful shacks beside the tracks where the passengers were given twenty minutes to eat, and the food consisted of rancid meat, cold beans, and old coffee. Because there wasn't one decent jewelry store in San Francisco, she'd been compelled to travel clear across the country to Tiffany & Company in New York. "My dear, I wouldn't dream of going anyplace else." This time around, she'd bought a hundred-piece china service, carefully packed and stored in the baggage car, and—she touched the butterfly brooch on her shoulder—"I love this. Eighteen-carat gold, and those are real diamonds in the center, all fifteen of them. And of course, my real pearl necklace and my rings." She held up her hands and wiggled her fingers, four of which bore expensive-looking rings. "These are all from Tiffany's."

Belle remained unimpressed. The snobbish woman had talked of nothing but herself and hadn't shown the slightest interest in why her seatmate was traveling west. Fine with Belle. Although she'd convinced herself no shame should be attached to being a mail-order bride, she didn't care to say so and was grateful her pretty much one-way conversation with her newfound companion helped pass the time.

Late in the day, a steward in a white jacket came through the car ringing a chime, announcing, "First call for dinner."

"Shall we go?" Mrs. Hollister inquired.

"Sounds wonderful." Despite the woman's snobbishness and pessimism, Belle was happy to go along. Who wanted to eat alone?

"You'll find the food is excellent," Mrs. Hollister said. "They don't give you a choice of table, though. In the past, I've highly objected, but it does no good. You must eat with whomever they put you with."

Belle suppressed a smile. After long hours of listening to Mrs. Hollister, she would love to talk to someone with a more positive view of life.

The dining car was situated ahead of the caboose, three cars back from their own. She soon discovered getting there was no easy feat. The cars were connected by an open passage, exposed to the elements. To get from one car to the next, she must step over a shifting plate between the swaying cars, nothing on either side but chain guardrails. She glanced downward at the ground flying by beneath her feet. One slip and she'd be gone forever. To make matters worse, soot, red-hot cinders, and ash from the exhaust of the locomotive constantly flew by. She turned to Mrs. Hollister who followed directly behind. "Dear me, this is dangerous." She was surprised the woman would even attempt such a treacherous undertaking.

Her seatmate had a determined look on her face. "It's better than rancid meat and cold coffee."

They reached the dining car, which Belle found to be far more elegant than she'd imagined with its plush carpet, wide windows, and murals on the walls. A row of larger tables seating four ran along one side of the aisle; tables seating two ran along the other side, all with white linen tablecloths and gleaming silver and crystal. When they arrived, they had to stand in a short line. When they got to the front, Mrs. Hollister spoke to the steward. "I would like a table for two."

"Sorry, madam, if you want a table for two, you'll have to wait. Only tables for four are available right now."

"Then we'd like one to ourselves."

The steward threw her a withering glance, as if he'd never heard of anything so outlandish. "Not possible."

Belle spoke up. She was starving. "We don't mind sharing a table, do we, Mrs. Hollister?"

The older woman frowned with annoyance. "Oh, very well. Lead the way."

The steward led them halfway down the aisle to a table where two men occupied the seats riding forward. One, a corpulent gentleman in his forties, wore a stylish suit and vest with a gold watch chain draped across the front. The other, who was somewhat younger and a whole lot thinner, wore a plain dark suit. With a flourish, the waiter indicated the two seats riding backward. "Enjoy your dinner, ladies."

Belle took the seat by the window, directly across from the younger, thinner man. As Mrs. Hollister seated herself, her lips pursed into their sour-lemon look. "I detest riding backward."

The heavier gentleman immediately spoke up. "Oh, say, we can't have that. We'd be happy to switch with you"—he looked to his companion—"wouldn't we, Yancy?"

Before the other one could answer, Mrs. Hollister raised her hand. "Never mind. I shall manage."

No surprise there. Belle hadn't known her seatmate long, but long enough to recognize she liked to complain for the sake of complaining. No doubt she didn't really mind riding backward. It was just something to complain about.

The older man chuckled. "Which is better? To see where you're going or to see where you've been?" He stuck out his hand. "I'm Ronald McLeish from San Francisco. I'm delighted to dine with two such lovely ladies as you."

Mrs. Hollister extended her hand reluctantly and gave him a quick, limp handshake. "Delighted to meet you. I'm Mrs. Edith Hollister from

San Francisco." Her words came out pinched, as if she begrudged each one as it left her mouth.

If the gentleman noticed, he gave no sign of it and extended his hand to Belle. "Pleased to meet you, little lady."

Belle took his hand and shook it with a firm grasp. "I'm Belle Ainsworth from Savannah, Georgia, and I'm delighted to meet you."

He glanced toward his companion. "This is my brother, Yancy McLeish."

The younger man had been sitting so quietly Belle had hardly noticed him. Now that she looked closer, she could tell they were brothers from the definite similarity about their mouths, and the same brown eyes. But other than that, the resemblance ended. Ronald's facial features had gone soft and pudgy, and he had a double chin, while Yancy's sharp cheekbones and angular jaw made his lean face almost too thin, and from what she could see of his sinewy body, he carried not one extra ounce of fat. He didn't appear to be as outgoing as his brother, either. "Pleased to meet you," he said with a short nod to each of them. Polite enough, but without his brother's excess joviality.

Belle returned a "Delighted," and for the first time gazed directly into his eyes. They weren't smiling eyes, nor were they cold, either. They just didn't have that spark of interest in them, like she remembered when she was the most popular belle in Savannah, and the young men's eyes carried that certain gleam that told her how smitten they were. Nice eyes, though, set deep, and at least friendly.

With a beaming smile, Ronald McLeish reached in his pocket and handed each a business card. "At your service, ladies, in case you're ever looking for a bank in San Francisco."

Belle glanced at the card. "So you're president of a bank?"

"That I am. Of course that doesn't mean I'm rich as the robber barons who live on Nob Hill." He gave a chuckle. "As you can see, I'm not riding in my own private railroad car."

Mrs. Hollister took a long moment to stare at the card. When she raised her eyes, an actual smile tilted the corners of her mouth, a sight Belle hadn't seen before. "Well, fancy that, a bank president." Her tone of voice had become all warm and friendly.

Ronald McLeish turned to his brother. "Yancy here comes from Maine. Lives out in the woods with the bears and Indians. Just wait. When we get to San Francisco, I'm going to show him what fine living is all about so maybe he'll stay." He slapped his brother so hard on the back he had to grasp the edge of the table. "What do you say to that, my boy?"

A slow grin crossed Yancy's face. His brother's excess cheeriness didn't seem to bother him. "We'll see, Ronald." He picked up a menu. "Time to order."

From then on, Belle began to enjoy herself, more than she thought she would. To begin with, she'd expected the food would be ordinary, but to her delight the menu listed such items as Braised Duck Cumberland, Lobster Americaine, Hungarian Beef Goulash with Potato Dumplings, and more. She chose the braised duck and soon found herself laughing and chatting, engaged in lively conversation with her newfound friends. The banker might be a bit bombastic, but he provided fascinating stories of what he called the "real" San Francisco and the shockingly wicked doings of what went on in the notorious Barbary Coast. Mrs. Hollister lost some of her rigid demeanor and gave them a description of the fancy mansions on Nob Hill and the high and mighty millionaires who lived there. Yancy didn't talk much, but when asked, he described his dealings with the friendly Indians who lived around Moose Lake. "People think they're savages, but they're more civilized than some white people I know."

Belle had finished her braised duck and had been served her dessert of chocolate mousse when a sudden sense of well-being struck her. Here she was, traveling with affable companions, enjoying a fabulous meal on a gently rocking train, watching the whole country roll by as she traveled in style to a new life and the wonderful man she was going to marry. What more could she ask for? Life was good. Surely she'd made all the right choices. She smiled and drew in a satisfied breath.

The banker was busy talking to Mrs. Hollister, but Yancy had been watching her. "You're smiling, Miss Ainsworth."

"Yes, I am. It's because…" How could she explain? "It's because I'm happy. I know that sounds silly, but—"

"Not silly at all. Seize the moment and hope that it lasts."

How surprising. She hadn't expected such a thoughtful answer from the quiet man in plain clothing who sat across. "I didn't think of it that way, but you're quite right. And what about you, Mr. McLeish? Have you seized the moment?"

He laughed in appreciation and was about to answer when his brother, who'd drunk several glasses of wine during dinner, slung an over-friendly arm around his shoulders. "Listen everyone, I'll have you know Yancy here is the family hero. Served four years in the Union Army and—"

"That's enough, Ronald." Yancy spoke in a soft voice edged with an overtone of uncompromising firmness. "These folks don't want to hear about a war that's long since over. Who did what doesn't matter anymore."

Mrs. Hollister bobbed her head in agreement. "Absolutely right. Let's change the subject."

Belle had been bringing a spoonful of her chocolate mousse to her mouth when the words "Union Army" stopped her halfway. After the briefest of hesitations, she continued as if nothing had happened. Never let it be said she'd create a scene in public, or private, for that matter, but she had to take a moment to absorb this startling information and laid her spoon down. Dear Lord! She was sitting across from a Yankee—sharing his table—chatting agreeably. If she'd thought about it, she'd have realized she wasn't in the South anymore, so of course this was bound to happen. She couldn't change her feelings, though. The Yankees had nearly destroyed her family, her home, everything she held dear in life. Yes, she'd survived, but she'd never, ever forget the terrible price she and her family had paid.

Ronald withdrew his arm. "All the same, my brother's a hero, I don't care what you say." Undaunted, he began chatting with Mrs. Hollister. "Have you ever been to the Tadich Grill? Best steaks in the world. You ought to try it sometime...."

While the banker rambled on, Belle directed her attention to her dessert. She felt, rather than saw, Yancy's gaze upon her and raised her eyes.

He was giving her a long, searching look. "Are you surprised?"

"That you fought on the Union side?" She paused to put her thoughts together. "Yes, but I shouldn't be. I'm not in the South anymore. The trouble is where I come from, the Yankees are gone now, and we very much like it that way."

He sniffed appreciatively. "And you thought you'd never see another."

She tilted her chin. "I'm not sure about that, Mr. McLeish. All I know is, for me the war will never be over. *Never.*"

If he took offense, he didn't let it show, and instead simply gave a brief nod. "Understandable," he said and returned his attention to his meal.

* * * *

At the end of dinner, the two ladies left first, the brothers gazing after them as they disappeared up the aisle. "Pretty little thing, isn't she?" Ronald remarked.

"Which one? Have you become smitten by the charms of Mrs. Hollister?"

Ronald guffawed and reached for a cigar. "You know who I mean. Well put together, I must say. Pretty face. I don't think she likes that you're a Yankee, though."

"She's from Savannah. How else would she feel?"

Ronald sighed. "I'd like to see you married someday. So would Mother."

"I don't need a wife, Ronald, so for God's sake don't try any matchmaking."

"Can't blame me for trying, although I've got to admit there's a certain merit in being single." He thought a moment and quickly added, "Except for the children, of course. What would I do without them? Wait till you meet them."

Yancy replied with an agreeable nod and said no more. From what he'd gleaned thus far, Ronald didn't have anything good to say about his wife, Bernice. He'd noticed that since they left Maine, her name hadn't crossed his brother's lips, although he'd heard plenty about his children, Richard and Beth. Plainly Ronald wasn't happy in his marriage. Hard to figure why, but Yancy supposed he'd find out soon enough and wouldn't pry. And in the meantime, he hoped Ronald would cease any further efforts to marry him off. In the future, he'd be more careful because somehow Ronald had sensed his attraction to Belle Ainsworth, even though he thought he'd concealed it pretty well.

He'd only known her for an hour or so, but couldn't stop thinking about her. So unlike him to have a woman on his mind, but the moment she sat across from him, something about her sent a jolt straight to his gut. He could hardly keep from staring at the delicate features of her face: those high cheekbones, full lips, perky up-tilted nose, the sweep of her lashes against her fair skin. She'd sat all ladylike and proper, dressed in the appropriate fashion, including that ridiculous feathered hat perched atop her head. But the severe cut of her suit hadn't concealed her full breasts and small waist, and he could easily imagine those long legs hidden beneath her skirt. But wait. The trouble was, his hands would never be exploring the intimate parts of Miss Belle Ainsworth, not when she knew the whole truth about him. He allowed a wry laugh to escape his lips. Lord no!

Chapter 5

That night, Belle didn't sleep well, and no wonder. Even though she could lower the seat back, it didn't go all the way down. It was better than sitting up all night, but the hard pillow provided by the railroad did little to alleviate the discomfort of having to lie halfway horizontally on a thinly upholstered seat. She must have slept some, though, and when she opened her eyes in the morning, she found Mrs. Hollister already awake with her mouth pursed.

"Good morning, Miss Ainsworth. I see you've survived the night, no thanks to those heartless millionaires who run the railroad. My rheumatism is killing me, but do they care? Now that they're rich, they don't give a fig we must practically sit up all night and end up with stiff necks and aching bones."

"Good morning." This early in the day, Belle didn't feel like arguing. She'd awakened in a good mood and wanted to keep it that way. "At least they gave us pillows."

"Ha! Who cares? Robber barons, all of them."

Belle chose not to answer, even though she was tempted to point out that judging from Mrs. Hollister's remarks and those Tiffany jewels, she herself was one of those heartless millionaires she supposedly despised. Instead, she hastened to the tiny bathroom where she washed up as best she could, combed her hair, and resettled the ostrich-plumed hat atop her head. When she returned and peered over her seatmate to look out the window, she got a surprise. "Where did the prairie go? Look, we're in the mountains. I've never seen such tall trees."

Mrs. Hollister didn't appear the least impressed. "They're only pine trees. At least we've left Nebraska behind. We're in Wyoming Territory now."

The train soon stopped for water at a place called Pine Bluffs. When Mr. Parkhurst, the conductor, announced they could get off the train for twenty minutes, Belle jumped at the chance to move around and stretch. Mrs. Hollister chose to stay on the train, but when Belle stepped to the platform, she found most of her fellow passengers taking a break from the narrow confines of the cars. She was watching a little boy racing madly from one of the platform to the other when she heard a shout.

"Good morning, Miss Ainsworth! Nice to see you again."

The banker's voice. She looked to see Ronald McLeish and his brother standing not far away. She could hardly avoid them, nor did she wish to. She moved toward them, waving a greeting. "Good morning, gentlemen. I trust you slept well last night."

Ronald appreciated her humor and guffawed. "That's a good one, Miss Ainsworth. Makes you appreciate your own bed, doesn't it? But things may improve soon. I've heard there's a fellow in Chicago named George Pullman who's started a company that makes sleeper cars. Think of it. Your own private bed on a train."

"That sounds almost too good to be true." She gazed around her. The small train station sat nestled amidst tall trees. She drew a deep breath, savoring the sharp scent of pine in the air. "So this is what the mountains are like."

Ronald started to answer, but suddenly his eyes lit. "Oh, say, I think I see someone I know." He drifted away, leaving her standing with Yancy McLeish, who so far, other than a nod of greeting, hadn't said a word.

She hadn't planned on having a conversation with this former member of the Union Army and therefore a hated Yankee. She could walk away, but again good manners intruded. "It's a lovely morning, isn't it, Mr. McLeish?"

He surprised her by breaking into laughter. "You don't have to be polite, Miss Ainsworth. Don't worry about hurting my feelings. If you wish not to talk to me, I completely understand."

His honest answer caught her unprepared. What next? She could simply walk away, but if she did, she'd come across as incredibly rude, and she wasn't raised that way. Better that she stayed. What would it hurt to exchange a few words with the man who played a part in her most enjoyable dinner last night? And besides all that, how nice to be standing in the sunshine, breathing in the delightfully sharp, pine-scented mountain air. At the moment, she couldn't make herself hate anybody, even a Yankee. "It's too nice of a day to argue, don't you agree?"

An easy smile played at the corners of his mouth. "I agree."

He was tall. Taller than she realized when she sat across from him last night. Unlike his portly brother, he had a lanky frame that appeared to be all hard, lean muscle. She liked the way he stood, not the least unsure of himself. Just like her father, he carried an imposing air of self-confidence that clearly announced he could handle himself well, no matter what, and nothing could rattle him. She could detect no flirtatious gleam in his eyes, but at least they were filled with interest and a bit of humor. "Have you taken this train before, Mr. McLeish?"

"Never, nor will I ever take it again, other than to go back where I came from, and that'll be soon."

"So your visit to San Francisco will be short?"

"Just long enough to say goodbye to my mother. She's dying."

"Oh." His answer hit her hard. Agonizing memories came flooding back. "I am so sorry, Mr. McLeish. It's never easy. I lost my mother back in '63, and I'm not over it yet."

"During the war," he said.

"Yes, during the war." She never thought she'd be talking like this, but something about this man caused her to open up in a way she'd never done before. "She died of typhoid during the blockade."

The moment the words left her mouth, she wished she hadn't said them. Not like her at all. What was it about this man that made her cut through all her carefully constructed defenses and reveal her personal life? "I apologize, Mr. McLeish. That was uncalled for. I didn't mean to burden you with my sorrows."

"You didn't. I also apologize. I shouldn't have mentioned my mother. It's a personal matter."

"Well, it looks like we got off to a bad start, doesn't it?"

He smiled. "It's nothing we can't fix." He gazed around him and pointed toward the train. "I was talking to the conductor. Did you know that's a three-hundred-horsepower engine?"

"Three-hundred-horsepower! My, my, fancy that." She wasn't the least interested in the power of a steam engine but gratefully welcomed the change of subject. They stood chatting of inconsequential things until a blast of the train whistle announced they would soon depart.

"It was nice talking to you," she said.

"Likewise." He sniffed the air. "I like your perfume."

Pleased, she answered, "It's called *Fleur de Bulgarie*. Queen Victoria wears it."

"Does she now," he said with a laugh. "I'm impressed."

They parted and climbed back on the train. When she got back to her seat, Mrs. Hollister remarked, "I was watching you and the thin Mr. McLeish out the window." She raised an inquisitive eyebrow. "Do I see the start of a romance? You seem to be hitting it off pretty well, and I know he was taken with you. I noticed last night at dinner."

What did she mean by "taken with you"? Belle would love to ask, but what would be the point? Robert Romano was waiting for her in San Francisco, and she mustn't forget that. Besides, how annoying. Could she not even talk to a man without this busybody jumping to conclusions? But then... *Calm down and don't be blaming Mrs. Hollister.* She herself was at fault. She hadn't revealed she was about to be married. Mr. Yancy McLeish might be extremely pleasant to talk to, but he was a Yankee, and she, loyal Southerner to the end, should have nothing further to do with him.

* * * *

The day passed slowly. Belle and Mrs. Hollister ate breakfast and lunch in the dining car but saw no sign of Yancy and his brother. The rest of the time, she helped a beleaguered mother, Mrs. Duffy, whose little boy, Billy, had begun to run wild up and down the aisle; and whose little girl, Alice, was driving the passengers wild with her nonstop whining. Belle welcomed the distraction and found pleasure in diverting their attention with simple entertainments such as cat's cradle. She yearned for all the books she'd bought for her nieces and nephew but had to make do with a tattered copy of *The Water Babies*, which little Alice insisted upon hearing over and over again. While with the children, Belle stayed away from her own seat. Mrs. Hollister would have thrown a fit if she'd brought squirming Billy to sit on her lap. Only in the late afternoon, while the children were taking a nap, did she return to sit next to her cranky seatmate.

"I don't see how you do it," Mrs. Hollister said. "If I hadn't had a nanny for my three, I would have gone insane."

Belle hid her surprise. Mrs. Hollister was a mother? Her children must be long since grown, but you'd think she would at least have mentioned them. That's what mothers did—talk about their children. Not her seatmate, though. "You have three children?" she asked to be polite.

"I *had* three children. Two of them died."

The poor woman. What could be worse than losing a child? "I'm so sorry."

"Don't be. It was a long time ago. I still have my son, Malcolm, and his dear wife, Eugenia."

Belle wondered if she was mistaken or was there a snappish edge to her seatmate's voice when she mentioned her son and his wife. Either way, she would intrude no further. She was looking for a change of subject when Mrs. Hollister cocked her head. "Why is the train slowing down? It's not supposed to slow down here."

"Perhaps for water?"

"No. It doesn't stop for water here."

Belle leaned past her seatmate to peer out the window. Sure enough, the train was gliding to a halt on a straight stretch of track. They were still in the mountains, a thick growth of pine trees bordering each side. She couldn't see much of the train, but nothing looked out of the ordinary. "That's curious. Why would it stop? There's nothing here."

Mrs. Hollister got a stoic look on her face. "It's probably bandits. Somehow they got on board, and now they're going to rob us and kill us all."

Belle started to laugh. "Oh, I hardly think—"

From out the window she saw a man leap from one of the cars ahead, or possibly the engine, she couldn't be sure. He stumbled and started to run, a desperate urgency in his movement as he headed toward the pine trees. Shots rang out, so many Belle couldn't count. The man staggered and collapsed on the ground. A group of masked men on horseback emerged from the trees and milled about the still body. They all carried guns. As she watched, one aimed a pistol and fired a shot into the man's head.

"Oh, my God." Belle fell back in her seat, hand pressed over her pounding heart. "You were right, Mrs. Hollister."

At the sound of the gunshots, pandemonium erupted in the car. Women screamed, children cried, men leaped from their seats. Some rushed from the car but soon returned. They could easily have stepped off the train, but the masked men aimed their pistols at them and stopped them cold. Nobody knew what to do. The men simply milled about the aisle until the arrival of Mr. Parkhurst, who'd been in one of the cars ahead. Looking cool and unperturbed, he held up both palms. "Calm down, everyone. Return to your seats." He waited until all passengers had cleared the aisles and a semblance of order had been restored. "Stay in your seats, ladies and gentlemen. Remain calm. Chances are you're safe here."

"What's going on?" a man shouted.

Someone shouted, "We've got robbers aboard!"

More screams and gasps erupted. Mr. Parkhurst stood patiently waiting until he could continue. "Judging from the number of horses, there's at least eight of 'em, maybe more. Looks like some of 'em sneaked aboard last time we stopped for water. They hid in the tender—that's the coal car behind the engine—until we got here, the middle of nowhere. My guess is they broke into the engine, got the drop on the engineer and fireman, and ordered them to stop the train at this exact spot. The rest of the gang was already here, waiting with extra horses. It was all carefully planned, that's for sure."

"Who was that man running away, the one who got shot?" asked a woman whose voice bordered on hysteria.

"Can't say for sure but looks like it was Tilton Evans, the fireman." The conductor's mouth set in a grim line. "A good man. Wife and five children."

"So what do we do now?" a man asked.

"Nothing to do but wait, folks. I can't get to the engine without getting off the train, and with all those masked men out there, I'd be wise not to try that. I can't tell you for sure what's going on, but I can make a good guess. The Wells Fargo express car sits back of the tender. It's got a safe that I know for a fact is carrying a big load of cash meant for payrolls up around the Sweetwater mines. I'd wager that's what they're after."

A panicked woman declared, "Then Wells Fargo needs to give them the cash so they'll let us go."

"I agree that would be the simplest solution. The trouble is, Wells Fargo keeps those doors to the express car locked tight on both ends. I can't get in there, and neither can anyone else. It's up to the men inside. If they're scared enough, or get tricked, they'll let the bandits in. If someone gets brave, they'll refuse to unlock the doors, and we could have a standoff for hours. I doubt it'll last that long, though. From what I've seen of these train robbers, they get impatient. That's when bullets start to fly."

Another passenger spoke up. "What if Wells Fargo lets them in? Will the bandits take the money and go, or will they rob us, too?"

Mr. Parkhurst took a long moment to ponder. "From what I've seen so far, this looks like the work of the Cooper Brothers Gang. Can't say for sure, though. If it's the Coopers, they've been known to go through the train and rob the passengers."

"What'll we do?" a woman wailed.

"Calm yourself, madam. Some try to hide their valuables, some don't. Whatever you decide, the best advice I can give you is if they come through the car, don't argue with them. If any of you men are carrying guns, and I'm guessing some of you are, don't think you're going to make a hero of yourself by taking on one of the most ruthless gangs in the region. Hide your guns. Jasper Cooper himself is wanted for murder in three states, so you don't want to tangle with him. He's got nothing to lose and would just as soon kill you as look at you."

A babble of frightened voices broke out. After admonishing them all to remain calm and think over what he said, the conductor returned to the car ahead. Belle turned to her seatmate. The older woman's face had turned deadly pale. "They're going to take my jewelry," she cried.

"No, they won't." Belle made sure she sounded more confident than she felt. "Like the conductor said, there's a good chance they'll just take the Wells Fargo money and go."

"But what if they want my pearls, my emerald earbobs? Oh, no, not my butterfly pin! I'll die before I give it up." Mrs. Hollister reached for the pin and tried to remove it, but her hands shook so much she couldn't manage.

"Here, let me do it." Belle reached to undo the pin. What a shame this woman placed such a high value on her jewelry. Didn't she realize her life was in jeopardy? Still, this wasn't a good time for a discussion on what one should value in life. She would do what she could to help. While she unfastened the butterfly pin and unhooked the string of pearls, her seatmate frantically stripped off her rings and removed the emerald and diamond earbobs. Soon a glittering pile of jewels from Tiffany's lay in her lap. "What do you think is a good hiding place?" Mrs. Hollister asked.

"I really don't know."

"Think! You've got to help me."

Belle was sorely tempted to say she couldn't help, and furthermore, why should she be responsible for someone else's jewelry? But somehow she couldn't. The poor woman looked so distraught over her jewels, she might break into a full-blown case of hysterics at any moment. "I could put them in my handbag, I suppose."

"No! That would be the first place they'd look."

"Well, then, there's my valise under the seat, but they'd probably look there, too." Belle peered up and down the aisle. Some women were removing their jewelry, but not all. The firm-jawed, middle-aged lady across the aisle had left her necklace and rings in place. "Let them have what they want," she called. "It's not worth my life."

Belle agreed. Her own jewelry couldn't begin to match the magnificence of her seatmate's, yet she treasured her gold locket that contained a strand of her mother's hair, and her gold ring with a small diamond that her father gave her when she was a little girl. She wouldn't hide them, though. Let the robbers take what they wanted and be gone.

Mrs. Hollister regarded her with accusing eyes. "So where are you going to hide them?"

Think, Belle, think! Not her handbag, not her valise, but somewhere on her person where the bandits wouldn't look. Ah! The perfect hiding place. She looked around to make sure no gentleman was watching and unbuttoned the top few buttons of her jacket. She picked up the butterfly pin and thrust it down the front of her blouse, not stopping until she found the warm space formed between her breasts and the top of her corset. She let go of the pin. As she hoped, it nestled safely within the confines of her secret hiding spot. This wouldn't be the first time. She'd used this place before, mainly for handkerchiefs but more than once for a note from an admirer, back in that long-ago time when she'd been the belle of the ball. But she'd certainly never used it for anything like this. She heard a gasp.

Her seatmate looked askance. "Miss Ainsworth! What are you doing?"

"What does it look like I'm doing? Can you think of a better place?" She scooped up the remaining jewels from her lap and quickly tucked them beside the pin. Giving them a pat, she remarked, "They fit." She re-buttoned her jacket and looked down. No bulge, no nothing. "See? The perfect spot. They'll never know."

Mrs. Hollister could only sputter.

Belle patted her arm. "Don't worry. It's going to be all right, you'll see." Suddenly she remembered the two hundred dollars from Bridger she'd tucked in a side pocket of her valise. Good grief! That would be the first place they'd look. She leaped to her feet, grabbed up the valise, and pulled out the money. "Look the other way, Mrs. Hollister." She yanked up her skirt and thrust the bills into her bloomers, clear down to where one leg gathered just below her left knee. She smoothed her skirt and sat down again. When Mrs. Hollister gave her a wide-eyed stare, Belle simply said, "It's the safest place I could think of."

Chapter 6

An eerie silence settled over the car. The passengers had made their choices. Some hid their valuables. Others did nothing, deciding their lives were more important than money or a piece of jewelry. Many fervent prayers were sent upward, including Belle's. *Please, God, make the bandits give up and leave. If you can't do that, let them get hold of the Wells Fargo payroll and then leave. Make them happy with what they've got and decide not to rob the passengers.*

From ahead, they heard a series of clanking sounds. "They've uncoupled the engine," a man shouted. He was right. Looking ahead, Belle could see the engine slowly moving forward, but the rest of the train stayed as it was. She couldn't take her eyes from the windows. So far, everything remained the same. Up ahead, the masked riders still milled about, ignoring the body of the fireman lying still on the ground. Tethered nearby, three riderless horses bolstered the conductor's theory that part of the gang had sneaked aboard the train earlier and had either broken into the express car or were still trying to get in. As Belle sat waiting, she could feel the weight of the jewels pressing between her breasts. The diamond pin scratched a little, but not too bad. She heard the car door behind them open and soon sensed someone beside her.

"Miss Ainsworth?"

She pulled her gaze from the window. "Why, Mr. McLeish, I'm glad to see you." And she was, maybe because he seemed so calm, as if nothing disastrous could possibly happen.

Yancy knelt in the aisle beside her. "How are you doing?"

"As well as can be expected, I guess. Will we be all right, do you think?"

"I can't say for sure, but if you ask my brother, he's expecting the worst."

"He thinks they're going to rob us?"

"You've noticed that big ruby ring of his? He's been considering places where he could hide it"—a little smile crossed his face—"some of which are best left unsaid."

He leaned across Belle toward Mrs. Hollister and earnestly inquired, "Are you doing all right, ma'am?"

The older woman grabbed his arm. "Oh, Mr. McLeish, do you think they'll kill us all?"

"Not likely. They're after the money, not your life."

"You don't think they'll come after my jewels?"

Yancy's gaze fell to her bare fingers, then to her shoulder where the butterfly pin once sat in all its sparkling magnificence. "You've hidden them?"

"If those bandits think they can steal from me, they have another think coming."

"Where have you put them?"

Mrs. Hollister shifted her gaze to Belle, who lightly touched the front of her jacket. "They're in here. Snug and safe where Jasper Cooper, or whoever he is, will never find them."

Yancy rolled his eyes. "Not a good idea, Miss Ainsworth. This isn't a game. These are ruthless men with nothing to lose. Why take a chance? Better to give them what they want."

A knot of fear formed in her stomach, but she'd made her decision and wouldn't change now. "Thanks for the advice, but I'm not worried in the least."

"But you…" He apparently thought better of what he was going to say, and his expression lightened. "Too late now. Be careful." He rose to his feet. "Gotta get back. Ronald doesn't do well in a crisis."

He'd been gone less than a minute when the whole car shook, and the sound of an explosion split the air, followed shortly thereafter by the acrid smell of gunpowder. "My God, they've broken in and blown the safe," someone shouted. A few women screamed, but many stayed silent, including Belle. She was beyond screaming. Like many others, she was ready—braced for the worst, praying for the best. She could not take her eyes from the window where the riders no longer were waiting, milling around. Now they had a purpose—catching bags marked "Wells Fargo" as they were tossed off the train, obviously from the safe they'd blown.

Everyone watched and waited. Soon what must have been the last bag was tossed and loaded onto the backs of the horses. A long pause followed. They seemed to be discussing something. In an agony of suspense, Belle waited. *Please just take the money and go. Just go.*

But they didn't. Nearly all the bandits dismounted and fanned out, one or two to each of the cars. So they were coming. Belle braced herself and turned to her seatmate. "I'm afraid they're going to rob us, but you have nothing to worry about. They'll never find your jewels."

The front door of the car burst open. Two masked men entered, each carrying a canvas bag in one hand, a pistol in the other. Belle cringed at the sight of the man in the lead, wearing a slouch hat, sack suit, heavy boots, all in black, and that included the black bandana that covered much of his face. His eyes made her blood run cold—flat and murderously hard, no trace of compassion in them. He pointed his pistol toward the ceiling and fired. As the deafening noise brought startled screams from the passengers, he yelled, "Throw up your hands. This is a robbery. As we pass down the aisle you will put your watches, jewelry, money, and anything else of value you've got into the bag. Is that clear?" He glanced at his companion behind him. "Go to the other end. We'll meet in the middle."

"Sure, Jasper."

"Damn! What did I tell you about names?"

"Sorry." The second robber hurried to the other end of the car.

"Oh, dear God," Belle whispered, softly so her seatmate wouldn't hear. Jasper was not a common name. This had to be the man who would just as soon kill you as look at you, like the conductor had said. Sick fear coiled in the pit of her stomach, but she couldn't let it show. She gave Mrs. Hollister's hand a comforting squeeze. "Don't worry," she whispered, "we're going to be fine."

Jasper Cooper started down the aisle, stopping at each seat, bag outstretched while terrified passengers tossed in their contributions without a murmur of complaint. At the fourth seat back, he stopped and addressed a young man in his twenties sitting in the aisle seat. "You got nothing to contribute?"

"Nothing."

"Stand up."

Belle watched as the man stood, face twisted in defiance.

The bandit waved his pistol. "Step in the aisle."

"Why? I don't have any money."

"We'll see about that." Using the butt of his gun, the bandit struck the passenger on the side of his head, swift and hard. He did it again, then again. Bleeding heavily, the man collapsed to the floor. The robber turned to the passengers. "See what happens when you don't obey my orders?" He gave the bag a good shake. "Cough up all of it, ladies and gentlemen, or you'll get the same."

He stepped over the groaning man and continued down the aisle. As he moved ever closer, Belle felt the blood drain from her face. What had she done? She should never have tried to hide those jewels but too late now. At least she had her own jewelry to give him, plus all the cash in her handbag, and that should be enough. He would never find her secret hiding place.

What seemed an eternity passed before the robber approached her seat. When he arrived, and silently held out the bag, she was ready, holding her locket, ring, and cash in her hand. She uncurled her fingers long enough so he could see what she was giving and dropped them into the bag. Surely that would satisfy him and he would move on.

"Is that all?" he asked.

"Yes, you have everything."

His hard eyes shifted to her seatmate. "What about you, lady?"

"I... I..." Mrs. Hollister's lips were moving but nothing was coming out. Belle spoke up. "She doesn't have anything. She doesn't wear jewelry."

"That right? You wouldn't lie to me, would you, little lady?"

Belle couldn't see Jasper Cooper's mouth but could tell from the way the corners of his eyes crinkled he was smiling, and not a friendly kind of smile. "No, sir, of course I wouldn't lie. My friend here has nothing. I've given you my jewels and all the cash I have. There is no more."

"Stand up."

She couldn't believe what she'd just heard. She pointed to herself. "You mean me?"

He loomed over her, dark and deadly. "I mean you." With a sudden reach, he grabbed the front of her jacket and yanked her to her feet. His forehead creased. "What's this lump here?" He pressed his big hand over the spot where she'd hidden the jewels.

She choked back a cry. "I... It's..." She couldn't move, couldn't think, and wasn't sure her legs would hold her up.

"Let's see what you're hiding under there." He gripped the top of her jacket and yanked with such force the buttons went flying. She looked down. Her jacket hung open. She let out a gasp and reached to close it, but before she could, he clasped her blouse at the neckline and ripped it all the way down.

The bandit's eyes lit. Without warning, he plunged his hand down the top of her corset. The feel of his fingers on her bare skin made her want to scream, but she pressed her lips together and remained silent. "Well, lookee here," he crowed. All she could do was stand there, watching in horror as he yanked his hand from the top of her corset, clutching all of Mrs. Hollister's jewels. Without thinking, Belle grabbed at them, sending the pearls, rings, and butterfly pin flying to the floor where they lay at the feet of Jasper Cooper.

"So the little lady was lying." A scornful laugh came from beneath the bandana. He pointed his pistol toward the diamond pin that lay beside his right shoe. "Pick it up. Pick it all up."

A soft gasp escaped her. Not only was her corset exposed, he'd torn open her blouse to where the edges barely covered her breasts. Ignoring his command, she reached to cover herself, but the bandit grabbed her arm. "Do you want to get hurt? Pick them up."

In her worst fears, she never thought he'd actually hurt her. She'd gone through life believing a gentleman would never strike a lady, much less do her injury. Even in the darkest days of the Union occupation, the Yankee soldiers had been cruel in many ways but never threatened bodily harm. Now she knew otherwise. Jasper Cooper was going to hurt her unless she picked up the jewelry.

Only the trouble was, she couldn't do it. Call it pride, call it stupidity, or maybe she was simply petrified with fear, but she'd rather die than lower herself to obeying his command. "No," she said.

His head jerked back as if she'd surprised him. He raised his pistol and pointed it directly into her face. "Pick them up."

"No."

His black eyes smoldered with fury. With a curse, he raised his arm, turning the pistol in his hand as he did so. Just as he'd done to the man up the aisle, he was going to strike her with the butt of his pistol.

She'd made her choice. Nothing she could do. She closed her eyes.

"No, you don't."

That voice! She recognized it. She opened her eyes in time to see Yancy McLeish appear directly behind the bandit. With a swift raise of his arm, he grabbed the pistol from Cooper's hand. Before she could comprehend what was happening, Yancy had the bandit's arm locked behind him. He'd knocked off the slouch hat and was pointing the pistol directly at Jasper Cooper's head. "Drop the bag. You're leaving now, and so is your friend."

He spoke in a savagely gruff voice Belle hardly recognized. Gasping, she ducked out of the way as Yancy, pushing Jasper Cooper ahead of him, started down the aisle. "Any man with a gun?" Yancy called over his shoulder as they headed for the exit. "Could use some help here."

At least three men eagerly leaped from their seats, drawing their up-to-now hidden weapons. Crowding behind Yancy, they followed as he shoved Jasper Cooper down the aisle toward the rear door. "What'll I do?" the other bandit yelled.

Cooper snarled back. "Can't you see he's got the drop on me? You do what he says."

Clutching the sides of her jacket together, Belle watched as Yancy shoved his captive clear down the aisle, gun to his head, the other bandit cringing along ahead of him. Three armed passengers followed close behind. The instant they disappeared out the rear door, she and every passenger in the car rushed to the windows.

"What's he going to do?" Mrs. Hollister cried.

Belle couldn't imagine. Yancy had cleared the car of the bandits, but the rest of the gang still controlled the train. She watched as the men got off the train, Yancy still holding a gun to the bandit's head. Somewhere along the way, Cooper had lost his bandana. Belle could see his whole face now, with its black beard, hawkish nose, lips twisted like a snarling animal. Yancy's expression hadn't changed. He looked the same as he had last night when they were discussing mundane matters over dinner. He looked as if he knew exactly what he was going to do, although Belle couldn't imagine what that might be.

* * * *

Yancy didn't think about it. There wasn't time, and even if there was, he knew what had to be done and didn't hesitate. He glanced back at those brave fellow passengers close behind. "Look sharp now. Keep your guns drawn and follow me." Pistol still pressed against Cooper's head, Yancy marched the bandit and his cohort along the track toward the front of the train. By now, most of the gang had finished and mounted their horses. Twenty feet away, Yancy halted. "Hey, boys," he called. "I've got your leader here. Drop the bags. If you're not mounted and out of here by the time I count to ten, he's dead."

The bandits milled about, uncertain what to do. Holding fast to his captive, Yancy began, "One... Two... Three..." His pulse held steady. He knew what he was doing. For a flicker of a moment he was Captain McLeish of the Massachusetts Second Infantry again, ready to lead his men forward, never wavering.

"Let him go. We're leaving," yelled one of the bandits. They began to throw the loot-filled bags to the ground. When they were done, Yancy released Jasper Cooper. Instead of fighting back, he ran to his horse like a scared rabbit and hightailed out of there with lightning speed, as if the devil himself was after him. His band of bandits followed. The Wells Fargo payroll went with them, but most of the loot collected from the passengers remained behind.

Yancy watched as the last horse disappeared. He turned to see passengers pouring off the train, smiling, issuing whoops of joy. Mr. Parkhurst came up and slapped him on the back. "By God, you saved the train!" A small crowd gathered, all applauding.

"I didn't do it alone." Yancy raised a hand in salute to those fellow passengers with guns who'd got their courage up and stood with him. "Thanks, boys."

The conductor raised his hand to get everyone's attention. "Without an engine, looks like we're stuck here for a while, folks. I don't know how far they took the engine, but the next telegraph station is only twenty miles from here. They should know by now something's wrong, so help should be coming shortly."

Nobody seemed to mind the wait. What with all the talking and laughing, the passengers were acting like they were on some sort of picnic, everyone calling him a hero, wanting to shake his hand. No need for thanks. He'd done what had to be done, and that didn't make him a hero. He was about to get back on the train when Miss Belle Ainsworth approached. She didn't look much like the fastidious, perfectly groomed lady he'd met last night. She'd lost her fancy hat. A few strands of hair had come loose and dangled around her face. Lucky for her she'd located some safety pins, so at least she'd regained her modesty and managed to pin her jacket closed.

Her grey eyes peered into his, all soft and filled with admiration. "Mr. McLeish, I want to thank you. You could very well have saved my life, and I'm extremely grateful."

Was she insane? Didn't she realize? He had to take a deep breath and let it out before he could continue. "I have a question for you, Miss Ainsworth."

"Yes?" She fluttered her eyelids, all innocence.

"Why did you refuse to pick up the jewels?" He could hardly get the words out.

"Well, for one thing, I didn't like the way he was talking to me."

"You do know you came close to having your head blown off."

His words must have given her pause, because she pursed her lips. "I suppose I was a bit stubborn. You think I should have done what he asked?"

Dear God in heaven. "You're lucky to be alive. Jasper Cooper is a ruthless killer. He could easily have blown your brains out or crushed your skull."

"Oh, dear." She hung her head a moment. "What you're saying is I made a big mistake."

He nodded wordlessly.

"I should have done what that bandit said and picked up the jewels."

"By far the wisest move."

"You think I'm an idiot."

"I wouldn't be that unkind, but for a lady who seems quite bright, you could have made a better choice."

"I see that now, and I see how stupid I was. Can you forgive me?"

Of course he could forgive her. He could tell from her voice and the stricken expression on her face she'd learned her lesson. "Whether I forgive you or not doesn't matter. Maybe you thought you were being brave to defy him, but brave gets you dead a lot more often than using your common sense."

She broke into relieved laughter. "I'll remember that."

He liked the sound of her laugh, not screechy like some women, but soft with kind of a soothing sound. He also liked her face with its tilted little nose and full red lips. He looked around. A few logs lay next to the tracks, some occupied by passengers, but he saw one that wasn't. "Let's sit over there."

"I would love to. Looks like we won't be going anywhere for a while."

She followed him to the log and sat next to him in the warm sunshine. Despite the earlier excitement, the peacefulness of the day made him instantly calm. He breathed deep of the pine-scented air, took a long, indolent look at a blue sky that stretched forever over the tops of the pine trees. They started to chat. She told him about her life in Savannah. He described his cabin in the Maine Woods; his friends, the Indians; what a fine thing it was to live on a lake where the best-tasting fish in the world were his for the taking. She seemed genuinely interested, gazing at him with those big grey eyes as if she was hanging on his every word.

"I'm so sorry about your mother," she said, when he talked about how he'd never wanted to make a trip like this.

"Thank you. How could I not have come? She's my mother, after all. And besides, my brother traveled clear across the country to bring me back. Over the years, we haven't seen eye to eye on a lot of things, but he has a big heart." Only half thinking, he inquired, "And why are you traveling to San Francisco?"

"Why, I..." A strange look crossed her face.

As she struggled for an answer, he heartily wished he could take his words back. Looked like he'd struck some kind of a sore spot. "Sorry, that was rude. You don't have to answer that."

She laughed uncomfortably. Just then, the *chug-chug* of an engine sounded from a distance. The passengers started applauding.

He smiled. "Sounds like it's here."

She stood and brushed her skirt. "I'd better get back aboard."

He watched her leave. He was about to follow when he spotted Mr. Parkhurst climb from the train and head straight for him with what seemed an urgency in his pace.

* * * *

With a lift in her step, Belle climbed back on the train. The day that earlier had gone so horribly wrong was ending well. The bandits were gone, and she would get her ring and locket back. She'd even managed to find all the buttons from her jacket and sewn them back on. She'd enjoyed her conversation with Yancy McLeish and would have elaborated on how grateful she was, but clearly he didn't want her gratitude. There was something about him she liked. For one thing, he wasn't bad looking at all with his tall, lanky build and the touches of humor around his mouth and eyes when he smiled. But beyond his attractive appearance—hard to explain with words—the force of his presence struck her anew. Just sitting and talking to him made her aware of his strength and determination. Yancy McLeish wasn't a man who dithered or dawdled, and that she greatly admired.

His question had caught her by surprise. Since she left Savannah, nobody had asked why she was traveling to San Francisco. She didn't expect Mrs. Hollister to ask. The woman was so taken up with herself she wouldn't have the least curiosity about anyone else. So why, Belle wondered, had she hesitated? She could easily have replied she was traveling to San Francisco to meet her fiancé, but if she had, Yancy would have figured out she was a mail-order bride who hadn't even met her husband-to-be.

For some reason, she didn't want him to know. Back home, her friends and family may have disapproved, but at least they understood, or pretended to. But she wasn't in the South anymore. Now she found the whole thing rather shameful and embarrassing, even though it shouldn't be.

She reached her seat and sat down, happy to see Mrs. Hollister had retrieved all her jewelry, the diamond butterfly pin in place on her shoulder. "I'm glad to see you got everything back." She readied herself for her seatmate's usual stinging reply.

Mrs. Hollister broke into a grateful smile. "My dear, how can I ever thank you? You could have been killed, and all because of me."

"I survived, didn't I? Think nothing of it."

"You're a very brave girl, Belle." Tears filled Mrs. Hollister's eyes. "I'm seventy-five years old. I've outlived my husband, my friends, and all but one of my children, and the one still living, well… I've no one left to care for, and no one who cares for me, so that's why I'm so deeply touched by what you did for me."

How surprising. So the old lady had a heart after all. "I'm glad you got your jewelry back. I know how much it means to you."

"Not really. It's only a substitute." The older woman heaved a deep sigh. "When you get settled in San Francisco, you must come see me. I live on the corner of Powell and California. That's on Nob Hill, not far from Leland Stanford's mansion. It's a Queen Ann Victorian-style house with lots of gingerbread. You can't miss it."

"Thanks, I'll remember that." Belle highly doubted she'd ever pay the old lady a visit, although she was nice to invite her.

"And if things don't work out, come to me, and I'll hire you as my companion."

Companion to this difficult old lady? Not likely. "Thanks, I shall keep that in mind."

Chapter 7

Something was wrong. As Mr. Parkhurst drew closer, he started waving. "Mr. McLeish, it's your brother."

Yancy started toward him, a sudden apprehension causing his heart to race. "What is it?"

"I don't know, but one of the passengers who's a doctor is with him. Better come quick."

Yancy raced to the train. He remembered now. When the robbers came through their car and shot bullets into the ceiling, Ronald turned pale and seemed to have trouble catching his breath. Yancy hadn't thought much about it at the time. Everyone was scared. Who wouldn't be with the threat of death so terrifyingly real?

He sprang up the steps and into the car. Ronald was lying motionless in the aisle on his back, shirt unbuttoned, bare chest exposed. A cluster of passengers crowded around. One woman held a hand over her mouth, eyes wide with horror. A man was shaking his head in consternation. Kneeling beside his brother, a well-dressed gentleman in his fifties with a neatly trimmed grey beard held a stethoscope to his chest.

Yancy raced up the aisle and knelt beside the doctor. "What is it? What's wrong?"

The doctor frowned. "He was clutching his chest in pain and then collapsed. Looks like his heart. Had he complained of not feeling well?"

Yancy had to answer over the lump that was forming in his throat. "He didn't say anything, but after the shooting started, he turned pale and complained of being tired. Had trouble breathing. He mentioned his left arm felt a little numb. I figured it was all the excitement."

The doctor gave a slight nod, as if Yancy had confirmed his diagnosis. He moved the stethoscope around on Ronald's chest, listening carefully. He raised his head, eyes full of sympathy. "I'm afraid he's gone."

Ronald is dead? Yancy sat back on his heels. He'd seen death many times and in the most horrendous ways, but had always managed to keep his composure. This was different. This was his brother and he couldn't think straight. "Was it his heart?"

"I have no doubt that it was."

Mr. Parkhurst pushed his way through the crowd. In a voice that rang with authority, he proclaimed, "Nothing more to see here, folks. Kindly get back to your seats." He bent over Yancy and spoke softly. "Mr. McLeish, I am terribly sorry. Don't worry, we'll handle everything."

"What will you do with him?" Yancy could hear himself talking, yet his words seemed to be coming from someone else, and he couldn't believe what he was hearing.

"We will immediately remove the...uh...remains to the baggage car. We will telegraph ahead, and when we get to Green River, we'll have a casket waiting, that is, if you approve."

Ronald is going home in a coffin. "That's fine, Mr. Parkhurst. Be sure to let me know whatever costs are involved. And meanwhile..." He was about to choke up.

The conductor placed a firm hand on his shoulder. "Don't worry, he will be treated with the greatest respect."

"Thank you for that."

The train began to move. At another time, the passengers would have given a cheer, but the jovial man from San Francisco was gone, and only a mournful silence hung over the car as two baggage car employees swiftly carried the remains of Ronald McLeish away. As the train began to sway and the *clickety-clack* of the wheels grew ever faster, Yancy returned to his seat, turned his back, and stared out the window, clearly sending the message he'd rather not talk. Everyone respected his wishes. Now and then, a hand touched his shoulder, accompanied by a whispered "sorry," but no one intruded on his grief. He didn't want to talk, didn't want to think, had no idea of the passage of time. Maybe he slept, he didn't know, but he slowly became aware of a faint scent of Belle's perfume filling his nostrils. *Her.* He raised his head and shifted in his seat. "It's you? I thought Queen Victoria was sitting next to me."

She smiled gently. "Bad news travels fast. The whole train knows about Ronald. I'll leave if you like. I didn't want to intrude."

"No, stay."

"I'm so very sorry. I liked your brother. I liked his laugh. He was a fine man."

"Yes, he was."

"If you don't mind, I'll sit here for a while."

"I don't mind."

As the train sped on through the thick forest and darkness fell, she continued to sit quietly beside him. He liked having her there. Not that he couldn't handle Ronald's death by himself, but he liked that she didn't ask questions and didn't get all weepy and sentimental. They rode in silence for at least an hour before the train began to slow down and Mr. Parkhurst appeared. "We're not at Green River yet. Just a stop for water."

She rose and looked down on him. "I'd better get back. Mrs. Hollister must be wondering where I am."

He had to smile. "Well, you certainly don't want to upset her."

"She's had a change of heart. She actually thanked me for saving her jewels. Maybe she's not so bad after all."

After she left, he kept thinking about her. The more he saw of Belle Ainsworth, the more he liked her. On that god-awful march through the South, he'd seen many a so-called Southern belle, many self-centered and boring to talk to, but Belle Ainsworth wasn't like that. She was smart. She had a compassionate heart. If she didn't, she couldn't have been so kind and tolerant of the miserable Mrs. Hollister. That showed a lot of character, and besides all that, she was a beautiful woman and he could hardly keep his eyes off her.

He had better get his thoughts together. There was much to do. Before they left, Ronald had sent a telegram letting his family know when he'd arrive. That meant when he reached San Francisco, they'd be waiting to greet him. Not Mother, who was bedridden, but Bernice would be there and possibly Richard, who was eight, and Beth, who was five and much too young to be greeted with such a shock. As for Bernice, from what he'd gathered, Ronald wasn't overly fond of her, nor she with him. Even so, God forbid Ronald's wife or his children should see him arrive home in a plain pine box unloaded along with the baggage. He would have to let them know, send another telegram. *Oh, God.* Yancy leaned back, shut his eyes, and tried to picture his cabin by the lake, his haven from the world, silent and peaceful, where he'd intended to spend the rest of his life. He couldn't see it. Could see nothing but who-knew-what turmoil lay ahead. At least he could count on the Indians to take good care of the place. It might be a while before he got home.

* * * *

When Belle got back to her seat, she found Mrs. Hollister sound asleep, her mouth slightly open, head resting against the window. Thank goodness. After a day like today, she wasn't sure she could handle the testy old lady, even though she'd taken a kinder turn. Belle sank to her seat and lowered the back. More tired than she could ever remember, she tried to sleep but couldn't. The terrible events of the day flooded her mind: that awful moment Jasper Cooper held a gun to her head, Ronald McLeish's sudden death, and Yancy's wrenching grief when he learned his brother was dead. What a shame men thought they weren't supposed to cry. Yancy would have been better off if he had, but he'd held it all in except for the unspoken sorrow so clearly showing in his eyes. He'd even made his little joke about Queen Victoria, and she admired him for that.

All the passengers were asleep. She needed sleep, too, and badly. Funny, before this journey, she'd never thought she could sleep partway sitting up, but the lulling sound of the wheels was making her sleepy. After such a terrible day, there must be something good she could think about. Ah, yes, her future. In only two more days, Robert Romano would be waiting on the dock in San Francisco. He would be every bit as handsome as she expected, kind and compassionate, with a fine sense of humor that would be slightly on the ironical side to match her own. In no time, their first child would arrive. Just think, in less than a year, she could be holding a baby in her arms. They would have at least three, no, four. Maybe five or six, the more the better as far as she was concerned. She would love them all and be the best mother any woman could possibly be.

She closed her eyes and tried to bring an image of Robert Romano into focus, but she couldn't. All she could see was the long, lank figure and troubled face of Yancy McLeish.

Early next morning, the train arrived at the town of Green River in Dakota Territory. As the train rolled into the station, Belle saw a long pine box resting on a baggage cart sitting next to the tracks. The instant the train came to a complete stop, Mr. Parkhurst appeared on the platform, Yancy following close behind.

"Look there," said Mrs. Hollister. "That box must be meant for poor Mr. McLeish."

"Looks like it," Belle said. Yancy shouldn't be alone at a time like this. She hastened to the tiny bathroom where she struggled to make herself presentable. She combed her hair, splashed water on her face, and washed up as best she could. By the time she stepped off the train, the coffin had been loaded into the baggage car. Yancy stood by himself at the edge of the platform, his face unreadable as always, yet Belle could easily guess the turmoil in his heart. "Good morning," she said. "I saw the pine box and guessed it was for your brother."

He nodded grimly. "At least he's got a decent coffin now. Good enough until we get to San Francisco."

He sounded all right, yet Belle easily caught the sorrow in his voice. "Have you eaten? We could get back on the train and have some breakfast."

"Not hungry." He looked toward a winding river that lay beyond the station. "Want to go for a walk? There's time. Mr. Parkhurst said we'd be here for an hour, loading water and coal."

"I'd love to."

They started walking, following a path that took them along the tree-lined river's edge. They didn't say much until they came to a bench overlooking the water and sat down. Belle looked toward the high buttes that overlooked the town. "Beautiful, isn't it? So different from Savannah."

Yancy nodded agreeably. "You won't find any moss hanging from the trees around here."

How did he know about the moss? Had he ever been in Savannah? Surely not, and she wouldn't bother to ask. She sought for something positive to say, anything to lift his spirits.

"By the way, I'm doing fine," he said. "You don't have to cheer me up."

Had he read her mind? She'd better think carefully before she spoke. Yancy McLeish had an independent streak a mile wide. The last thing he would want was someone's shoulder to lean on. "I can see you're doing fine, but even so"—a small smile touched her lips—"I thought you could use some company, and, frankly, after yesterday, I could use some, too."

He leaned forward, elbows on knees, and clasped his hands. "Yeah. Matter of fact, I'd like your opinion." He went on to relate his concerns about sending a telegram. If he didn't send one, Ronald's wife and maybe his children would be waiting in San Francisco at the ferryboat dock, all eager and happy to see their beloved husband and father again. Imagine how shocked they'd be, especially if they saw the coffin unloaded—a sight much too grim for the eyes of young children. But on the other hand, what if he did send a telegram to Ronald's wife, Bernice? What would he say? Wouldn't the cold, impersonal words of a telegram be just as shocking, not only to her but to his mother? "Only two more days and we'll be there. I've got to decide."

She immediately knew the answer and didn't hesitate. "There's another answer to your dilemma. Yes, you send a telegram, but why not send it to someone who can break the news more gently? Maybe someone at the bank where Ronald was president? Surely your brother was close to some of the people who worked there, someone who could break the news to his family."

Yancy closed his eyes a moment, deep in thought. "I remember. Ronald often talked about his good friend, Leighton Canfield, who's the vice president. Yes, that's it. I'll send him a telegram. I've got the address of the bank on Ronald's card. Thanks, Miss Ainsworth. You've hit upon the perfect answer."

"Call me Belle. Don't you think it's about time?"

"I do." For the first time that day, he smiled. "Call me Yancy. You've been very kind."

"Kindness has nothing to do with it. I wanted to help. I…" How strange that feelings she never talked about, the ones buried deep inside herself to escape the pain, had not only surfaced but for a reason she didn't quite understand, she was about to reveal. "I, too, lost a brother."

He frowned in sympathy. "You did? What was his name? Tell me about him."

"Gregory was five years older than I. He was everything a brother ought to be—handsome, smart, successful, and such a tease." She laughed, remembering. "Back then, I was such a vain creature. Thought I was the belle of the ball, but whenever I got too full of myself, he'd bring me down to size. Then the war came along. He joined up, of course. You should have seen how handsome he looked in his uniform. Lieutenant Colonel Gregory James Ainsworth of the Fifth Georgia Infantry. Ladies nearly swooned at the sight of him. He fought at the Battle of Murfreesboro and came home a hero. Then his regiment went off to the Battle of Chickamauga and…" She had to talk over the sudden lump in her throat. "He never came back." For a time she sat in silence, gazing at the slow-moving flow of the river. "They say he was killed instantly. Shot through the heart. That's what the letter said, but I suspect the colonel who wrote it was just being kind, and…" She could go no further. "Sorry. You have enough on your mind without having to hear my heartaches, too."

"Not at all. Didn't you say you had another brother?"

"Yes, Bridger." Up to now, she'd never realized how deeply she'd buried her grief. But in those awful days of the war, death was so commonplace that like everyone else, she hid her sorrow and carried on. She never thought she'd reveal her hidden anguish, lay her deepest feelings bare, but never had she had a listener like Yancy McLeish. With that attentive look on his face, he was giving his attention to every word she said, his eyes brimming with sympathy. She told him all of it— about her brother, Bridger, so badly wounded that his life would undoubtedly be cut short; about Jeremy, her fiancé, killed at Gettysburg; about the father she adored who was killed at Antietam; about how her beloved mother died supposedly of typhoid, but in reality, after losing her husband, one son dead, another badly wounded, she'd died of a broken heart. When Belle finished, she sat back on the bench, drained, yet somehow vastly relieved that for the first time ever, she'd spoken of the constant pain she carried in her heart. "I didn't mean to dump all my grief on you," she said. "Please forgive me."

"Nothing to forgive." He turned toward her. His hands gripped her shoulders. "It's good to let it all out. My God, you've gone through hell, haven't you?"

What was happening? She'd just poured out her deepest grief, yet the feel of his hands had caused a lurch of excitement within her. So unexpected. One minute she'd been baring her sorrow to a sympathetic listener. The next, that sympathetic listener had turned into a man so desirable he was making her heart hammer. She must stop this immediately, but his presence was so male, so appealing, all she wanted was to lean closer. But he was only being nice. She'd better pull away before she made a fool of herself. But wait, he'd just taken a quick breath, then another. Her gaze locked with his. The sympathy was gone. Now an unmistakable desire shone in his eyes. She moved toward him, hearing herself make a little humming sound as his arms encircled her and his mouth hungrily covered hers. She wrapped her arms around him and found herself returning his kiss with passion. When at last he lifted his lips, she leaned forward for more. "Ah, Belle," he whispered. He planted kisses on her forehead and cheek before returning to her lips again.

A blast of the train whistle caused them to break apart. For a moment, they simply looked at one another in surprise, as if neither could believe what had happened. Yancy took a deep breath. "We'd better get back."

Her heart hammering, she reached to smooth her hair. "Guess we better had."

In silence, they hurried back to the train. "We'll talk later," Yancy said as he handed her up the step to her car.

She thanked him, climbed into the train, and returned to her seat. Everything seemed so normal. Passengers looked idly out the windows; Mrs. Hollister worked on her crocheting. On the outside, she supposed she looked normal, too, but on the inside, she still reeled from the effect of Yancy's kisses. Men had kissed her before, but never had a man caused such a lurch of excitement within her and made her ache for more. What happened by the river had been the last thing in the world she'd expected, but now that it had, how could she forget? How could she look at Yancy McLeish and not feel this overwhelming attraction?

But what was she thinking? She had better get her head out of the clouds and face the facts. In all good faith, Robert Romano had offered to marry her, paid her fare, said he would give her a good home and good life in San Francisco. What kind of a fickle, deceitful woman would she be if she broke her promise? She could never do such a thing. She might not have much, but nothing on this earth would cause her to give up her honor and the respect of her friends and family. She might be falling in love with Yancy McLeish. Surely she'd never forget him, but without question she would marry Robert Romano as planned.

Chapter 8

For the rest of the day, Yancy sat alone. Belle didn't join him like she had the day before, but even so, when he wasn't thinking of Ronald, he was thinking of her. Too bad she'd chosen not to sit beside him. He would have liked to share the spectacular view as the train crossed the Wasatch Mountains into Utah's Emigration Canyon, past places with curious names like Thousand Mile Tree and Devil's Slide. It stopped at Ogden where the Union Pacific Railroad became the Central Pacific Railroad, and from there entered the Valley of the Great Salt Lake. In the late afternoon, the train stopped for water at a desolate spot so small it didn't have a name, only a big water tank sitting next to a rickety wooden platform. He saw her get off and followed to where she stood.

Belle took a step back when she saw him but quickly recovered and smiled. "Hello, Yancy." She looked out over the vast, salt-crusted expanse of the Great Salt Lake desert. "Not much of a view, is it?"

"We need to talk." Passengers milled about. He took her arm. They walked past the water tank to the edge of the platform where no one was around. "About what happened this morning. Perhaps I—"

"You can stop right there, especially if you're going to apologize. I…" She bit her lip in thought. "It was my fault as much as yours. You didn't see me pushing you away, did you? Only the thing is…"

"Is what?"

"You and I—it won't work."

"Why not? When we get to San Francisco, I'd like to see you again."

"That's not possible because…" She sucked in a deep breath, as if she'd need all her strength to get her next words out. "I'm betrothed, Yancy. When we get to San Francisco, my fiancé will be waiting. I'm sorry I haven't

been honest. That's because I didn't want to admit I'm a mail-order bride."
She laughed wryly. "Yes, that's right. So desperate to get married I got
betrothed to a man I haven't even met. I'm beholden to him, though. He
paid for my train fare. I could hardly—"

"Go no further." He forced a smile and tried to ignore the ache that had
settled behind his heart. "Of course you must keep your promise. As for
you being a mail-order bride, I can't imagine what's wrong with that." He
could hardly get the words out, but he'd be nice if it killed him. "I wish
you the best. May you and your fiancé have a long and happy life together."

"Thank you for that. I…"

He could see she wanted to say more, but thought better of it. He also
wanted to say more, but what was the point? Besides, he hadn't thought
it through. Maybe this was for the best. What if she'd said yes, that she'd
like to see him in San Francisco? Then what would he have done? He,
Yancy McLeish, the loner, the man who lived isolated and alone and liked
it that way. But then…

An unfamiliar tenderness swept through him. Would she be all right?
Wasn't she taking a risk marrying a man she'd never even met? So much
could go wrong, but why should he care? He hardly knew her, and she
wasn't his concern. Tomorrow they'd come to the end of the line, and he'd
soon forget about her, even her name.

* * * *

Belle had assumed that once she told Yancy she was betrothed, not only
would she be filled with relief, she'd resume her daydreaming about Robert
Romano and the wonderful life she was going to have in San Francisco.
The problem was, Yancy stayed on her mind as much as ever. Try as she
might, whenever she tried to picture her fiancé, she saw Yancy instead, felt
his hands on her shoulders, heard his passionate whisper, *"Ah, Belle,"* as
he pulled her into his arms. But she must stop thinking about him. Must
forget him. Much as she yearned to be near him, most definitely she'd need
to avoid him the rest of the journey.

Despite her mixed-up feelings, Belle looked forward to what Mrs.
Hollister described as the fascinating scenery they would pass on the
last leg of their journey. "You might as well sit by the window," the older
woman suggested in an amazing moment of generosity. "I've seen it all
before and could not care less."

So they switched seats, and Belle sat with her nose practically pressed to the glass as the train left the Great Salt Lake desert and began its trek over the Sierra Nevada Mountains. From Reno, the train made a slow, serpentine climb around the east end of Lake Tahoe until it reached seven thousand eighteen feet at Donner Pass. Mr. Parkhurst passed through the car occasionally, imparting interesting bits of information. "Laying the tracks across these steep mountains was an amazing engineering feat," he told them as they started a 105-mile descent to Sacramento. "Be glad it's summer. In winter, this section is always treacherous. Sometimes they've got to clear as much as fifty to sixty feet of snowfall as well as ice from water dripping in the tunnels."

The miles of snowsheds needed to keep the line passable made Belle think she was traveling through a long, continual tunnel. In between the tunnels, there were times she had to hold her breath as the train crept along a grade literally carved out of the side of a mountain.

At last they left the mountains behind, stopped at Sacramento, and started on the very last leg of their journey to San Francisco.

"We're almost there," Mrs. Hollister said.

Belle's spirits fell the closer they got to San Francisco. Since that painful talk when she told Yancy she was betrothed, he'd avoided her, as she had avoided him. But she couldn't let it end that way. She would talk to him one more time before—her heart ached at the thought—she'd never see him again.

As the train pulled onto the dock at Oakland, Mrs. Hollister, who seemed to have reverted to her usual unpleasant self, sniffed her displeasure. "You'd have thought they would lay the tracks clear to San Francisco, but they didn't, and now we have to take a ferryboat. Most inconvenient, I must say."

Belle didn't think it inconvenient at all. She looked forward to a ferry ride where surely she'd find Yancy so they could say their final goodbyes.

As the ferryboat, *El Capitan*, pulled away from the pier, Belle stood on the upper deck, both hands on the railing, and got her first look at the city of San Francisco. Bathed in sunlight, it sat on a series of hills that overlooked the entrance to the bay. The Golden Gate, they called it, and that seemed the perfect title. The day seemed golden, what with the sun sparkling on the water, seagulls soaring gracefully over the ship, and passengers in a happy mood, glad their long journey was coming to an end. She searched among the passengers who crowded the upper deck. Where was Yancy? She must find him and there wasn't much time. But before she could move from the railing, he appeared beside her. "Nice, isn't it?" he said. "Reminds me of Boston Harbor, the same salty smell."

He'd found her. Her heart took a leap, but forcing herself to stay calm, she looked out over the white-capped waters and breathed deeply of the crisp, bracing air. She turned to him and remarked, "Savannah's a port city, too, but it's different. The air's not salty, it's muggy."

"Will you miss it?"

A pang of longing shot through her. "More than words can say."

"Ae you excited?"

"Of course! I'll be meeting my new husband today." What a lie. Her excitement at becoming a new bride had vanished, and it was all Yancy's fault. Up until he kissed her, she'd been so excited over her impending marriage she hadn't given a thought to what could go wrong. Yancy had changed all that, filled her full of doubts. No longer did she daydream of Robert Romano. Now she could only hope she hadn't made a horrible mistake.

"He'll be waiting at the dock?" Yancy asked.

"I suppose so." She heard the doubt in her voice and made herself brighten. "I mean, of course he will. We'll be married right away. Did I tell you he owns a restaurant?"

"That so? I'm glad." He reached into his pocket and pulled out a card. "Here's one of Ronald's personal cards. It's got his address on it, where I'll be staying. I want you to take it, just in case."

"Thanks, but I'm sure I'll be fine. I'll take it, though." She reached for the card and tucked it into her handbag. "Just in case," she echoed, wanting to make light of it, but sounding more serious than she'd intended. "So is someone meeting you?"

"I took your suggestion and sent a telegram to the vice president of Ronald's bank. He'll be meeting me."

"Again, I am so sorry about your brother." She had to force herself not to place a comforting hand on his arm, but she mustn't touch him. "This is going to be an ordeal for you, I know. Your mother will need you, and I should imagine Ronald's wife and children, too. Then there's the funeral—all of that. I wish I could help in some way, but—"

"There's nothing you can do." His smile held a touch of sadness. "Don't worry, I'll be all right. I'll do what has to be done, then head for home."

"Ronald wanted you to stay in San Francisco, remember? He had big plans for you."

Yancy shook his head decisively. "I'll be counting the days until I'm back in my cabin again."

"I can see you mean it."

While they continued their light chatter, Belle yearned to tell him how much she'd like to see him again, but her good sense kept her quiet. She'd made her choice. Nothing more should be said. Only minutes passed before the ferryboat's shrill whistle sounded loud and clear. They were nearing the dock in San Francisco. Passengers who'd lined the railing started down the stairs, getting ready to disembark. "So this is goodbye." She gazed deep into his eyes, aware of him in every pore of her body—his nearness, the air he breathed, the heat from his skin.

"Goodbye," he said.

Just like that it was over. What had she expected? She sensed he felt the same, though. Knew it from the regret in his voice, the aching hunger in his eyes, and the frustration on his face, knowing this was how it had to be. She raised her chin and remarked, "Good luck to us both."

A thoughtful smile curved his mouth. "I have a feeling we're going to need it."

Nothing more to be said. He gave her a quick, silent salute as she turned away and headed for the stairs.

* * * *

Coming down the gangplank, Yancy scanned the people waiting on the dock. A few held small signs with names on them, obviously looking for someone they wouldn't recognize. He started to read the names but stopped when he spotted a tall gentleman dressed in a double-breasted frock coat, derby hat, and gold chain looped over his vest. He didn't hold a sign, but he didn't need to. This had to be a banker if ever there was one. Yancy walked to the gentleman and inquired, "Leighton Canfield?"

The man smiled with relief. "Why, yes. You must be Ronald's brother."

"I am."

"And is the body...?" Canfield seemed to be searching for a way to put his words discreetly. "I mean..."

"It was transferred to the ferry. They should be unloading it shortly." Hearing himself, Yancy reflected on how calm he sounded, how detached, as if this wasn't Ronald he was talking about.

Canfield cleared his throat. "Fine, then. I've engaged the services of Duggan's Mortuary over on Valencia Street. They'll take care of everything. The funeral itself will be at Ronald's house. Bernice is arranging it. She's bought a casket, solid copper, all velvet inside. Thing cost a fortune." He looked toward the ferry. "I don't suppose you already—?"

"He's coming home in a pine box."

"Fine then." Canfield shook his head in sympathy. "We were all shocked. Ronald was an exceptional man whom we all admired. Not only did we like him personally, he was first-rate at what he did, making the bank one of the most profitable in the city. But"—he frowned, as if displeased with himself—"what am I thinking? It must have come as a terrible shock, having your brother die on the train like that. I'll drive you home right now, but tell me, what else can I do? I'm standing by to help any way I can."

Yancy liked this man and how he quickly got to the point and expressed his sympathy without overdoing it. "About my mother—is she all right?"

"As well as can be expected. As I'm sure Ronald told you, she's been bedridden for quite some time, and quite fragile. When I got your telegram, I wasn't sure I should give her the bad news. Thought I should wait until you arrived, but..." The banker's lip curved slightly with disapproval. "Bernice thought otherwise, so I told your mother myself. She took it well, or at least I think she did. She's a brave woman, your mother."

Thank God she was still alive. "And Richard and Beth? My brother talked about them all the time."

"They know."

Yancy detected a trace of disapproval in the banker's expression. "They're all right?"

"Let's just say I'm glad you're here," Canfield replied. "Let's be off, shall we? The children are eager to meet you."

Yancy chose to ignore the banker's reluctance to answer his question. He'd find out soon enough what was going on. As they left the dock, he caught sight of Belle. She appeared to be walking toward someone with a purposeful step, as if she'd found whom she was looking for. He glanced ahead and saw a man holding a sign that read BELLE AINSWORTH. So, she'd found him. He looked closer at the man she was going to marry. Tall and dark with a full head of black, curly hair—young, with a muscular build—face handsome as the devil.

How foolish he'd been with his ridiculous hope that she'd take one look at her mail-order husband and run the other way. But of course he was glad for her. At least now he could concentrate on whatever lay ahead. Why did he have this uneasy feeling that he'd soon have more than enough troubles of his own?

* * * *

There he was! Belle walked toward the man holding the sign with her name. He smiled as she came toward him. How young he looked, much younger than thirty-three, with even, white teeth that contrasted pleasingly with his olive skin. He wasn't blond, as she'd expected, but his full head of black curly hair added greatly to his gorgeous good looks. He wasn't dressed formally, wore simple clothing, but oh my! He was better looking than she'd ever imagined. She touched her hair, looked down, and smoothed her skirt. When she reached him, she extended her hand, acutely aware of this momentous occasion when she and her about-to-be husband would speak for the first time. "Robert Romano? I believe you're looking for me. I'm Belle Ainsworth."

He took her hand and gave her a big smile. "Pleased to meet you, but I'm not Robert. I'm Tony, his brother. He was too busy to meet you, but he said to tell you he'd try to break away as soon as he could. Come on, I'll take you home."

Chapter 9

During the minutes after Belle met Tony Romano, she had to concentrate on searching for her trunk from the pile of luggage on the dock. Not easy when every other passenger was doing the same. When she found it, Tony easily hoisted it to his shoulder and shoved his way through the crowd, she following close behind. When they got to the street, he loaded the trunk into the back of a delivery wagon with big red letters on the side that read ROMANO BROTHERS FISH COMPANY. "Climb right in," he cheerfully remarked. "Need a hand?"

"I can manage." Everything had happened so fast, she could hardly think straight. Now, as Tony eased the wagon into a street teeming with traffic, she had time to wonder why Robert hadn't met her himself. Was she that unimportant to him? Her nose caught an aroma of not-so-fresh fish. Was that all he thought of her? Letting her ride to her new home in a smelly fish wagon? They started off. As Tony drove along a wide street that bordered the bay, he was rattling on in a friendly fashion, something about what sights to see in San Francisco. He seemed an affable young man, not more than twenty-five she guessed. If he noticed how quiet she was, he refrained from commenting. "My brother was sorry he couldn't meet you," he said. "He's never been busier, what with the restaurant and all. He hardly ever goes out with us anymore."

"Goes out to do what?" she asked.

He threw her a glance of disbelief. "To fish of course. He's a fisherman, or he was before he started the business. He said he'd try to get home early, though. So will my brothers, unless they get becalmed."

"Becalmed," she numbly repeated, trying to think clearly and make sense of it all.

Tony chuckled. "I guess you don't know much about the fishing fleet. They go to sea early every morning except Sunday. Sometimes there's no breeze and the boats can't get back in. They've got to wait till there's a breeze again. It takes hours sometimes, unless they get out the oars and row. Or sometimes they'll throw a grappling hook into the rudder chain of a steamer passing by. That way, they get an easy ride home."

"Do the people on the steamer mind?" she asked.

"Hell, yes, they do. Excuse the language, ma'am, but if you think that's bad, you should hear what they holler at us. They don't like it. Slows 'em down. Roberto—I mean, Robert—never lets go. You should hear what he hollers back. It would make your ears burn. He's got a bit of a temper, you know."

Dear God, what had she done? Was this really happening? But despite everything, she'd be polite like she always was. "So you're a fisherman, too, Mr. Romano?"

"Nobody's a mister around here. I'm just plain Tony. Sometimes I go out on the boat. Sometimes I deliver the fish, like today. My brothers and me work for Roberto now. The whole family works for him. We pretty much do what he says. You've never been in San Francisco?" She shook her head, and he gestured toward the water. "Well, that's the bay. This roadway is called the Embarcadero. It runs along the seawall and leads to all the piers, and that includes Meiggs Wharf, where the fishing boats are moored. You'll be spending a lot of time there."

"Really? Doing what?"

"Mainly the wives do the light stuff like gutting the fish and packing 'em in crates. Then we load up the wagons and deliver all over town. Dungeness crab, shrimp, oysters, salmon, and the like. Those fancy seafood restaurants buy all we've got, not only from our own boats, but we handle the catch from some of the other boats, too."

Gutting the fish? Surely she hadn't understood correctly, but she had no wish to pursue such a revolting subject. "Where are we going now?"

"I thought I'd drive you past Meiggs Wharf—that's where the fishing fleet comes in—and then straight home. The family wants to meet you. Maybe Roberto will be back by the time we get there."

A dark, unthinkable suspicion began to grow in her mind. "When you say 'home,' you mean Robert's home?"

"I guess you could say that. He owns the house, but we all live there."

She had to close her eyes a moment. Clear her head. Take a deep breath. "So how many are in the family?"

"Well, let's see now. There's Mama. She's by herself now. Papa died two years ago. There's me and my brothers, Marco, Lorenzo and of course Roberto. Marco has a wife, three kids, and one on the way. Lorenzo and Giana have only the one. That's Bruno. He's thirteen and nothing but trouble. I'm single but not for long. I've sent for my bride, and she'll soon be arriving from Sicily, where my parents came from. That's where all the wives are from, too." He threw her a cheerful grin. "Except you. I don't know what got into Roberto, but he does things differently sometimes."

This latest revelation left her momentarily speechless. She could only come up with a mindless answer. "It must be a pretty big house."

"You don't need to worry. Roberto has his own bedroom."

They continued around the perimeter of the bay. To the right lay an assortment of rickety piers mixed in with solidly built wharves, some with large ships berthed alongside. Huge warehouses lay to her left, along with shops, businesses, and along one stretch, shabby-looking hotels, boardinghouses, and a large number of bars with names like the Salty Dog and the Old Ship Saloon.

"That's the Barbary Coast we're passing," Tony remarked. "You won't get closer than this, though. Nice ladies like you wouldn't be caught dead there."

When they started out, they'd been traveling north. Now the roadway curved around the water's edge, taking them west toward the Golden Gate. They passed a row of piers until finally they came to a pier extending far out into the bay. Boats and ships of all kinds were moored on either side. A throng of people strolled along the walkway. "This is Meiggs Wharf," Tony explained. "See all those sailing boats? That's the fishing fleet. I guess you could say the Italian fishing fleet because we're all Italian. The boats are mostly green, like in the old country. They paint the names of the patron saints on the hulls. Ours is the *Florian*."

"Why is the wharf so crowded?" Belle asked.

"There's shops and amusements, and the housewives come here to buy their fish. Some of the restaurants do, too. And people come to eat here." He pointed toward a two-story building, one of several built at the edge of the pier. "That one belongs to Roberto. He just opened it. See up there?"

She could hardly miss the sign atop the roof, stretching the entire length of the building, announcing ROMANO'S FISH GROTTO.

"That's where you're getting married, so you'll be seeing it soon enough." Tony turned off the Embarcadero, drove a block, and stopped the wagon in front of a large, two-story frame house that stood on a slope with a fine view of the bay. No sooner did he announce, "We're here," than the front door burst open and a short, plump woman came hurrying down the steps.

Wiping her hands on her apron, she called, "Welcome, Belle, so glad you got here safe." She spoke with a heavy Italian accent. "Come on in and meet your new sisters. They're in the kitchen."

What new sisters? Robert hadn't said anything about sisters. Belle smiled. She might be confused, but she'd never ignore the social graces she'd been raised with. "Are you Robert's mother?"

"Robert?" For a moment, the older woman looked perplexed. "Oh, you mean Roberto. That boy! I told him not to put on airs. Yes, I'm his mother."

"I'm pleased to meet you, Mrs. Romano."

"Call me Mama. Everybody calls me that, and you can, too. He's not home yet but should be soon."

Leaving Tony to unload the trunk, Mama led her inside and straight to the kitchen, a large, cheerful room with bright-colored curtains, wooden sink with a pump, and a delicious aroma from something cooking on the big cast-iron stove. Two young women sat at a table drinking coffee. One broke into a smile. The other, a thin-face woman around thirty or so, remained unsmiling, although her sharp eyes assessed Belle with keen interest as she walked in.

Belle wished she could hide. She'd done what she could to make herself presentable, but after four days on a train, she suddenly felt wilted, wrinkled, and desperate for a bath.

Mama proudly pointed toward the smiling woman at the table who was dark haired, around thirty, and obviously expecting a baby. "This is Rosa, who's given me three grandchildren and another on the way."

Rosa came around the table and gave Belle a hug. "Welcome to the family! You're going to love it here!"

Mama pointed to the woman with the thin face. "This is Lorenzo's wife, Giana. She only has Bruno, but she'll catch up, won't you, Giana?"

The thin-faced young woman, also dark haired, uttered a barely civil, "Pleased to meet you," not bothering with a hug. "So you got here," she added, a faint thread of hostility in her voice.

Before Belle could think how to respond, Mama declared, "Don't mind her. She gets cross sometimes. Sit down. Do you want some coffee? Milk? Have you eaten?"

Belle replied she wasn't thirsty and had already eaten, but Mama soon had a glass of milk and a plate of cookies on the table. Belle became the center of attention, as Rosa's three small children trooped through the kitchen, shyly staring. Giana's only child came in. Bruno, a boy of thirteen, wasn't shy like the others and made Belle feel uncomfortable with the brazen stare he was giving her. After a brief stay, he grabbed some cookies and left. During the lively conversation around the table, Belle hardly had to say a word. Mama and Rosa did all the talking, making her feel welcome, assuring her Roberto himself would be home soon to greet her.

Giana sat quietly listening, face set in lines of disapproval. Finally, looking as if she could stand it no longer, she addressed Belle. "Why did you come here? Were there no men left in the South?"

Mama bristled. "Giana! You will be nice to Belle. Don't forget, she's going to be your new sister."

The thin woman rolled her eyes and muttered something in Italian.

Mama glared at her. "That's not polite. Speak English."

"Gladly." Giana tossed her head. "I still think Roberto was out of his mind. He could have sent for a nice Italian girl. But no, he changes his name so he sounds more American. Orders up this little *cagna* from God knows where."

Apparently Giana had said something so outrageous that Mama stood abruptly and pointed toward the door. "You will apologize this minute or out you go, and Lorenzo with you."

Giana's face fell. With obvious reluctance she turned to Belle. "All right, I apologize. It's not your fault, I suppose. Every woman wants to get married."

Belle was trying to form an appropriate answer when Mama looked toward the door and her face lit. "Roberto! Your bride is here."

Belle looked toward the door. A man in a finely tailored suit, tall derby hat, and black leather brogan boots stood in the doorway. *Oh, no.* This was Robert? Where was the tall, incredibly handsome man she daydreamed about? Surely not this man. He wasn't the least appealing with his stocky build, heavy jaw, and large, hawk nose. And he wasn't much taller than she was, either. As he stepped into the room, his gaze fell upon her. "Belle?" Before she could even nod, he strode to where she was sitting, lifted her to her feet, and planted a wet kiss on each cheek. "My bride! Welcome to San Francisco." He held her at arm's length and gave her body a raking gaze. "*Bellissima!* We'll be married tomorrow." He threw a glance at his mother. "Right, Mama?"

Mrs. Romano beamed. "The wedding's all planned. Wait till you see, Belle. It'll be at the restaurant in the banquet hall. We've hired a band. The whole neighborhood will be there. We've planned it for late afternoon, so everyone from the fishing fleet can be there, too."

"Uh, that sounds very nice." Belle had only half listened to Mama. The disgusting feel of the two wet spots on her cheeks was all that concerned her. She wanted to wipe them off, but he'd be offended, so she'd better not. She took a step back and asked, "You're Robert Romano? The one who sent the letters?"

He threw his head back and let out a big peal of laughter. "I'm Roberto, not Robert. My bookkeeper has a way with words, so he wrote that ad. He said I'd attract more women with 'Robert' than Roberto. Sounds more American." He stuck his hand under her chin and gazed into her eyes. "You're here now, sweetheart, and that's what counts." He glanced over her shoulder at his mother. "What do you think, Mama? Did I do good? Isn't she a pretty one?"

Belle didn't want him near her. If he touched her again, she'd run out the door. She backed away. "Would you mind? I've been traveling for days and must freshen up."

Mama shot a warning gaze at her son. "Don't be so pushy, Roberto. Give her time to settle in." She came around the table and took Belle's arm. "Come along. I'll see you get settled in and fix you a bath. We have a real bathroom now. It's got a big copper bathtub and a water closet. Isn't that nice? No more privy in the backyard." Talking nonstop, she led Belle upstairs to a large bedroom crowded with heavy mahogany furniture. "This is Roberto's room. We put your trunk in here, even though tonight you sleep with the children." She sighed and went on, "I hope you don't disappoint me like Giana did. I can never have enough grandchildren. I'll show you the bathroom. It's down the hall." She got a sly grin on her face and nudged Belle in the arm. "You'll have to wait till tomorrow night to sleep in Roberto's bed."

For the next hour, Belle concentrated on ridding herself of the dust and grime from four days of travel. She took a long, languid bath in a big copper bathtub, washed her hair, and dressed in the new rose silk taffeta she'd retrieved from the trunk. Ah, so good to be clean again and looking her best. She was staring into the mirror in Robert's bedroom, putting the finishing touches on her hair, when he walked in without knocking. Arms outstretched, big smile on his face, he walked toward her. "Come kiss me, Belle." His booming voice rang with confidence, as if he couldn't even imagine she wouldn't find him desirable.

She threw up her hand. "You have some explaining to do, Robert, Roberto, whatever your name is. I want to know why you lied to me in your advertisement."

His eyes widened in surprise. "Why should you care? You're here now, aren't you? What does it matter?"

"But I don't like that you deceived me. Why did you do it?"

He shrugged as if her question was hardly worth answering. "Blame my bookkeeper, not me. I paid your fare, didn't I? Tomorrow we get married and everything will be fine."

Why couldn't he see why she was angry? She might as well be hitting her head against a brick wall, but she had to make him understand how very upset she was. "Everything is not fine. You said you were from Virginia, that you graduated from William & Mary College with a degree in law. You did no such thing, did you?"

He shrugged again. "Maybe my bookkeeper got a little carried away, but it's not important, is it? I live in San Francisco. I own a restaurant, so what more do you want?"

"But you led me to believe…" The words stuck in her throat. True, he had lied, but she could see how stubborn he was, and there was no use arguing. Also, he hadn't mentioned she'd be living with his family, but even bringing it up would be a waste of time. "You weren't completely honest with me," she finished lamely.

"Is that all?" He was laughing again, unbelievably unconcerned. "You're tired. You need a good night's sleep. You'll see things differently in the morning."

Maybe she would, but she highly doubted it. One thing she already knew: She might marry this man, but she could never love him. For now she would say nothing more. Not her nature to be rude and ungrateful. She wasn't raised that way. She had to decide what to do, but later. "Perhaps you're right."

"I know I'm right. Now come downstairs. Mama's fixing dinner and you can help. One thing you'll learn about this family, we all pitch in."

"Does that include gutting fish?"

"Looks like Tony's been talking to you. Well, don't worry your pretty head about that. You won't have to do it every day, only when a big catch of salmon or herring comes in."

* * * *

Yancy had never seen a place like San Francisco. The air was different, unexpectedly cool and crisp even in the middle of summer. When they started out, the streets were flat, but now the two horses pulling Leighton Canfield's fine carriage were straining as they ascended a steep hill.

"We're almost there." Canfield lightly flicked the reins. "You'll get used to these hills. We're in Pacific Heights now. Other than Nob Hill, it's the classiest neighborhood in town. Ronald didn't care much where he lived, but nothing but the best for Bernice. Had to have a house that looked like one of those fancy French chateaux, so that's what she got. Ronald pretty much gave her everything she asked for. If he didn't, she..." Canfield frowned in annoyance. "Forgive me, Yancy. I shouldn't be criticizing any of your family at a time like this."

"Quite all right. Actually I've never met Bernice or the children." *Or even knew of their existence*, he thought wryly. But of course, now that he was here, he'd do what he could to help. His plan remained the same, though. See Mother. Go home.

Ronald's home sat on a ridge with an outstanding view of San Francisco Bay, including the entrance they called the Golden Gate. Small islands jutted from the water here and there. Oakland and the eastern shoreline stretched beyond. Canfield called the house a French chateau. Whatever it was, Ronald must have sunk a fortune into this sprawling two-story structure with its steeply pitched roof and so many towers and pillared balconies Yancy couldn't even count. Two wagons and several carriages sat in front. From the wagons, both marked "Duggan's Mortuary," workers were unloading stacks of chairs, obviously meant for the funeral.

Leighton Canfield pulled to a stop. "If you don't mind, I won't go in. Got to get back to the bank. Go right in. Bernice will be there, and her many friends."

There went that look on Canfield's face again. What was it? Dislike? Disgust? Whatever it was, the banker had made it plain he didn't care much for Ronald's wife. "I'll be fine, and thanks for the ride." Yancy grabbed his valise—he hadn't bothered with a trunk—and walked up the fancy stone walkway to the double-wide stained glass door. A frowning, middle-aged woman in a black dress answered when he rang the bell. She took one look and smiled. "You're Yancy, aren't you? Thank God you're here." She ushered him inside and took his valise. "I'm Mrs. O'Brien, the housekeeper. I'll put your valise in your room upstairs. Mrs. McLeish, Ronald's wife, wanted to see you the minute you arrive. She's in the parlor fixing up for the funeral."

"I'd like to see my mother first."

The housekeeper sighed. "Of course. She's not doing well, I'm afraid. I'll take you up there right now. She has a nurse with her, Miss Willoughby."

When he entered his mother's bedroom, the nurse, a stern-faced woman in her forties, took him aside. "You're Yancy?" she whispered. He nodded. "Good. I was afraid you wouldn't get here in time. She's very weak. Don't stay too long."

The nurse slipped out the door. He walked to the bed to where his mother lay with her eyes closed. How old and frail she looked. Smaller, somehow, and her hair had turned white. She opened her eyes. Her face lit when she saw him. "Yancy, you've come." She lifted her arms to him.

"Mother." He went into her arms, buried his head on her shoulder, sniffed the familiar smell of the lilac cologne she always wore, and got tears in his eyes. Had to wait till they were gone before he lifted his head. "I'm so sorry about Ronald."

Her eyes moistened, but she didn't cry. "He was a good man. Always kind and considerate. Maybe a bit too boisterous at times, but you know Ronald. *Knew* Ronald, I mean. Tell me, did he suffer?"

"Not a bit." He sat on the edge of the bed and told her all of it: Ronald's visit to the lake and the great conversations they'd had, Yancy's agreeing he would come to San Francisco, the train trip, the robbery. "The bandits were shooting up the car. Everyone was frightened out of their wits, and that included Ronald. He started feeling bad. His stomach hurt. His left arm was numb. Afterward, they said it was his heart. It happened fast, really fast."

"How shocked you must have been."

"God, yes. I thought of you and how sick you were, and how his death couldn't have come at a worse time."

"Losing a son—is there ever a good time?"

He shook his head and couldn't answer. He took her hand—so wrinkled and fragile—and sat holding it for a time, waiting until he could speak again. "I'm here now, and don't worry, I'm not leaving until…"

"I'm as good as dead," she said, managing a faint smile. "It won't be long, I'm afraid. The doctor was here this morning. You know about the tumor, I suppose. The pain's worse, but he gives me a lot of laudanum. I'm fine, but I sleep a lot."

He hid his sorrow at her words and gave her a smile. "Tell me what I can do for you. I mean, right now."

"You can go see the children, Richard and Beth. They've lost their father and they're devastated."

"Of course. Anything else?"

"Well perhaps, one more thing."

Mother had always had a wicked sense of humor. Now she'd got that same mischievous little grin on her face that he remembered so well. "You can go downstairs and toss my daughter-in-law out of this house and into the street, and tell her never come back."

"What?" He sat back, at a loss for words. Mother was the most peaceful woman in the world. Never talked any sort of violence.

She patted his hand. "Don't worry. I didn't mean it literally. I think the reason I've hung on so long is because I had to tell you. She's a horrible woman. If only for the children's sake, you've got to do something about Bernice. I've known some selfish people in my time, but her? Grasping and greedy. She made Ronald's life a misery."

"He never said, but I gathered he wasn't happy with her."

"Ronald had his head in the clouds. He never knew the half of it. She never loved him. What I hated the most was how she made fun of him behind his back. For some unfathomable reason, he kept trying to make her love him. He was always showering her with presents, but the more he gave her, the more she despised him. Now he's gone, and Bernice gets everything." She had to stop and catch her breath. "So unfair."

"Mother, you need to rest," he said.

"No, I need to finish this. You know me. I've never been one to pass judgment on others, but I hate that woman. I hate what she did to Ronald, and now it's the children who will suffer."

"She neglects them?"

"She hardly knows they're in the house. They've suffered a terrible loss, especially Richard. He adored his father. I've tried to console them both as best I could, but what can a sick old woman do?"

He was trying to come up with a suitable answer when she spoke again. "And not only that, she drinks too much, and she has a lover on the side."

For a time, words failed him. "You surprise me. I've never heard you talk this frankly before."

"I never had a daughter-in-law like Bernice before." She clutched his hand. "I know you want to go home, back to that cabin of yours and your beautiful life, but you can't go yet."

He would not argue. "I can see that."

"You've got to do something."

But what? "I'll do what I can, Mother, but I'm not sure—"

"You'll think of something. You always do."

Chapter 10

Belle liked Robert's family. Even Giana had lost her sullenness and become friendlier. Everyone did their best to make her feel at home, and for a while she almost did. When she mentioned she wanted to let her family know she'd arrived safely, they hastened to provide her with pen, paper, and even a stamp. Dinner was delicious. The Romanos ate well, what with Mama's special chicken cacciatore and spumoni ice cream for dessert. Afterward, Mama washed the dishes while Belle dried, and Rosa and Giana cleaned the kitchen and dining room. They laughed and chatted, Belle feeling like part of the family and having a good time. Wisely she refrained from mentioning she'd never dried a dish before. Or hardly ever stepped into the kitchen. The servants had done all that.

The problem was she'd been born and raised in a family far different than this one. The Ainsworths loved one another but showed their affection in a more restrained manner, not nearly as boisterous as the Romanos. Maybe she could manage, but living with a noisy family this size would take a lot of getting used to. She'd always assumed that when she married, she'd be in charge of her own household, in her own house, with her own garden. She'd never have that here unless Robert decided he wanted a home of his own, but would he? He seemed so contented with the way things were that she highly doubted he'd ever want to leave. That meant the only privacy they'd ever have would be their bedroom.

One good thing if she stayed: She'd surely have children, and wasn't that what she'd yearned for?

But then…

How many times had she dreamed of her wedding night when she'd know the bliss of being in the arms of the man she loved? Like Yancy. Yes, she'd feel that way about Yancy. But Robert? How could she share her bed with a man she didn't even like? Feel his hands all over her, groping her wherever he wanted, doing whatever he pleased. Ugh! And he'd want to do it all the time, she had the feeling. He'd be her husband, and she'd have to do what he said for the whole rest of her life. Oh, God, how could she do it?

But then...

What if she backed out of the wedding and returned to Savannah? Would that be so hard? Bless Bridger's heart for giving her that two hundred dollars. She could repay Robert for what he spent for the train fare and have enough left for her fare home. She would hate to disappoint Robert's family after they'd been so nice to her, especially Mama, but there were times when hurt feelings couldn't be avoided. That would be the easy part. The hard part would be when she got home and faced her friends and family. Only Bridger would understand. As for the rest, she'd have to come crawling back. How many times had Victoria told her not to go before she grudgingly gave her her approval? Doubtless her sister would never stop reminding her. Worst of all would be her humiliation when she walked into her first meeting of the Georgia Ladies of the Confederacy, heard the snickers and I-told-you-sos, looked into the scornful eyes of Mrs. Beauregard Bedford Stuart.

But then...

The wedding was tomorrow. If she was going to make up her mind, it had better be soon.

* * * *

Yancy sat by his mother's side until she dozed off. Mrs. O'Brien poked her head in. "Everything all right?"

"She's asleep," Yancy said. "Where's her nurse?"

"Miss Willoughby has gone home." The housekeeper glanced behind her, stepped inside, and shut the door. "Up to yesterday, your mother had a full-time nurse. Mr. McLeish insisted upon it, but as of this morning she's working days only. Now I'm supposed to take care of your mother at night, which I'm happy and willing to do, of course, but she also let one of the maids go, so I've got my hands full.

"*She?*"

"Mrs. Ronald McLeish, Bernice. That's who." Mrs. O'Brien's eyes narrowed in disgust. "Needs to cut costs, she says. I'll do what I can for your mother, though. She's a lovely woman, and I love her dearly. Everyone does."

"Is Bernice still downstairs?"

"Yes, she is, still busy setting up for the funeral, which will be quite elaborate, from what I understand."

He should have talked to Ronald's wife by now. She must be in a state of shock, anxious to hear the details of her husband's death. He didn't look forward to telling her, especially since he'd just gone through the painful details with Mother, but it had to be done. "She must be anxious to hear what happened. I'll go downstairs right now."

Mrs. O'Brien's mouth tightened. "I believe she can last a few more minutes. Why don't I show you to your room first? After your journey, you must be tired. You could rest up. The maid could draw you a bath."

"Good idea, thanks."

And it was a good idea, Yancy thought, as he looked around a room larger than his whole cabin, with fancy French-looking furniture, a carpet so thick his boots sank into it, and a stone fireplace that looked like it had never been used. Yeah, old Ronald had done well for himself, but maybe not in all areas. Leighton Canfield had clearly let it be known he didn't think much of Bernice, and so had Mother and Mrs. O'Brien. What was going on? He'd have to see for himself because he always formed his own opinions. Never went by what other people said. Best to meet Bernice McLeish with an open mind.

The deliverymen from the funeral parlor had left by the time he came downstairs. Mrs. O'Brien met him in the foyer and pointed toward closed double doors. "They're all in there. I've informed Mrs. McLeish you have arrived."

The sounds of laughter met his ears as he opened the doors and walked into what was ordinarily a drawing room but was now set up for a funeral with big bouquets of flowers everywhere, rows of empty chairs, black crepe bows and streamers hanging from the chandeliers, draped on the walls and pretty much everywhere they could be put. The casket had arrived. It sat at the front, open. Hands across his chest, Ronald lay inside. A small group of men and women sat relaxed and at ease in front of the casket, each with a wineglass in hand. A young woman, somewhere in her thirties, saw him and fairly leaped from her chair. "Yancy, at last you're here! I'm Bernice, your sister-in-law." She set her wine glass down and rushed to embrace him. Before he could hardly move, she'd hugged him, kissed him on both cheeks, clasped his arms, and held them out wide. "You're all Ronald ever talked about. For years I've been dying to meet you." She turned to her friends. "He's here! Ronald's brother, Captain Yancy McLeish who fought four years in the Union Army. Our hero!"

He kept an agreeable look on his face while Bernice's guests broke into applause and came to greet him and shake his hand. He hated being the center of attention, but he was in for it now, and no escape. Bernice stood by his side all the while, her hand on his arm as if she owned him. She didn't look like what he'd expected. The way Ronald had described her, he'd assumed she wasn't much to look at, but he was wrong. Bernice was a beautiful woman with a nicely curved figure, fine-featured face, and thick auburn hair piled atop her head in a big mass of curls. She wore a black satin dress with a bustle in the back, decorated with black satin bows. Her hand still clasping his arm, she gazed up at him, searching his face intently. "Look, everyone, you can tell he's Ronald's brother. He has the same eyes and mouth but taller and a whole lot thinner." Someone tittered and she looked amused. "This is my husband before he fell in love with the chocolate cream pie at the Palace Hotel."

Everyone laughed. What the hell? Why were they laughing when Ronald was lying in his casket a few feet away? He'd braced himself for the sad task of describing her husband's death, but Bernice and her friends didn't seem interested. She wasn't a grieving widow, that was for sure. He'd had enough. Would make a quick excuse and leave. He glanced toward the door. She must have read his thoughts because her face clouded and she let out a tragic sigh. "Oh, Yancy, you must forgive me. I'm only joking to cover my grief. I can't believe Ronald's gone. Such a shock. I am brokenhearted."

He would give her the benefit of the doubt. "I understand, Bernice."

"And I want to hear all about what happened, but first you must come and meet my friends." Bernice led him to her friends, all on the young side, well dressed, sitting at ease with their wineglasses. If they were aware of Ronald lying in his casket, they showed no signs of it. She introduced them, one by one. All of them dear friends, it seemed, come to console her in her grief, although judging from their expressions, none looked the least mournful.

"Please do sit down, Yancy. Would you like some wine?" He sat and said no to the wine. She continued on in a voice that often sounded bright and bubbly. "As you can see, I've spared no expense. The funeral will be tomorrow. All of San Francisco will be here." She threw a triumphant glance at a blond young man dressed in a cutaway coat with velvet trim. "Isn't that so, Reggie? Did I not invite the mayor himself and he said he'd come?"

Reggie sat slumped in an indolent posture in his chair, legs sprawled before him. "Everyone who's anyone is coming, my dear. Ronald had a million friends."

For a while, the conversation centered on who was coming to the funeral and how important they were, what refreshments would be served, and the excessive cost of Ronald's casket. The more Yancy listened, the less he thought of her friends, all of them frivolous at best, more interested in lively chatter and the supply of alcohol than anything else. Fine wine and brandy appeared to be the beverages of choice. Bernice preferred *Courvoisier L'Esprit*. Pretty fancy. Considering the red spots on her cheeks and her slightly slurred words, she'd had more than enough.

Yancy's thoughts soon drifted. Much as it pained him to think about it, Mother would be gone soon. The minute she was, he'd be on the train home, to his cabin, his lake, his contented life free of fools like Bernice and her friends. He'd about had enough of the mindless chatter when Mrs. O'Brien came in and spoke to Bernice. "About dinner, I need to know how many are staying."

They were all staying.

"And what about the children?" Mrs. O'Brien asked.

Bernice gave an indolent wave of her hand. "They'll have dinner upstairs, Mrs. O'Brien, like they always do."

The children. Richard and Beth. He could still see that proud gleam in Ronald's eyes when he spoke of them. Where were they? He should have seen them by now. He got up and spoke to Bernice. "I want to see them." Not waiting for her answer, he spoke to Mrs. O'Brien. "Can you show me the way?"

A slender boy of around eight was sitting by a window looking out when Yancy walked into his room. *A fine-looking boy*, Yancy thought. Straight brown hair. Big brown eyes. Nicely dressed in a wool tweed suit with a vest and short pants.

Yancy strode across the room. "Hello, Richard, I'm your uncle, and I wanted to meet you."

The boy immediately got to his feet and held out his hand. "It's an honor to meet you, sir. My father talked about you all the time. He was proud of what you did in the war."

Yancy bent to shake his hand. "I only did what I had to do. I'm sorry about your father, Richard. He was a fine man. I was always proud to be his brother."

The boy gulped. His eyes watered. He made a quick swipe at them in an effort not to cry. "My dad was the best dad in the world."

"Yes, he was, Richard."

"My dad..." His voice broke. The tears spilled over, and he began to sob.

Yancy knelt, gathered the small, trembling body of his nephew and pulled it firmly against him. For a time he remained silent, holding the boy tight. When the sobs let up, he reached in his pocket. "Looks like you could use a handkerchief."

Richard took it and blew his nose. "I'm sorry, sir. Men don't cry. It's not manly to cry."

"Whoever told you that? I've cried many a time."

His eyes widened. "You have? Even when you were a soldier?"

"Especially when I was a soldier. Bravery has nothing to do with tears. You just lost your father, so of course you're going to cry. I'd think less of you if you didn't."

The boy actually managed a faint smile. After a time, they sat on the bed together, Richard listening intently while Yancy racked his brain, bringing up all the good things about Ronald that he could remember from when they were boys. Eventually they talked of other things. To Yancy's surprise, Richard knew all about every battle he'd fought in, and that included all the generals' names, who won, and who lost. "Father knew in detail every battle you fought in," Richard said.

Eventually Mrs. O'Brien appeared, holding the hand of a little girl. "This is your niece, Beth," she said.

So this was Ronald's daughter. No wonder he was so proud. Yancy felt a tug at his heart as he looked at the pretty little girl with blue eyes, rosy cheeks, and hair the color of corn silk. "Are you my uncle Yancy?" she asked.

When he said he was, she threw her arms around him and hugged him tight. "Daddy loved you, and I do, too. Please don't go away."

Mrs. O'Brien reached for Beth, but Yancy stopped her. "That's all right." He swung the little girl to his lap. She cuddled against him. "Let her stay. We should get better acquainted."

"I'll be bringing their dinner soon," the housekeeper said. "Mrs. McLeish wants you downstairs."

He didn't hesitate. "Please inform her I'll be dining with the children tonight."

"Of course." Mrs. O'Brien didn't lose her straight-faced expression. A spark of pleasure lit her eyes, though, and Yancy didn't miss it.

Chapter 11

That night Belle slept in a small bed with Angeline, Rosa's ten-year-old daughter. She didn't sleep well, partly because the little girl tossed and turned all night, but mostly because the wonderful new life she'd dreamed of had become a disaster, and she didn't know which way to turn. *I keep going around in circles*, she thought, *like a dog catching its tail.* When morning came, she dreaded getting up. This was her wedding day. In hours she would become Mrs. Roberto Romano, reluctant wife, part-time fish gutter, third-in-line daughter-in-law expected to produce babies without delay. She hadn't unpacked her wedding dress from the trunk. If she was going to wear it, it needed to be pressed, also the veil. She'd better go to Robert's bedroom and get the dress right now. That is, if she was going to go through with the wedding, and maybe she should. Wouldn't that be the easiest thing to do by far? No big scene. No awful confrontation with Robert. She'd gotten herself into this mess, and it was far too late to get herself out. She should just keep her mouth shut until she said, "I do," and let the rest of her life take care of itself.

So fine, she'd made up her mind. This *would* be her wedding day. In approximately ten hours, she was going to marry Roberto Romano. Mother used to say, "You've made your bed, now lie in it," and that's exactly what she was going to do. She retrieved her wedding dress from her trunk in Robert's room, relieved he wasn't there, and carried it downstairs. The kitchen was a busy place, what with Rosa setting the table for breakfast, Giana squeezing oranges, and Mama stirring a big batch of eggs in a skillet. Seeing the dress, she waved toward the pantry. "Good morning. You'll find the ironing board and flatirons in there."

If Belle were home, a servant would have taken her dress to be pressed, but that wasn't going to happen here, and she'd better get used to doing things for herself. So how did one iron? She retrieved the board and two flatirons that were way heavier than she'd thought. She watched as Mama tossed more wood into the stove and set the flatirons directly on two of the burners. So that's how it worked. Use one iron until it cooled; set it back on the burner and pick up the other one. As if she knew what she was doing, she draped her dress over the board and began to iron, not an easy task, what with the row of tiny buttons on the bodice that must be avoided, and the dozens of small satin bows that circled the skirt, each surrounded by white satin rosebuds, fastened in a circle of delicate lace. A big white satin bow decorated the bustle in the back, surrounded by more of the small ones. She did her best but soon her wrist began to ache. Ironing was harder than she'd ever imagined, but she wouldn't dream of complaining. She was a Romano woman now, ready and willing to do her part, as she would be for years and years and years to come. Best not to think about it.

During the morning, Mama and her soon-to-be sisters-in-law talked about nothing but the wedding. San Francisco had never seen such a grand wedding, they declared. The banquet room had been more beautifully decorated than ever before. Wait till Belle saw it! The two hundred guests would swoon with delight when they drank the specially ordered French champagne and were given a choice of stuffed lobster tails or porterhouse steaks.

Belle listened quietly and couldn't keep her eyes off the clock on the wall.

In ten hours she would be married....

In eight hours she would be married...

In six hours....

In the early afternoon, she bathed, took a nap in Rosa and Marco's bedroom, and actually slept. She awoke to find Rosa and Giana standing by the bed, carefully holding the wedding dress between them. "Only two more hours," Rosa said. "It's time to put it on."

By now, she was beyond all thought. She would do what she had to do, and the less she dwelled upon her miserable fate, the better. Her about-to-be sisters-in-law helped her into the dress. Giana, who seemed to have a knack for it, swept her hair atop her head, fastened it with a big pearl comb, letting a few tendrils dangle fetchingly around her face. When the two stood back and took a look at her, they seemed beyond delight at what they saw. How beautiful she was, how stunning. No bride in the world could ever be more gorgeous. Roberto would be speechless with joy when he saw her. Belle took a good look at herself in the full-length mirror. The dress fit to perfection. The bustle in the back made her waist look tiny and gave elegance to the sweep of the train. Not that it mattered. She didn't care what Robert thought. If it were Yancy, she'd feel totally different, but it wasn't Yancy. She'd been a fool and her fate was sealed.

Roberto walked in. His sisters-in-law shrieked when they saw him dressed for the wedding in full formal attire. How elegant he looked, they exclaimed. How very handsome. Belle didn't think so. He could dress up all he wanted, but with his thick, stocky body and arrogant expression, he was not an attractive man and nothing would make him so.

He nodded with satisfaction when he saw her. "Very nice. I like the dress." He jerked his head toward the door and spoke to his sisters-in-law. "I want to talk to her."

They left immediately. No surprise there. Easy to see who ruled the roost in that household. After they left, she remarked, "You look quite elegant, Robert."

"It's not every day I get married," he said. "By the way, my name's not Robert. It's Roberto, and you may as well start calling me that right now."

She'd decided to say nothing more about how he'd deceived her, but the words flew from her mouth before she could stop them. "All right, but I do not appreciate how you—"

"You can stop right there. It doesn't matter now, does it? This is your wedding day, Belle. Be happy. Make the most of it."

How galling, but she let it go. Had to let it go. She'd made the commitment and by God, she'd stick to it. "I shall do my best, Roberto. I want to make you a good wife. We're practically strangers now, but who knows what the future holds? In time, it's possible an affection might grow between us, and—"

"Love? Forget about love, Belle. Stay in your place and give me lots of sons. That's all I care about."

She gasped. Stay in her place? Like some kind of obedient servant? "This is not what I bargained for. We need to talk."

"Why? There's nothing more to be said." He rolled his eyes upward and spoke again, looking amused. "You Southern belles are all alike, so desperate for a husband, you'd crawl clear across the country to find one. I've spared no expense to give you a wedding to be proud of, and believe me, you'll find nothing finer in all of San Francisco. Isn't that what every girl dreams of? What else matters? We leave for the restaurant in an hour."

After he left, Belle turned back to the mirror, too stunned to cry, too stunned to do anything except stand unmoving, gazing at the foolish woman in the fancy wedding dress who had just ruined her life. All her own fault. Her incredible stupidity had led her to this, and she deserved her fate. But did she? What had she been thinking? What, really, had she done wrong? She'd been honest and forthright, and she didn't deserve this. The undeniable fact was, Robert Romano was a callous, thick-skinned tyrant who would make her life a misery. No way in the world would she marry him.

"I've got to get out of here," she whispered and reached for the fancy, satin-covered buttons of her wedding dress.

* * * *

Yancy found his sister-in-law alone in the small parlor across from the dining room. She was sitting on a settee. Judging from the full glass in her hand, she'd just poured herself a sizable slug of cognac. She smiled when she saw him and patted the cushion beside her. "Do come sit down, Yancy." She held up her glass. "Would you like some?" When he shook his head no, she pursed her mouth into a little moue. "I suppose you think I drink too much."

He chose to sit across from her. "It's not for me to say."

She gazed down at the black silk dress she was wearing. "I hate black. It's not the right color for me. I'll wear it for the funeral, but after that, out it goes. I don't care what people say." She tipped her head in that flirtatious, attention-getting manner she had. "Are you shocked?"

"Why should I be? You're free to wear whatever you want."

"Well, that's a relief. I value your opinion more than you know. Ronald idolized you. He had you up on a pedestal. I can't tell you the number of times I heard about your exploits during the war and what a hero you were. So of course I want you to think well of me."

"Why would I not?"

"Because..." She hiccupped, giggled, and daintily touched two fingers to her mouth. "Excuse me, it's the cognac. For one thing, I'm not the best mother in the world."

Apparently she wasn't. He would choose his words carefully. "Ronald loved his children. He was proud of the both of them, and now that I've met them, I see why. Their father's death has disturbed them deeply, especially Richard. The boy seems lost without his father and could use some special attention."

"Well, my goodness, he gets plenty of attention, and so does Beth. Mrs. O'Brien sees to all that."

He refrained from pointing out Mrs. O'Brien was a busy woman and only a servant. "My mother was concerned—"

"*Her*." Bernice bristled but caught herself and gave him an apologetic smile. "Forgive me, but your mother isn't too fond of me, I'm afraid. She thinks I neglect my children. I love her dearly, don't get me wrong, and I know how very ill she is, but I think she should mind her own business, even though she's right."

"What do you mean?"

"I mean, I do neglect my children, and I don't intend to change."

He must have looked surprised because she laughed and declared, "Oh, I know I've shocked you, but you don't understand."

"I guess I don't."

"Then I shall explain. I have no reason to hold back now."

"Go ahead." He couldn't imagine what she was going to tell him, but it couldn't be good.

"You need to understand how I felt about Ronald. When he first came to San Francisco, my father took him under his wing, taught him the banking business. Ronald was his special pet, although to this day, I never knew why. Daddy's gone now, so I'll never know. To me Ronald was always— well, I know he's your brother and all, but to me he was always so loud and obnoxious there were times when I could hardly stand him."

"Then why did you marry him?"

She took a healthy swig of her cognac. "My mother died when I was only four, so my father pretty much raised me. I was an only child, and it seemed as if he spent all his waking hours ordering me about, telling me what to do. I resented it, of course. I was a teenager when I turned rebellious. Sometimes I'd sneak out at night to meet men I knew he'd disapprove of. One thing led to another, and I got myself in a spot of trouble, if you know what I mean. I had to tell Daddy. He gave me two choices. Either marry Ronald McLeish or"—her nose wrinkled in distaste—"he'd pack me off to one of those horrible homes for unwed mothers where you're treated like dirt, and then they take your baby away. So what could I do?"

"You married Ronald even though you didn't love him."

"Exactly. What choice did I have?"

The entire truth dawned. Yancy was hard put to keep his jaw from dropping open. "So Richard is not—?"

"Not Ronald's child." She smiled, as if she found her revelation amusing. "Poor man, he never knew. I always intended to tell him, but from the day Richard was born, he made such a fool of himself bragging about his son, I couldn't do it. I'm not entirely heartless, you know." She leveled a piercing gaze at him. "Now I suppose you really are shocked."

He wouldn't lie to her. "Pretty much, yes."

"Well, you may as well hear all of it."

"There's more?"

"Lots more." She got a serious look on her face. "I spent ten miserable years living with a man I didn't love. He's gone now. It's a shame and all that, but the truth is, as of two days ago, when Mr. Canfield read me your telegram, I have felt like a bird let loose from its cage. I'm still young and pretty. I have all his money now, and I'm free, free!" She swooped her hand through the air, nearly spilling the contents of her glass. "Not that I've been deprived of companionship. Reggie is madly in love with me, and I with him. I'm spreading my wings, Yancy. In three days, we leave for New York. From there we'll sail to Europe. They call it the grand tour, and grand it will be. London, Paris, Amsterdam! I plan to see it all." She sat back, a gleam of defiance in her eye. "So what do you think?"

He could hardly believe this woman. Poor Ronald, living in a fool's paradise, never knowing the truth, which was probably for the best. "What about the children?"

"They'll be fine. Mrs. O'Brien will be here. Between her, the maids, and the cook they'll get plenty of attention. And Richard has his private school, of course. For which Ronald paid a fortune, I might add, so I can't see a problem."

"When will you be back?"

"I have no idea." She set her glass down and earnestly bent forward. "I've done my duty, Yancy. You can condemn me if you want, but frankly, I've never had a great love in my heart for my children. From the day he was born, I've resented Richard because he ruined my life. When I look at Beth, I see Ronald. They look very much alike, you know. Same eyes, same chin. I just can't bring myself to love her like I should."

He had thought nothing could shock him anymore, but that was before he met Bernice. What could he say? No sense trying to dissuade her, she'd made up her mind. Nor would he stand in judgment. At least Ronald never knew, he'd give her that. "I'm glad you told me, Bernice. At least you were honest."

She looked pleased and said, "I suppose you want to go home as soon as the funeral is over, but you're welcome to stay as long as you like." She fluttered her eyelids at him. "I'm so glad you understand."

He did not understand, would never understand a woman like this. Before he joined the Union Army, there'd been a girl he was interested in, but he never knew her well enough to learn why women did what they did, and he still didn't know. He hurt for his brother. Ronald had known some of the truth about Bernice, but at least had never known the extent of his wife's trickery and deception. Yancy stood and looked down at her. "Good night, Bernice. You've made your mind up, and I wish you well."

He had reached his room and shut the door before he asked himself, *What do I do now?*

* * * *

Belle had managed to unbutton half the small satin buttons when Rosa, flowers in her hair, all dressed up in a pink satin gown, burst in. "Are you ready? Mama and Roberto have already left for the restaurant. Marco and I will bring you and—" Her lips parted in surprise. "Why are you taking your dress off?"

"I'm not going to marry him."

Rosa gasped and slapped her hand to her mouth.

"I don't have time to talk. Can you help me with these buttons?"

"But... But... What are you doing?"

"Isn't it obvious? Now please come help me."

At least Rosa had sense enough to look into the hallway, peer both ways, and close the door. Looking thunderstruck, she took over the unbuttoning. "Have you lost your mind? I can't believe I'm doing this. Do you realize the guests are already arriving? The flowers, the French champagne, the lobster. All those porterhouse steaks! Roberto's there waiting. Oh, dear God, he's going to be furious."

She'd try to explain. Of them all, Rosa was most likely to understand. "You think I don't know how awful this is? After you've all gone to so much trouble? But I just can't marry him, that's all. I've made up my mind. Nothing can change it, so don't even try."

An expression of understanding spread over Rosa's face. "You don't have to explain. I wouldn't want to marry him, either."

"You wouldn't?"

"He's a horrible man. All right, that's the last button. Let's get your dress off, quick." As Belle pulled the dress over her head, Rosa asked, "What will you wear?"

The brown wool suit she'd worn on the train was the handiest. At least she'd given it a good brushing and had a fresh blouse to wear. While she dressed, Rosa asked, "What are you planning?"

Belle could almost laugh. "I haven't quite figured that out yet. I suppose I should go to the restaurant. Somehow I could get Roberto aside and tell him the wedding's off. That would be the honorable thing to do."

"No! You can't do that. Don't you understand what kind of man he is? You've wounded his pride. You'd be lucky if he doesn't kill you."

"Then I'll just go."

Rosa nodded emphatically. "You've got to get out of here, and the sooner the better."

"I've made a mess of things."

"Don't worry about that now." Rosa cast an urgent glance around the room. "What do you need?"

"I can't take the trunk. Maybe I can send for it later."

Rosa laughed. "Knowing Roberto, I wouldn't count on it."

"I'll just take my handbag and my valise then. I have money enough. I'm going to pay him back for the train fare."

"Why should you bother? He'll still be furious."

"Even so. It's the honorable thing to do." She opened her valise. She'd been keeping the two hundred dollars Bridger gave her in a side pocket. She dug it out, took three twenty-dollar notes, and set them on Roberto's dresser. Thank goodness, that left plenty for her fare home and other expenses. "Now I feel better."

"Roberto won't. You must hurry."

What to take? She hated to leave her new dresses behind but had no choice. That was the least of her worries, even though Rosa was right, and she had little chance of ever seeing her trunk and its contents again. She ended up packing her valise with only the essentials: a change of underwear, clean blouse, brush and comb, and some handkerchiefs. "Do you know of any good hotels?" she asked. "Nothing too expensive."

"You could stay at the Baldwin Hotel. It's not too expensive, and there's a horse car you can catch a block away that will take you right to it."

She could do it! Thanks to Rosa, everything was falling into place and she could actually see her way clear of this awful predicament she was in. She wasn't out of trouble yet, but at least she could see her path of escape. If all went well, she'd be long gone before Roberto discovered she'd fled. But what if he did and she wasn't gone yet? Just thinking of it caused an icy fear to twist around her heart. "I've got to get out of here."

"Yes, you do," Rosa said. "When you're ready to go downstairs, I'll go down first and make sure nobody's in sight. We've got to be careful, though. Marco's still here, down in the kitchen, I think, and I don't know who else. You can't let anybody see you." She stepped back and scrutinized Belle with a sharp eye. "Don't you have a wrap? This is San Francisco. You're not going to be warm enough if you're out at night."

Belle shook her head. This was the middle of summer, and she hadn't thought to bring a coat.

"Come to my room, and I'll find you something." Rosa opened the bedroom door. There, suspiciously close, stood Giana's unlikeable son, Bruno. She scowled at him and asked, "What are you doing lurking in the hallway? Were you spying on us?"

The boy got a sour grin on his face. "No, I wasn't, Aunt Rosa. I'd never do that." He looked over Rosa's shoulder and spied Belle. "Weren't you wearing your wedding dress a while ago? How come you're not wearing it now?" His gaze fell to the valise sitting in the middle of the bedroom floor. His mouth dropped open. "Are you leaving? Does Uncle Roberto know?"

Rosa pointed a warning finger at her nephew. "You're to keep your mouth shut. Don't you dare tell your uncle. Do you understand?"

With a sense of urgency, Belle laid a hand on Rosa's arm. "Let it go. There isn't time. Let's get that wrap."

Rosa wagged her finger one more time at Bruno. "You heard me. You'd better keep your mouth shut or you'll have me to deal with. Now wait downstairs. You can come to the restaurant with Marco and me."

They hurried to Rosa and Marco's bedroom where Rosa found a wool shawl. Belle threw it over her shoulders. When they stepped into the hallway again, Bruno was gone. Rosa snorted with disgust. "That sneaky little weasel is going to tattle to Roberto. I doubt he's waiting downstairs and is probably halfway to the restaurant by now. You've got to go now, Belle."

As if Belle needed to be told. Her heart was pounding as she returned to Roberto's bedroom and picked up her valise. She took one more look at this room that would have been hers and Roberto's for the next, who knew? Maybe fifty years? She cringed at the thought. No question she'd made the right decision, but no time to think of it now. She left the bedroom and fairly flew down the stars. "I hope I haven't got you into trouble," she said to Rosa, who stood by the front door.

"You let me worry about that." Rosa opened her arms and gave her a big hug. "I'll be thinking of you and hoping you're all right. When you get home, be sure to write." She pointed toward the bay. "You walk one block that way, and that's where you'll find the horse car. It costs a dime."

"Wish me luck, Rosa, and thank you." Carrying her valise, Belle started walking. A mist was falling. It was turning dark. The guests would all be at the restaurant by now. They'd be laughing and talking, drinking that specially ordered champagne, waiting for the big moment when the bride would arrive and the ceremony would begin. Her heart ached when she thought how hurt and disappointed Mama would be when she realized her about-to-be daughter-in-law had fled. The rest of the family, too, except Roberto. Rosa was right. Belle had only caught a glimpse of his temper when she'd looked into his cold eyes, but she'd seen enough to know if she stayed, she would have regretted it for the rest of her life. She would go directly to the Baldwin Hotel. Maybe they'd have a restaurant, so she wouldn't need to go out again. Tomorrow she'd find where to buy her train ticket and how soon she could leave. Very soon, she hoped. She didn't like paying for a hotel any longer than she had to. How very satisfying to know she had a plan, and everything was falling neatly into place.

She reached a street with a set of tracks running along the middle. This must be where she'd catch the horse car. She looked down the street. Here it came, two horses pulling what looked pretty much like a Savannah streetcar. She looked behind her, picturing Roberto racing toward her, hands outstretched, ready to strangle her. No one coming. The horse car stopped. She climbed on board, dug in her handbag, and dropped a dime in the coin box. As she took her seat, her heart lifted. He couldn't catch her now. Fortune was shining upon on her, and she'd soon be home. She thought of Yancy and what could have been. He was somewhere in this city. Maybe she should try to find him, but this was hardly the time. All she wanted was to get home to her beloved Savannah, but maybe later on, somehow she'd find him again.

* * * *

Yancy sat by his mother's bedside. She was gone. "Gone to a better place," she whispered in her last moments, and he believed it. If anyone deserved to go to heaven, it was Mother.

Miss Willoughby, the nurse, stood by. "I'm so sorry, Mr. McLeish," she said. "I've never worked for a finer woman. She didn't want a big funeral, you know, not like"—she tipped her head toward the door—"all that fancy business downstairs. Just say a few words over her grave, she said, and that will be enough."

"Yes, simple is best." Ronald was gone. Mother was gone. A grief, the likes of which he never felt before, hit him hard. He thought of Belle, what a comfort she'd been on the train, how he would have wanted her to be here. But she could be married already, starting her new life. By now she'd forgotten his name. A burst of laughter came from below. Ronald's funeral. He would go downstairs for one reason only—to honor his brother. The rest of them could all go to hell, as far as he was concerned. Nothing was keeping him from going home now except the children.

Chapter 12

Just what she wanted. Located at Powell and Market Streets, the four-story Baldwin Hotel had a respectable look about it without appearing to be overly expensive. Carrying her valise, Belle stepped inside a large lobby filled with tasteful furniture, potted palms, and oil paintings on the walls. She walked to the front desk and spoke to a thin, balding man in his forties, neatly dressed, who peered at her through a monocle. He gave her a thin-lipped smile. "Yes, madam?"

She didn't like the quizzical way he was looking at her. Had a woman alone never asked for a room before? Did he think she was one of those women who earned her living on the streets? "I'd like a room for one, please."

He stared down his nose at her. "For how long?"

She lifted her chin and stared right back. "It would be for one or two nights. Perhaps more, but I'm not sure."

"Hmm, let's see. We're almost full." He gave a reluctant shrug and spent some time perusing something behind the counter, a list of rooms she assumed. She suspected he was trying to decide whether or not to turn her away, but finally he took a key from the rows of cubbyholes behind him and placed it on the counter. "I can give you room 334."

"That's fine."

"We'll need the first night in advance. That'll be one dollar and fifty cents."

"Of course." She had at least two dollar bills in her handbag, more than enough. She opened it and peered inside. Where were they? Had she put them in her coin purse? She checked but the bills weren't there, only a few coins. She thought she had more than that, but apparently not. "Just a moment." She bent, opened the valise, and dipped her hand into the side pocket where she'd placed the remaining $140. Empty? How could that be? She distinctly remembered carefully folding the seven twenty-dollar notes together and placing them in that very side pocket. Somehow they must have slipped out. "Excuse me, this will take a minute," she told the clerk. She picked up the valise and walked to an upholstered, wing-backed armchair where she set it on the seat and opened it wide.

The money was nowhere in sight and must have somehow slipped toward the bottom. She started digging through her belongings. Nothing. Up to this moment, she hadn't been concerned, but a sudden unease seized her. Where had her money gone? She picked up the valise, dumped its contents into the chair, and pulled another chair close. She picked up each item she'd packed, examined it carefully, and placed it in the other chair. That way, she couldn't possibly miss anything. By the time she reached the bottom of the valise, anxiety griped her heart. The seven twenty-dollar notes she'd so counted on had disappeared. Aware of what a futile gesture it was, she ran her hands across every inch of the bottom, up the sides, into the side pocket she already knew was empty.

It's gone. My money is gone.

But how did it happen? Clearly she remembered taking three twenty-dollar notes from the two hundred and leaving them on Roberto's dresser. The rest she'd put back in the side pocket, she was sure of it, and the only time the valise was out of her sight was when she went to Rosa's room to get the shawl. So who...?

Bruno.

He'd been standing in the hallway, no doubt snooping. Rosa had referred to him as "that sneaky little weasel," and how right she was. He would have had just enough time to look in her valise and take her money. Had he stolen from her handbag, too? He probably had and could even have taken the sixty dollars she left on the dresser for Roberto. She would never know, though. She'd burned her bridges and could never go back. So what was she going to do? Without money, she couldn't buy food, couldn't pay for her train fare, couldn't pay for her room.

"Madam?" the hotel clerk called. With dragging feet, she returned to the counter. He'd tilted his brow and looked at her inquiringly. "Well? I can't hold the room forever."

"I...I ..." She would throw herself on his mercy. She couldn't think what else to do. "It seems my money has been stolen. I didn't discover it until now. Would it be possible? What I mean is, could I pay you later? I'm from Savannah and could send you the money as soon as I get home. I'm good for it, I assure you. It's just at the moment I find myself without funds."

"Pay later?" The clerk compressed his lips as if trying to keep from smiling. "We don't extend credit to anyone. Sorry, it's the rule of the house."

He didn't look sorry. "Oh, I see," she murmured. The tempting sight of the key still lying on the counter added to her despair. She had so counted on that room. It would have been her refuge, a place where she could walk in, lock the door, and feel safe from Roberto and the world, at least for a little while. She could try again to persuade the clerk, but it was plain to see he wouldn't bend, and she'd only further humiliate herself. She stood straight and pulled her shoulders back, assuming all the dignity she could muster. "Then I don't want the room." She stepped away before he could answer and returned to the chair where her belongings sat in a pile for the world to see. Hastily, she repacked them in the valise. Feeling the clerk's eyes drilling into her back, she picked it up and was about to walk out the door when the clerk called out, "Why don't you try Western Union? They've got a new service now. Someone in Savannah could wire you some money."

There was hope! "Where is it located?"

"Just down the street. You can't miss it."

She thanked the room clerk. He wasn't so bad after all. She left the hotel and hastened to the Western Union Telegraph Office only a block away, as the clerk had said. She walked to the counter and spoke to a young man in his twenties who wore an eyeshade and rubber bands on his rolled-up sleeves. "I understand I can have money sent to me by telegram?"

He smiled. "You certainly can, ma'am. It's a new service we're offering. Whoever sends the money must go to their Western Union Office and pay the amount requested. The clerk sends us a telegram, and we pay you. Simple, huh? That's progress for you."

"Indeed, that's wonderful." Suddenly buoyant, she set her handbag on the counter. "So I must send a telegram first, of course."

"Of course. Where to?"

"Savannah, Georgia."

The clerk did a quick calculation. "That'll be four dollars and seventy cents for ten words."

"What!" She couldn't have heard correctly.

"Four dollars and seventy cents for ten words, ma'am."

"Oh, dear." She looked in her handbag, took out her coin purse, and plucked out the few remaining coins: seven dimes, five nickels, three pennies. Altogether, counting the pennies, she had exactly ninety-eight cents to her name. "I'll send two words then. That should be enough." Actually two words would really be enough: *send money.*

The young man regretfully shook his head. "Sorry, the minimum is ten words."

"You mean even if I send two words I have to pay for ten?"

"Sorry."

"Could I go ahead and send it, and they could pay at the other end?"

"Sorry."

"I see." She picked up her handbag and valise. "Thank you anyway." She walked out the door with her head held high. Night had fallen. The light mist had turned into a fog that seemed to be getting heavier. In a daze of disbelief, she started up the street, not knowing or caring which way she was going. A chill in the air caused her to shiver, and she pulled the shawl closer around her. *Thank you, Rosa.* She had walked she didn't know how many blocks before she realized how hungry she was. At least ninety-eight cents would buy her a meal.

She searched for a cheap restaurant and found one with a tattered awning and a faded menu posted in the window. The food was good: roast beef, bread, and vegetables. It cost only forty-five cents, so she splurged and bought a glass of milk for ten cents and piece of apple pie for fifteen cents. The rest she left as a tip for the waiter, so when she stepped onto the street again, her stomach was full, but her coin purse was empty. So now what? She must try to think clearly, decide what to do. She looked around. The street sign said Market Street, but that didn't mean a thing. A steady stream of people passed by. She envied how they all walked with a determined step, secure in the knowledge they had a destination, knew where they were going. *Except me.* For the first time in her life, she had no place to go. Even worse, nobody would miss her. Nobody would start searching for her, concerned she was gone. For a terrible moment, a panic like she'd never known swept through her. Her knees went weak, and she wasn't sure she could go on. People started staring at her as they passed by. What was she going to do, collapse on the sidewalk? Make a spectacle of herself? She must keep going, but where?

One direction was as good as another, she supposed. She started walking, taking determined steps like the rest of the crowd, so no one would notice her. Such an awful thing as this had never happened to her before. All her life, she'd been loved and cared for. Even during the darkest days of the war, she'd had a roof over her head and food on the table, although at times it wasn't much. There must be something or someone who could help her. Whom did she know in San Francisco? Allegra lived here now, but where? Belle hadn't bothered to remember her address. What about Mrs. Hollister? When they parted, her seatmate had described where she lived: "…on the corner of Powell and California. That's on Nob Hill, not far from Leland Stanford's mansion. It's a Queen Ann Victorian -tyle house with lots of gingerbread."

But even if Belle could find it, she wanted nothing to do with that cranky old woman, despite her more friendly attitude in the end. And besides, where was Nob Hill and how was she supposed to get there?

The same with Yancy. He'd given her Ronald's card, so she had his address. But even if she had the means to get there, she couldn't imagine anything more humiliating than standing at his door all bedraggled, begging for shelter, having to admit her horrible mistake. So here she was, alone in a strange city, penniless, and no one to turn to. She trudged on. What else could she do? After a while, her legs began to ache and her breath was coming short. She needed to sit down, but where? The nature of the street had begun to change. Market Street had been a respectable area with tall business buildings and reputable stores, but now she was passing vacant lots filled with weeds and a scattering of dilapidated-looking buildings that housed saloons with music booming out the door and hotels that looked on the sleazy side. Not that she wouldn't have rented a room from any one of them, but without a penny she didn't dare try. Some buildings were vacant, with shadowy doorways she hated to pass. The people looked different. Instead of the respectably dressed shoppers she'd seen on Market Street, now she was encountering men in seaman's clothes, some of them staggering, and once she passed a group of women dressed in bold, gaudy dresses who didn't seem to be going anyplace, simply standing around. The women stared at her as if she'd invaded their territory. Some of the seamen whistled and made comments as she passed by. "Hello there, sweetheart, want some fun?" She shrank away and kept on walking.

She was passing a lonely stretch along a vacant lot covered with weeds when a big man with hulking shoulders appeared out of nowhere and leaped in front of her. "Where are you going?" he asked.

He was blocking her way, and she had to stop. "Let me pass." She tried to step around him.

He blocked her again and grabbed her arm. At his touch, she jerked away, but he grabbed her again, his foul, whiskey-laden breath nearly causing her to gag. "Let me go," she cried, but he tightened his grip and started to drag her off the sidewalk. She dropped her valise and tried to claw at his face, but he grabbed her other arm, and she was helpless. Dear God, something horrible was going to happen to her, that unspeakable thing that every woman dreaded. She twisted and turned, using every bit of strength she had, but his grip was so powerful she had no chance of breaking away.

He dragged her clear off the sidewalk into the weeds, and was still dragging her when she felt a jolt and a young voice was yelling, "You let her loose!"

It was all a blur, but she had the impression that someone had jumped on the man's back. The powerful arms suddenly let go. She fell to the ground amidst tall, rough weeds that scratched her face. "Run, run!" The urgency of the voice spurred her to scramble to her feet, sprint to the sidewalk, and keep on running. Her lungs were about to burst, but not until she reached a saloon that had music blasting out the door did she stop in a circle of light cast by a streetlamp. One arm braced on the lamppost, she bent over, gasping for breath, heart pounding in her chest. Dear Lord, now she'd lost her valise. What was the use? Her knees grew weak. Despairing and hopeless, she was about to crumble to the ground when a boy of fifteen or so emerged from the darkness. "Are you all right?" he called. He was carrying her valise.

She pulled herself straight. "I think so." In the dim light she couldn't see much of him except he was taller than she, thin and gangly, with long, sandy hair, and a concerned look on his face. He might have reached full height, but his shoulders and chest hadn't filled out yet, so he had a scrawny look about him. "You're not the one who saved me, are you?"

The boy shrugged. "It wasn't hard. I jumped on his back and he lost his balance. He was pretty drunk, so that helped." He handed her the valise. "This is yours."

She took the valise. "How can I ever thank you?"

The boy frowned back at her. "Ma'am, what are you doing here?"

How could she possibly explain? "It's a long story."

"You shouldn't be here. Don't you know where you are?"

"I have no idea."

"I didn't think so. You're on Pacific Street. If you go one block more, you'll find yourself square in the middle of the Barbary Coast."

Tony's words about the Barbary Coast came back to her: *Nice ladies wouldn't be caught dead there.* What had she done? "I didn't intend—"

"I'm sure you didn't, ma'am, but all the same, you're headed for what some call the wickedest place in the world. If you go any farther, you're going to find block after block of gambling houses and opium dens, and men and women doing stuff I can't even tell you about. I can see you're a nice lady, and I hope you'll go back where you came from."

The gravity of her plight struck her full force. She held back tears, embarrassed to think she might actually break down in front of a teenage boy. "I can't go back. I don't have any money, and I don't know where to go." The second her words left her mouth, she was sorry she'd said them. All she had left was her pride. This boy had done enough for her, and she didn't want him to think she was asking for more. "I shouldn't be bothering you with this. I'll start back where I came from. I'm sure I'll find"—she gulped and her voice trembled—"something."

The boy didn't hesitate. "You're not going back. You need a place to spend the night, and I'll find it. The name's Luther, by the way, Luther Allen."

"I'm Belle Ainsworth from Savannah. How can you find me a place? I have no money for a hotel."

"Not a hotel. I meant a place off the street where you can be warm and safe. That is, as safe as you can be on the Barbary Coast. Let's see…" He thought a moment. "There's a tunnel where I sleep sometimes. You might not like it, though. It's damp and it's got rats."

She hadn't entirely lost her sense of humor and laughed in reply. "I would rather collapse and die on the street than sleep where there's one single rat."

He bit his lip, deep in thought. "Come with me. It's a place that's close."

They started walking along Pacific Street, past more saloons than she could count, past small theaters and dance halls. The Midway, the Bella Union Dance Hall, the Hippodrome theater where life-size figures of naked women shamelessly pranced about. *Who is this boy?* she wondered. He spoke well and had good manners. Why was he living on the streets? "Don't you have a home, Luther?"

"I used to. I lived with my parents and two little sisters back in Nebraska. Then Pa decided to come west. He thought he could get a better job out here, but all he could find was a job on the docks. We got by, though. Then he and my mother got the cholera and died. The neighbors took us in. They didn't treat us very well. The father used to beat me all the time, so I finally up and left. We turn here."

Luther led her about half a block off Pacific on a small side street and stopped in front of a dark, two-story building. A sign hung over the entrance, but the letters were Chinese, and she couldn't read them. "We're here," Luther said. "You have to be quiet."

The first thing Belle noticed when they entered was how sultry and oppressive the air seemed to be. They were in a large room, lit only by feeble yellow lights coming from small lamps. As her eyes adjusted to the light, she could see people lying about, some on beds, others on couches. They weren't lying down as if sleeping. Instead, most were in various stages of recline. They all looked as if they were asleep, though, but were they? How very strange they looked, some of them just staring off into space. "What is this place?" she whispered to Luther as they crept through.

"You're in an opium den," he whispered back. "Keep moving. They don't mind. They don't even know you're here."

Opium den? Despite her desperate plight, what popped into her head was, she'd like to see the faces of the Georgia Ladies of the Confederacy if they could see her now. "Where are we going?" she asked. Surely Luther didn't expect her to join these strange people who stared into space and uttered not a sound.

"Upstairs. There's rooms up there they don't use." He found a candle and lit it. "Just keep going. You'll see the stairs."

They climbed the stairs and found a room bare of furniture that was small, warm, and mercifully empty. Although the candle didn't shed much light, she could see the walls were almost black. "It's from all the smoke," Luther explained. "I hope you don't mind sleeping on the floor."

She was warm again, and she had a roof over her head. After a day like today, that was all that mattered. "I don't mind."

"Wait here and I'll find us some blankets."

When Luther returned, he handed her a blanket. She hoped it was clean, but if it wasn't, she didn't want to know. Her muscles ached from exhaustion. Her eyes kept wanting to close. How wonderful to lie down, even if it was on a wooden floor. She wadded up her shawl and used it for a pillow. Grateful for the blanket wrapped around her, she instantly fell asleep.

* * * *

"Good morning, ma'am, I brought you some breakfast."

Belle opened her eyes, wondering why she had such a heaviness in her chest, as if something dreadful had happened. It all came back. She had no money, no place to go, and she'd spent the night in an opium den. She struggled to sit up. "Good morning, Luther."

He sat cross-legged beside her, fresh faced and smiling. He had clear, sky-blue eyes she hadn't noticed before. "Look what I found us." He pointed toward a newspaper he'd spread on the floor. Two apples sat upon it, along with a bottle of Old Crow whiskey that looked full, a pile of crab legs that looked untouched, and a loaf of bread with a small portion torn from the end.

"Where did you get all this?" she asked.

"The garbage. That's how we eat, my friends and I. First thing in the morning, we find all kinds of good stuff behind the restaurants like the Midway and the Hippodrome. That's water in the whiskey bottle. I just filled it myself."

"So there are more of you?"

"Oh, yes, there's lots of homeless people around here. Mostly men, but women, too. And there's children, lots of them younger than I. They've lost their parents, like I did. Some have no place to go, or like me, whoever takes them in is only looking for servants to do the work. It's usually the father who beats on 'em, so they run away. I was twelve when I couldn't take it anymore and had to leave home. I get along all right, but I wish..." A muscle quivered in his jaw. "I worry about my sisters. Susan, she's six now, and Helen, she'd be eight. When I ran off, I hated to leave them for fear the family wasn't treating them right. I can get a job on the docks soon as they'll have me. Then I'll go after them."

She hated the thought of cruelty to a child. What a shame those children had no decent place to go. "I hope you'll find something soon."

"Do you want to wash up?" he asked. "There's a bathroom downstairs. Be careful, in case one of 'em wakes up."

Holding her breath, she crept down the stairs. No one in sight, thank God. The bathroom was disgusting—she'd expected nothing less—but at least she was able to wash up and smooth her hair. When she returned, she sat on the floor again and gladly shared Luther's breakfast offering. "This is sourdough bread, and it's delicious," she remarked after her first bite. She cracked open a crab leg. "Crab, sourdough bread, and an apple—who could ask for a nicer feast?"

They both laughed. He frowned and asked, "If you don't mind, I'm curious. How did a nice lady like you end up here?"

"I don't mind at all." She told him all of it: the train ride; Yancy and the bandit; how she decided she didn't want to be a mail-order bride and took flight; her shock at discovering a terrible boy name Bruno stole her money.

When she finished, Luther shook his head. "I don't blame you one bit for running away. I'd have done the same."

When they'd done eating, she picked up the Old Crow whiskey bottle and held it high. "A toast to you, Luther Allen. You saved me last night, and I'll not soon forget it."

He smiled and said thank you, but his smile soon disappeared. "What do you plan to do now?"

She sighed and didn't answer for a while. "Well, it's plain to see I've got to do something."

"Yes, ma'am."

"I can't stay forever on the second floor of an opium den."

"No, ma'am."

"There was a lady on the train, Mrs. Hollister, who gave me her address. She said it's on Nob Hill."

"That's not far, but it would be a steep walk."

She didn't think she could face a steep walk this morning, and besides, she really didn't want to go to Mrs. Hollister. "There's someone else. I told you about the man who saved me from the train robber. I have his address."

"You do? Then let's go find him."

"No, I can't. I would hate standing on his doorstep, begging for help. It's a matter of pride, but I just couldn't do it."

"That's all very well and good, ma'am, but pride won't fill your stomach or put a roof over your head. And besides, you're not safe on the streets here."

She mulled over what Luther had said, and it made sense. She never thought she'd be taking advice from a fifteen-year-old, but he was wise far beyond his years, and she'd be foolish not to listen. *Yancy.* She had thought she'd be too humiliated to go to him, but that was before she truly realized how dangerous the streets were and how she'd never survive unless she reached out for help. She opened her handbag, found Ronald's card, and read off the address on Franklin Street. "It's in a district called Pacific Heights, I believe. Is it far?"

"Not so very. Only a mile or two. You could walk it."

Chapter 13

The funeral was over. Yancy had honored his brother as best he could. He'd given one of the eulogies at the service. He'd accompanied Bernice and Richard to the Yerba Buena cemetery in a fancy carriage with a black-suited driver, first in the long procession following the elaborate, glassed-in hearse. He'd stood by the grave. Watched his brother's remains lowered into the ground. Listened as the minister said the final prayer. *Ashes to ashes, dust to dust…*

The crowd began to disperse. Leighton Canfield came up and placed a hand on his shoulder. "My deepest condolences. I understand your mother passed away last night."

"Yes, she did." It was hard to talk. "She wanted a simple, gravesite service. Nothing like this."

"Of course." The banker nodded with understanding. "Ronald had a lot of friends, Yancy. Did you notice how many are here? Not only employees from the bank but people from his church and his club. Waiters from his favorite restaurants are here, and horse car drivers…everyone who knew him loved him."

Not quite. Yancy looked to where Bernice stood chatting with the indolent-looking young man she called Reggie. At the funeral, she'd done a fine job of acting the grieving widow, but it must have been too much of a strain because she was laughing again, fluttering those eyelids. He thought of Ronald and had to look away.

Canfield must have noticed Bernice and her lover, too. "She's only getting half, you know."

"Half of what?" Yancy had no idea what he was talking about.

"Ronald's estate." Canfield bent close. "This is no time to discuss it, but his attorney will be contacting you soon. You get the other half, and that includes the house."

He hadn't given it a thought. "You mean Ronald mentioned me in his will?"

"Indeed, he did. Ronald talked to me about it many a time. He set up trust funds for the children and provided for your mother. Half of the rest he left to you. Quite frankly, you'd have gotten it all, but according to California law, it's community property. Bernice gets the other half and there was nothing he could do."

Yancy didn't want to hear anymore. "I hope you understand, but right now—"

"I've picked a poor time to bring it up. I shouldn't have bothered you with all this, what with you standing by Ronald's newly dug grave. Just keep in mind he wanted you to stay in San Francisco. You could, you know. There's a job waiting for you at the bank any time you want it. Of course, with the money you'll inherit, you can do pretty much anything you please."

"What I please is to get back to Maine, Mr. Canfield."

"I understand that, but would you do me this one favor? Allow me to give you a tour of our beautiful city tomorrow afternoon. No pressure involved, I assure you, but before you go, I would like you to understand why Ronald so loved San Francisco. You may not have another chance to see it."

How could he refuse such a well-meant offer? "Of course I'd like to go. I'll look forward to it."

"One o'clock then." Canfield gave him a sympathetic pat on the back and drifted away as friends of Ronald's approached and offered their condolences. Yancy lost track of how many hands he shook, how many "thank yous" he murmured. When he finally returned to the carriage, Bernice wasn't there, and only Richard sat waiting, looking quiet, pale, and sad. He barely nodded when Yancy climbed in, and seemed to be fighting back tears. "Where's your mother?" Yancy asked.

"She said she was going to ride with Mr. Hammersmith."

"You mean Reggie?"

"Reggie," Richard replied, a clear thread of resentment in his voice. "She said to tell you she wasn't coming right home. She's going over to his house, I think." As the carriage began to roll, he shrank back in his seat and looked disconsolately out the window.

Dammit! Bernice ought to be here, but apparently she had better things to do than comfort her grieving children, especially Richard, who seemed deeply disturbed by his father's death. Little Beth seemed okay. In a surprisingly wise decision, Bernice had decreed her daughter too young to attend the funeral. But Richard? Yancy racked his brain. How could he help? What did eight-year-old boys like to do? Hadn't Ronald mentioned something about chess? When Yancy was that age, he and his father played the game, too. "I understand you like chess, Richard."

The boy pulled his gaze away from the window. "Father and I played it all the time."

"Is that so? I used to play chess with my father. Of course, that was a long time ago before I went off to the war."

A faint light of interest appeared in Richard's eyes. "Do you still play?"

"Not anymore. I'm so rusty no one would want to play with me."

A long silence followed. Yancy waited patiently until Richard sat a little straighter and spoke again. "I wouldn't mind. If you've forgotten, I could teach you."

"Is that so? Fine, then. Let's set up a board after dinner tonight, but you've got to promise to go easy on me."

The hint of a smile crossed the boy's face. Good. He needed attention, and Yancy would do his best. He looked out the window and caught a glimpse of the sparkling bay. Everyone agreed San Francisco was a beautiful city. So did he, but it wasn't home. Nothing could compare to home, even though he realized it wouldn't be the same as when he left. He could never go back to what he used to think was his perfect life. Belle had changed all that. What was she doing right now? But why ask when he already knew the answer? No doubt by now she'd married that young stud with that fine head of curly dark hair who'd met her at the dock. At this very moment, she could be in bed with him, blissfully happy, those days on the train forgotten.

Why torture himself? He would never see her again. If he could erase her from his memory, he would, but he couldn't. The beautiful Miss Belle Ainsworth had disappeared from his life forever, but never would he forget her.

* * * *

Belle and Luther left the opium den the same way they'd come in—creeping unnoticed past the sprawling bodies of men and women who looked as if they hadn't moved from the night before. Once on the street again, Luther announced he was coming with her. "I've got the time, and I want to make sure you get there safely."

Relieved, she thanked him. She'd had quite enough of being alone in a strange city.

They started walking and soon left the Barbary Coast behind. They began to pass decent-looking homes on large lots with spectacular views of the bay. When they came to the address on the card, she wasn't surprised to see an elaborate two-story French chateau, or maybe three stories if you counted the two tall towers with conical roofs that sat on either end. Obviously Ronald McLeish had done well. She started up the paved walkway but stopped short when she saw a large black wreath hanging on the door. How could she inflict herself upon a family that must be horribly upset? "They're in mourning. I shouldn't disturb them."

"After you've come all this way?" Luther asked with a scornful sniff. "Just go up and knock. Either they'll let you in or they won't, but from what you told me about your friend, you won't be turned away. What have you got to lose?"

Nearly her last hope was what she would lose. Luther made a lot of sense. She should at least try, and if they turned her away, she couldn't feel any more embarrassed and humbled than she already was. "Let's go up to the door."

Luther took a step back. "This is as far as I go. I'll wait here. Soon's I know you're safe inside, I'll be on my way."

He'd taken her by surprise. "You can't go yet."

"You'll be fine."

"But I haven't thanked you yet. I don't know what would have happened to me if you hadn't come along."

He shrugged in mock resignation. "All right, you've thanked me. You don't need me now, and I'm going."

"But I want to make sure I can reach you. I want to give you something for your trouble, only it might take a while."

"Forget about that. I don't need a reward. Besides, finding me would be hard to do, considering I sleep in a different place every night."

She gave him a hug. "Then I thank you with all my heart, Luther. I don't think I would have survived without you, and I wish you well." She looked down at her bedraggled self. The brown wool looked as if it had been slept in, which, of course, it had. Somewhere along the way, she'd lost her hat, and her hair must look like a rat's nest. She hated that Yancy would see her this way, but unless she wanted to keep roaming the streets, she had no choice.

She pulled her shoulders back, walked up to the front door, and rang the bell. A middle-aged woman answered. Dressed all in black, she had the look of a housekeeper about her. She took one look at Belle and frowned. "If you've come for the funeral, you're too late. They've all gone to the cemetery. Or was it something else you wanted?"

Belle's courage was fading fast. Only sheer desperation kept her from fleeing back down the walkway. "I'm not here for the funeral. I would like to see Mr. Yancy McLeish. I'm a friend of his. We met on the train, and I very much... I mean, it's important that I speak to him." She held her breath waiting for an answer.

The woman's gaze swept over her and seemed to soften. Pity for her bedraggled appearance perhaps? Whatever the reason, the housekeeper swung the door wide. "They should be back soon. Come in."

What a relief. Belle looked back to where Luther stood at the end of the walkway, "Are you sure you must go?" she called.

"So long, ma'am. You'll be fine now." Luther touched his hand to his cap in a final salute and began to walk back the way they'd come, back to the ugly, sinful Barbary Coast. Tony had called it "the wickedest place in the world," and now Belle had seen firsthand it was true. She hated to see him go. What a shame a boy so bright, so generous and full of heart, had to live that way. She turned back and stepped through the door.

The housekeeper smiled. "Follow me. I'll put you in the library." She led Belle to a carpeted room with mahogany paneled walls and shelves full of books. "I'm Mrs. O'Brien. Would you like some tea while you're waiting?"

After a day of drinking nothing but water from a whiskey bottle? Belle wanted to shout, "Yes! A cup of hot tea would be wonderful." She refrained, though, and managed a polite, "If it's not too much trouble, Mrs. O'Brien." She sat to wait for Yancy.

* * * *

No matter what happened, ordinarily Yancy remained at ease with the world, but by the time the carriage brought Richard and him home from the funeral, his spirits had sunk to an unfamiliar low. He'd just lost his mother and brother. Belle was gone forever. He couldn't begin to deal with Bernice. He'd told her he wouldn't stand in judgment, but the woman so disgusted him, he wanted nothing to do with her. At least she'd be gone soon, but come to think of it, so would he. Meantime, he'd remain polite and that was all. So Ronald had left him some money? Mr. Canfield expected he'd be overjoyed, but he couldn't care less. What would he do with a big inheritance? He lived a simple life and had more than enough for all his needs, which were simple at best. As for a job in the bank—God, no.

Now that the funeral was over, he was free to return home. He wasn't sure about the train schedule, but if not for Canfield's invitation, he could leave tomorrow. The next day then, only he probably wouldn't. What was wrong with him? Why couldn't he leave yet? For one thing, he worried about the children. Bernice said they'd be all right, but would they? Bernice was a selfish fool, so self-centered she couldn't see her children needed help, especially the boy. He'd need a lot more than Mrs. O'Brien, the maids, and the cook to remove that unspoken pain and sorrow from his eyes.

He and Richard climbed from the carriage and walked to the front door. He'd think about returning home tomorrow. As for now, he would do his best to shake this miserable mood he was in and have a pleasant dinner with Richard, and of course play chess.

Mrs. O'Brien let them in. "There's a lady waiting to see you in the library," she said.

"There is?" He couldn't imagine who.

"She says her name is Belle Ainsworth. She seems most anxious to see you."

* * * *

After she finished her tea, Belle couldn't sit still and began wandering around the library. Eventually, she was drawn to a large window that framed a clear view of San Francisco Bay and stood quietly watching the progress of a steamer headed for the Golden Gate. The library door opened. She turned toward it. Yancy stood in the doorway, his brow furrowed in puzzlement.

Her breath caught at the sight of him. "Hello, Yancy. I suppose you're a bit surprised to see me."

"Belle, is it really you?"

"Oh, it's me all right." She looked down at herself and frowned. "I look a mess."

He shut the door and walked toward her, still with that questioning look on his face. "What happened? Didn't you get married?"

"No, I did not."

"You didn't?" Now he looked astounded.

"It's good to see you, Yancy."

His face relaxed, and he started to laugh. "And it's good to see you, Belle. What happened? How did you get here?"

"It's a long story that you wouldn't believe."

"Try me."

They settled upon a settee, and she told him what happened after she left the ferry, beginning with her insulting reception when Robert, whose name was really Roberto, didn't meet her at the dock and sent someone else instead.

Yancy's mouth twisted wryly. "So that good-looking fellow with all that hair wasn't—?"

"No, he wasn't. That was Tony, his brother. He drove me home in real style, in a delivery wagon. It had a big sign on the side that read Romano Brothers Fish Company."

He tried to stifle a chuckle and failed. "Did it smell like fish?"

"Actually, it did." For the first time, she saw the humor of it all and couldn't suppress a giggle before she got serious again. "From there I went from bad to worse. I met his family, and they were fine, but when I met Robert, I knew in less than a minute I could never love him." She hadn't known Yancy long, but well enough to know he'd never understand why she simply didn't walk out, so she skipped the part about her inner struggle, how she'd agonized over whether she should simply flee or do the honorable thing and marry Robert anyway. She continued with her story: how finally she'd fled from the family home only an hour before the ceremony; how she found a good hotel and thought she was safe; how shocked she'd been upon discovering that little weasel, Bruno, had stolen her money; how she'd wandered the streets, penniless and alone, ending up on the notorious Barbary Coast where a drunken man had attacked her.

Yancy had listened with growing concern. "I'm almost afraid to ask. What happened next?"

"I'm pretty sure they'd have found my dead body in the weeds if a boy named Luther hadn't saved me. He was wonderful. He found me a place to stay for the night and in the morning brought me breakfast."

"So where did you stay?"

Belle hesitated. Who would believe it, but the truth was best. "An opium den."

Yancy, usually so unflappable, sat back in amazement. "Did I hear you right?"

"Yes, you did, but we didn't have a problem because the... I guess you could say *customers* were all just lying there and staring into space. I doubt anyone knew we were there. Luther knew of this vacant room on the second floor, so that's where we spent the night."

"Oh, my God, I don't believe this."

"But it was all right," she tried to reassure him. "I slept well, even if it was on the floor, and had a lovely breakfast in the morning that Luther collected from the garbage. Bread, an apple, some delicious crab legs, and some water." Seeing Yancy's appalled expression, she decided not to mention the Old Crow whiskey bottle. "I'm fine now, really. I came to you because I had nowhere else to turn." That wasn't strictly true. She could have gone to Mrs. Hollister, but the truth was, she'd yearned for Yancy. Pride prevented her from saying so, though. "I feel like a beggar, and I guess I am, but if you could loan me enough money to get home, I would repay you immediately, as soon as—"

"Of course you can have all you need." His eyes brimming with concern, he took both her hands in his and held them tight. "You're a brave woman, trying to make light of it, but it must have been a nightmare. I wish I'd been there to help."

"After I'd done a fine job of getting rid of you?"

"We'll discuss all that later. You'll be staying here, of course. There's more bedrooms than you can count in this place."

"How is your mother, Yancy?"

A flash of sorrow crossed his face. "She died last night."

"I am so sorry."

He nodded his thanks. "At least I got to say goodbye to her, and that means a lot." Obviously not caring to dwell on the subject, he looked around and spied her valise. "The housekeeper can help you get settled in. Where are the rest of your clothes?"

"The last I saw of them, they were still in my trunk. Unless he's moved it, my trunk is sitting in Robert's bedroom."

"Then we'll go get it."

She drew back in alarm. "Never! How could I face Robert after what I did? He must still be in a rage."

"Then you don't have to go. I will."

"But you can't."

"I can and I will. They're your clothes, aren't they? Do you think I'm afraid of your Robert Romano?"

She knew better than to argue. Yancy could be warm and congenial, but she'd never forget that steely, unyielding look in his eye the day he tangled with the Cooper Brothers and sent them packing. "Then I would be most grateful." An understatement if ever there was one. She was so sick and tired of the brown wool suit, she'd burn it at the first opportunity.

"Then it's settled." He started to say more, but Mrs. O'Brien knocked and came in the room. "Sorry to bother you, but Mrs. McLeish isn't here, and Cook wants to know how many for dinner."

"I don't know when Mrs. McLeish will be back," Yancy replied, "but Miss Ainsworth will be here for dinner. She'll be staying with us, so she'll need a bedroom."

If the housekeeper was surprised, she didn't let on. "I'll get to it right away. So two for dinner then?"

"Four. Let's not forget the children."

"But they don't usually—"

"They do now, Mrs. O'Brien."

"Fine then. I'll tell Cook."

Belle didn't fail to notice the little smile that crossed Mrs. O'Brien's face as she left the library. "So I won't be meeting Ronald's wife tonight?"

"Apparently Bernice has more important things to do."

How strange. What could be more important than her children? They had just lost their father. Why would their mother not want to be with them every minute? Belle didn't know all the circumstances, though, so she wouldn't dream of offering her opinion. "I shall very much look forward to dinner." A huge wave of relief swept through her. She was safe and secure now. With Yancy's help, she could return to Savannah, her family, her comfortable life. Her spirits soared, but the more she thought about it, the more they began to fall. Comfortable life? Or was it more like her boring, unexciting life where she'd be attending the bi-weekly meetings of the Georgia Ladies of the Confederacy for endless years into eternity. Where she'd be the poor relative again, living with a sister who resented her. Where she'd be sleeping lonely and alone in her spinster's bed for the whole remainder of her miserable life.

But wait. Now was no time to be brooding over her dismal future. She should count her blessings that she wasn't lying dead in the weeds, thanks to a brave young man who had no obligation to help her. She should be grateful for Yancy's support and ignore her unexpected letdown. How foolish she'd been to expect he'd immediately take her into his arms when he walked into the library. He'd obviously been delighted to see her and genuinely sympathetic to her ordeal. That was all, though. If she'd been counting on their one kiss beside the river to bring on a proposal of marriage, she'd been sadly mistaken. Yancy was attracted to her, but he, smart man that he was, had thought things through, which was a lot more than she had. He'd come to the very wise decision that their romance, or whatever it was, didn't have a chance. He lived in Maine and could hardly wait to get home. She lived in the Deep South and could hardly wait to get home, despite all her pessimistic thoughts. What if he did propose? She could not imagine herself living in a tiny cabin beside an isolated lake in the woods of Maine. Nor, she was sure, could he imagine becoming a Southern gentleman, engulfed in a culture of plantations and magnolia blossoms.

But she shouldn't be thinking of her future right now. She should be grateful that whatever was going to go wrong had already gone wrong. From now on, everything was going to be fine. Her father used to say, "The successful people in this world take life as it comes," and that's what she planned to do.

Chapter 14

Yancy couldn't remember a more enjoyable dinner, served by a maid in the large, elegantly furnished dining room. Belle couldn't have been more charming, despite the ordeal she'd been through. Both Beth and Richard acted as if eating in the dining room was a rare and special treat. "Don't you ever eat here?" Yancy had asked.

"No, sir, never, except Thanksgiving and Christmas," Richard replied. "Father always wanted us to, but Mother said no."

Yancy's opinion of Bernice dipped even lower. Judging from the fleeting expression of displeasure that crossed Belle's face, she felt the same. She loved children, he could tell. Instead of ignoring them, she'd given them extra attention all evening, making Beth giggle and Richard occasionally smile. Yancy still hadn't gotten over his astonishment that Belle had fled from her mail-order husband and found her way here. He could hardly keep his eyes off her. She'd claimed she was "a mess," but a very pretty mess as far as he was concerned. The brown wool suit needed pressing, but he liked how it clung to her curves. Her hair might be a bit disheveled, but that didn't keep him from wanting to reach out and brush back the little strands that had escaped her hair clasp and twisted around her delicate face. What a beautiful woman. Brave, too, although she modestly didn't think so. Spent the night in an opium den? Good Lord. He liked that she hadn't gone all hysterical, like a lot of women would have done, and had even laughed at the worst of her predicament. He would like to see more of her, but what was the use? She'd be gone soon, and so would he. And besides, since when did he need a woman in his life? Or anyone? He, Yancy McLeish, the man who wanted more than anything else to be left alone. Only...

An idea popped into his head. He looked across the table at her. "I suppose you'd like to leave for Savannah tomorrow."

"I suppose." She arched an eyebrow. "Unless? Did you have something in mind?"

"Matter of fact, I did. Leighton Canfield, the vice president of the bank, is taking me on a tour of San Francisco tomorrow afternoon. You're welcome to come along. That is, unless you're anxious to get back."

She didn't hesitate. "I'm not that anxious. I could wait a day or two."

"Fine, then, we'll do it." He spoke with just the right amount of casualness in his voice, as if he really didn't care whether she came with him or not. But the trouble was, he did care, and where all this was leading, he didn't know. "I'll be picking up your trunk in the morning. You might appreciate having something different to wear."

She didn't smile. "I suppose I should be grateful, but you know how I feel. Since it's during the day, I doubt Robert will be around, but you must be careful."

"Don't worry, I will." Of course, he'd be careful. He always was. But if she thought he couldn't handle a bully like Romano, she should think again.

* * * *

That night after dinner, Richard set up his bone-and-ivory chess set. To Yancy's relief, he soon remembered the fine points of the game. In the end, he won, but not before he discovered the boy had a keen mind and wasn't easy to beat. They could have played all night but had to stop when Mrs. O'Brien firmly announced, "It's way past the child's bedtime."

The boy was smiling as he said good night. "I enjoyed playing chess with you, Uncle Yancy. Do you suppose we can play again?"

"We certainly can, Richard. I enjoyed it, too." And he had. Times like this, he didn't even want to think about leaving.

* * * *

In the morning after breakfast, Yancy took Richard with him to the carriage house. Happy to be included, Richard had jumped at the chance when Yancy asked if he'd like to come along when he picked up Belle's trunk.

The housekeeper's husband, Linus O'Brien, a husky Irishman with a friendly, open face, served as both the gardener and stableman. After hearing the address, Mr. O'Brien said he knew exactly where it was and would be happy to help pick up the trunk. In the carriage house, he gestured to where three carriages—a high-flying runabout, gleaming black coach, and a brougham—were lined up side by side, reminding Yancy yet again of how wealthy his brother had become. Mr. O'Brien pointed at the brougham. "We'll take this one. There's room for you and Richard in the cab, and we can tie the trunk onto the back."

The address wasn't very far, and soon Mr. O'Brien, sitting upon the high seat in front, pulled to a stop in front of a large two-story house not far from Meiggs Wharf. "I know this area well," he called back to them. "The missus likes to come here to buy her fish." He hopped from the carriage, and Yancy followed.

Richard started to climb down, too, but Yancy stopped him. "Stay in the carriage. We won't be long." Not that he expected any trouble, but why take a chance? With Mr. O'Brien beside him, he walked to the front door and rang. A young woman with an abundance of dark hair answered. "Yes?"

Yancy introduced himself. "I've come to collect Miss Belle Ainsworth's belongings. That would be a trunk and anything else she might have left."

The young woman gasped. Her eyes went wide. "Is she all right?"

"She's fine, ma'am."

"I was so worried." The young woman looked swiftly behind her, stepped outside, and pulled the door shut. "I'm Rosa Romano, Roberto's sister-in-law. Did she mention me?"

"She did. You're the one who helped her."

"She was scared to death, and so was I."

"I suppose your brother-in-law was pretty upset."

"Are you joking? Upset is hardly the word. After Belle left, I went to the restaurant. By then, Roberto was getting impatient. I couldn't bring myself to tell him, but I didn't have to. He'd sent Lorenzo to check on her, and when Lorenzo came back…" Rosa squeezed her eyes shut a moment, as if to blot out a bad memory. "It was terrible. There we were at the wedding. Two hundred people—family, neighbors, friends, employees. The band, the flowers, the food. I cannot describe the look on Roberto's face when he found out Belle wasn't coming, but I would sooner have faced a grizzly bear or a shark in the ocean. I've never seen him in such a fury. He wasn't shouting or cursing or stomping around in a rage. It was just the opposite. He got very quiet—too quiet. Only his eyes gave him away, so full of rage and hatred I got a chill down my spine. By then, the guests had sat down to eat. He ordered everyone to leave in this low, awful voice that supposedly was calm, but I could tell he wasn't calm at all. Everyone—the band, waiters, guests, family had to go. I was glad to get out of there. The last I saw of him that night, he was standing with his fists clenched, about to explode. From what I heard later, when he finally left, he closed the door, locked it, and hasn't let anyone in since."

Yancy shook his head with sympathy. "I'm sorry you had to go through all that. I don't want to cause you any trouble. All I want is Belle's trunk and whatever else is hers. We'll be in and out in no time."

"I guess… Mama and Giana have gone out shopping. There's nobody home except me and the children."

"So Roberto isn't here?"

"Gone for the day, far as I know."

"I hope he's calmed down since then."

"No, he hasn't, and I doubt he ever will. It's a good thing you've come for her trunk. He said tomorrow he's going to put it in one of his boats, take it out to the deepest part of the sea, and dump it." She placed a hand over her heart and paused to catch her breath. "That's not all he said. He vowed to find Belle, put her in the trunk, and dump her, too. I can't say for sure he didn't mean it. So you can see why the whole family's upset. Roberto doesn't know where she is, but I'm scared to death just thinking what he'll do if he finds her."

Yancy was having second thoughts. "I don't want to get you into any trouble."

"Belle needs her clothes, doesn't she?" Rosa squared her shoulders. "You let me worry about Roberto. I'm his sister-in-law, not the woman who jilted him. He won't kill me when he sees the trunk is gone. At least I don't think he will." She opened the door wide. "Come in."

"Just show me where. We won't be long."

Yancy and Mr. O'Brien stepped inside. With a finger to her lips and a "shh," Rosa led them upstairs. No one in sight. She led them to Roberto's bedroom where they found the trunk. They picked it up and were halfway down the stairs when a voice came from below.

"Aunt Rosa, what are these men doing?" A boy with a smirking face stood at the bottom of the stairs.

Rosa uttered a curse under her breath. "You shut your mouth, Bruno. You didn't see a thing, understand?"

"Yes, Aunt Rosa, if you say so."

Yancy recognized a sarcastic reply when he heard one.

Rosa spoke again. "Pay no attention, Mr. McLeish. That's Bruno, my nephew." She threw a menacing glance in the boy's direction. "He won't tattle to his uncle because if he does, he'll have me to answer to."

Bruno made a face and disappeared. Rosa followed as they hauled the trunk to the brougham where Richard sat waiting. They tied it to the rack on the rear and were ready to leave when Rosa asked Yancy, "So Belle is really all right?"

"She's fine now and plans to return to Savannah as soon as she can." A pang of regret shot through him. He must get over that.

"Well, give her my love, will you? She made the right decision." Rosa cast a leery look at the house. "Sorry about Bruno. The little weasel will probably tell Roberto everything. I don't worry for myself, but I want Belle to be safe."

"She will be," Yancy answered confidently. "Roberto has no idea where Belle is staying. She'll be gone soon anyway."

"Fine then. I won't worry." Rosa waved a goodbye and returned to the house. On the way home, Mr. O'Brien entertained them with fond memories of his employer. "You'd never find a finer man than Ronald McLeish. Always a smile on his face and an outstretched hand willing to help."

Richard clung to every word he said and asked for more. Yancy was glad he'd brought the boy along. This was just what he needed, to get out in the world and talk to people, instead of sitting and brooding in his room.

They reached the house. Turning the horses into the driveway, Mr. O'Brien had to come to a near-complete stop. Richard had been looking out the window. "Did you see that?" he asked.

"See what?"

"There was a boy riding on the back. I saw him jump off and run away."

Mr. O'Brien chuckled. "I wouldn't worry, It's one of the street kids. They're always hitching rides."

"This wasn't a street kid," Richard solemnly replied. "I saw him at the house where we got the trunk. He was sort of sneaking out the front door."

Bruno. Had to be the thieving little weasel. No doubt he'd tell Roberto, but no sense spreading an alarm. "I don't suppose the boy did any harm," Yancy said. "He was probably just hitching a ride."

* * * *

Belle kept telling herself not to worry. If ever there was a man who could take care of himself, it was Yancy McLeish. At first, she kept herself busy by writing a long letter to Bridger in which she described the train robbery, her harrowing escape from the terrible Roberto, and her amazing night in the opium den. Bridger was always on her mind, and she especially wanted him to understand why she couldn't marry Robert Romano. When the letter was done, she could find nothing else useful to do and began looking out the drawing room window, hoping for Yancy and Richard's safe return from the Romanos'. And the trunk, too. She could hardly wait. Even though she'd protested and told Yancy not to go, she'd be overjoyed to see her clothes again.

As she looked out the window, a coach with a driver dressed in gold-buttoned livery stopped in front. An attractive woman in her thirties descended, leaving a well-dressed man waiting in the coach. Judging by the servants' excited murmur and scurrying footsteps, this had to be Bernice. She wasn't in black, though, and instead was wearing a stylish blue gown with a bustle decorated with a huge blue velvet bow. *How awkward*, Belle thought. Should she present herself to the widow of Ronald McLeish? Should she wait until spoken to? Bernice solved her dilemma by immediately sweeping into the drawing room and studying her with an icy gaze. "Mrs. O'Brien said you were here," she commented, none too cordially. "May I ask who you are?"

"My name is Belle Ainsworth, and I'm from Savannah. I'm a friend of Yancy McLeish. I shall be leaving shortly." She could have said more, but Bernice's snooty attitude put her off.

The icy gaze grew icier still, if that was possible. "So you're leaving today?"

"Tomorrow." She would not say one more word than she had to.

"Is Yancy here?"

"No."

"Do you know where he's gone?"

"He and Richard are out on an errand."

Bernice breathed a sigh of annoyance. "My friend and I will be leaving for Europe tomorrow. I've already sent my trunk ahead, but I thought I'd say goodbye to the children before I left. Too bad Richard's not here, and Yancy, too. If they don't get back soon, will you tell them goodbye for me? I'll run upstairs and say goodbye to Beth."

Bernice exited the drawing room, leaving Belle staring after her with amazement. She would never understand a woman like that. How could she leave her children? At least little Beth was home, but would Richard get back in time to say goodbye to his mother? Belle spent the next few minutes anxiously peering out the window.

They didn't make it. Soon Bernice was back down the stairs again and out the door. Belle stood away from the window. She didn't even want to look at a woman so despicable she'd leave her children. Although she was practically a stranger and shouldn't interfere, she had to know how Beth was doing. She left the drawing room and encountered Mrs. O'Brien on the stairs. The housekeeper grimly shook her head. "I hope you're on your way to see Beth. She needs some attention right now. Perhaps you could read to her like her father used to do."

When Belle entered Beth's room, she found a disconsolate little girl sitting in a child's rocking chair hugging a doll. "Hello, Beth," she quietly said. "Do you remember me from dinner last night? I told you about my niece, Ellen, who's the same age as you."

Beth stared up at her, her big blue eyes glistening with tears. "I remember."

"I used to read to her a lot, and I'd like to read to you, too. Would you like that?" After a solemn nod from Beth, she looked around the room and found a shelf stacked with books. "What have we here?" She picked up a book and read the title. "*Cinderella and the Glass Slipper.* That's one of Ellen's favorites." She picked up another book. "*Puss in Boots.* Ellen liked this one, too. Which do you like the best?"

"Cinderella," the little girl mumbled.

"Good. That's my very favorite." She spied a large rocking chair, probably where Ronald used to sit, and settled into it. "Would you like to sit on my lap? Then we could look at the pictures together."

The little girl came willingly and snuggled into Belle's lap. She didn't say a word but followed closely as Belle began to read. "'Once upon a time there was a beautiful girl called Cinderella and she had two ugly stepsisters who were very unkind and made Cinderella do all the hard work....'"

Beth quietly listened as Belle read clear to the end. "'And then there was a happy wedding. Everyone who had gone to the ball was invited, even the ugly stepsisters. And the prince danced every dance with Cinderella. He would not dance with anyone else.'"

Belle put the book down. Beth looked up and asked, "What happened to the ugly sisters?" Her tears had dried.

"They decided to not be unkind anymore, so they found good husbands, too."

Holding the child close, seeing her smile, feeling the warmth of her, Belle was engulfed in a rush of emotions that made her throat ache. This sweet little girl didn't deserve to be hurt and it must never happen again. She so reminded Belle of the child she'd always wanted but would never have. A return to Savannah meant the end of her dreams. She'd make the best of it, though, like she always did.

Yancy and Richard arrived home shortly after. Yancy found her still in Beth's room. "We got the trunk," he said.

Belle wanted to hug him but settled for a heartfelt "thank you." She led Yancy back to the drawing room where she told him about Bernice, and how quickly she'd come and gone. Although tempted to express her low opinion of a woman who would run off and leave her children, she knew she didn't have to when Yancy's eyes flashed with anger. He didn't lash out at Bernice, though. Instead, he thought a moment and said, "I'd like to take the children along when Mr. Canfield takes us on that tour."

"I think that's a fine idea."

"Good. It's settled then." After a pause, he continued, "There's something you should know." He told her about his talk with Rosa, and how she feared Robert Romano might try to harm her. He went on to describe how Richard had spied a boy who had hitched a ride on the back of their carriage, a boy he was sure was Bruno. "So by now Roberto knows where you're staying."

Oddly enough, she wasn't the least worried, maybe because she so trusted Yancy to protect her. "I appreciate your telling me, but Roberto doesn't scare me."

He nodded approvingly. "And besides, you'll be going home soon anyway."

His words stabbed at her heart. Yancy had been wonderful to her. Generous, compassionate, and caring. But the thing that hurt was, he hadn't tried to talk her out of leaving. Obviously, he didn't want her to stay. But how foolish could she get? He, too, was going home, back to his beloved cabin in the woods where he could be alone. So there was nothing she could do. She would certainly not throw herself at him and make more of a fool of herself than she already had. She looked forward to the outing this afternoon, but tomorrow she would buy her return ticket to Savannah.

* * * *

Belle had informed Mrs. O'Brien she'd take care of getting Beth dressed for the outing. They had fun picking a dress from the little girl's full closet. "Father liked to buy me dresses," said Beth, all smiles as she stood before the mirror admiring herself in her pink dimity dress with lace frills and a silk sash that encircled her waist and tied in a large bow in the back.

Belle was more than happy to help. The children truly needed an outing. Mrs. O'Brien had reported that Richard had taken the news of his mother's departure in silence and had hardly spoken since.

For herself, Belle loved sorting through her trunk. How wonderful to have her clothes back! For the afternoon tour, she chose a royal-blue walking suit with a black flounce around the bottom and a small hat of dove grey.

Leighton Canfield arrived promptly at one o'clock. When told he'd have not one but four passengers, he jovially declared, "The more the merrier. It's a perfect day. You'll see San Francisco at its very best." He addressed Yancy. "Of course, you know my motive is to entice you to stay."

Yancy smiled agreeably but didn't reply. They settled themselves in the banker's luxurious coach with its top-hatted driver perched on a high seat in front. With six in the coach, seating was tight. Belle hadn't planned it, but she ended up next to Yancy, her thigh pressed against his. She could try to ease away, but if she did, he would notice, so she stayed where she was, acutely aware of the man who sat beside her. Had he noticed? A quick glance at his expressionless face told her he hadn't.

"To Woodward's Gardens," Canfield called to the driver.

Beth clapped her hands. Richard, who'd remained solemn faced up to now, actually smiled. "It's the zoo. Father used to take us there."

The "zoo" at Woodward's Gardens proved to be more of a small menagerie, but by the time they finished their stroll past the grizzly bear grottos, black swans, deer, and aquarium, Belle found herself in a surprisingly buoyant mood. Bridger once said, "All you really have is now." So true, and on a beautiful day like this, how could she not enjoy it? She loved being with these adorable children. How delightful to see them both smiling and having a good time. She loved being with Yancy. His quiet strength, his unconscious charm drew her like a magnet. Probably she'd never see him again after tomorrow, but only for today, she wouldn't look back, and she wouldn't look forward. All she had was now, and she'd make the most of it.

"Where next, Mr. Canfield?" she asked when they all piled back into the coach. She sat next to Yancy again, her thigh touching his, but this time she didn't think of pulling away. He'd made no effort to move away, either.

"We shall drive through Golden Gate Park," their host replied. "Then the best of all—Land's End and the Cliff House." He cast an inquiring glance at Yancy. "Like it so far?"

"You have a beautiful city, Mr. Canfield."

They drove through Golden Gate Park, admiring the thousands of recently planted eucalyptus, pines, and cypress trees. "It's only the beginning," bragged their congenial host. "Before long this park will be one of the finest in the nation."

The children showed only a mild interest in the park, but their excitement grew when they reached the Cliff House, a two-story rambling building that hung on the side of a cliff overlooking the sea. "We've never been here before," Richard said. "It used to be too far, but now they've got the toll road."

They went inside and looked out the windows. "What a view!" Belle exclaimed.

Richard pointed toward some tall rocks just offshore. "See? Those are sea lions."

Belle had never seen such a sight as the huge creatures sunning themselves on the jagged rocks. She could hear their loud honking.

Richard continued, "They're very big, you know. We studied them in school. Some weigh as much as eight hundred pounds. Have you ever seen them before, Uncle Yancy?"

"No, I haven't." Fondly, Yancy placed a hand on Richard's shoulder. "You know a lot for a boy your age."

Richard blushed with pleasure. "My father taught me a lot. He pretty much knew everything."

Belle and Yancy exchanged amused glances. She laughed to herself. They were acting like proud parents, finding pleasure in the unintended humor of their child.

When they finished looking at the sea lions, Mr. Canfield treated them all to ice cream. After that, he took them to the beach below the Cliff House where a number of people, mostly families, had gathered. Some simply sat on the sand looking out at the sea. Some had taken their shoes off and were wading in the surf. Children played in the sand.

"Ocean Beach it's called," Mr. Canfield said.

"Why is no one swimming?" Belle asked.

"Because of the riptides, but it's a fine beach anyway."

Soon, they all had their shoes off, excepting the dignified Mr. Canfield, who chose to remain fully clothed. They waded in the surf, the children giggling as they ran from the remains of a wave, and then chased it back again. "The water's freezing cold," Belle called, but she didn't care. She had to hold her skirt up but wasn't the least concerned Yancy might catch an improper glimpse of leg. How nice to see him so relaxed after what he'd been through. He'd rolled his pant legs up and was laughing as he romped with the children. Once, while holding Beth's hand, he grabbed hers, too, and she liked the feel of her hand in his.

For a while, they sat on the beach and talked while they kept an eye on the children. Once, when Belle gave a pensive sigh, Yancy asked what she was thinking about.

"Watching the children play reminded me of Luther," she replied. "He never had a childhood. Had to run away from home when he was twelve years old. I never had a chance to thank him properly, and that bothers me. Lord knows what would have happened if he hadn't come to my rescue. I wish I could find him. I'd want to do something to help him after all he did for me."

"Would he be so difficult to find?"

"Maybe not, but I'd hate to go back to that opium den."

The children ran up. Richard pointed toward the ocean. "Can I get to China from here?"

"Yes, you can," Yancy replied with a laugh. "It's just over the horizon and maybe a little bit more."

As the afternoon wore on, Belle grew more and more aware of Yancy, and by the time they were back in the carriage and on the way home, her body tingled with awareness of the long, hard, muscular body beside her. Neither by his words nor his actions had Yancy been other than a perfect gentleman, yet the heat of him flowed through her, stirring an aching hunger deep in the center of her being.

Richard and Beth had both fallen asleep. Mr. Canfield, pleased at the success of the outing, half dozed, his hands folded over his ample belly. Belle could almost laugh. Here she sat all ladylike, hands primly folded in her lap, expression a picture of unruffled serenity, when inside she yearned for the feel of Yancy's arms around her, the warmth of his lips on hers. She wanted him like she'd wanted no other man, not even Jeremy, whom she could hardly remember.

Thank God no one could read her mind. First thing tomorrow, she'd purchase her train ticket for home.

Chapter 15

After they returned from the outing, Yancy excused himself, claiming he needed a nap. What a joke; he never took naps. In truth, he needed to be alone for a while. Cool off. Get himself in hand after being close to Belle Ainsworth all afternoon. Sitting next to her, his thigh pressed against hers, he'd done his best to act as if he hadn't noticed. She would never have guessed how aware of her he was in every pore of his body—her nearness, the scent of her, the way she breathed. From the moment he saw her in the library yesterday, he'd been hard put to act as if he was just a friend. He hadn't forgotten that kiss by the river, how the heat had curled inside him, stirring to life a nearly forgotten hunger for a woman. Not any woman, though. He wanted Belle, and that was wrong for a whole lot of reasons. She would soon leave for Savannah, back to her beloved home and family. Any day now he'd be leaving for Maine, back to his cabin and the lake, the salmon, the loneliness. Was that really what he wanted? Somehow he was looking at things differently now. Just the same, he was wasting his time thinking about her and had better put her out of his mind.

Mr. Canfield had been invited to stay for dinner, and he graciously accepted. Now, as they all sat around the dinner table, Yancy remarked, "It was a fine day, Mr. Canfield. Your San Francisco is a beautiful city."

"Then you might consider staying for a while," the banker replied. "At any rate, you must come to the bank tomorrow. Ronald's attorney will be there." He threw a cautious glance at the children. "Certain matters need to be discussed."

The will. Yancy hadn't given it much thought, but for the children's sake, he'd better go. Now that he knew them better, and the kind of mother they had, he must make sure they were well provided for and that Ronald had taken the proper precautions. "Of course I'll come, Mr. Canfield."

So he wouldn't be leaving for home tomorrow after all. Perhaps the day after, although his need to return didn't seem quite so urgent anymore. Maybe that was because he really did have a fine day. What a pleasure to see Ronald's children happy and enjoying themselves, a blessing after what they'd been through. Belle had been a big help. On the train he'd recognized her natural love of children and her gift for making them smile. She'd used that gift with Richard and Beth, drawn them out of their gloom and transformed them into the two happy children he saw today. She'd make some man a fine wife, be a great mother. Whoa, he didn't like that idea. The thought of her being with another man was like a kick in the gut. There he went, thinking about Belle again. What was wrong with him?

The boy was talking to him, and he hadn't been listening. "What did you say, Richard?"

"I asked if you'd like to play chess later on."

"Of course I would." He enjoyed playing chess with Richard. And besides, he needed something to get his mind off Belle Ainsworth, if that was possible, and he was beginning to think it wasn't.

* * * *

It was late. After a pleasant evening, everyone had gone to bed. The day had been so full that Belle expected she'd fall asleep the moment her head hit the pillow, but that didn't happen. All Yancy's fault. She couldn't stop thinking about him, and that wasn't only stupid and foolish, it was a waste of time and would lead nowhere. Perhaps she could find something to read in the library. She highly doubted Bernice was much of a reader, but even so, perhaps she'd find something by Jane Austen or the Bronte sisters. She got out of bed and threw on her white lace peignoir, the one meant for her wedding night with Roberto. What a horrible life she would have had if she'd gone through with it. Thank God she'd made the right decision. The house was middle-of-the-night quiet. She lit a candle and placed it in a brass candleholder. Raising it high, she slipped downstairs and into the library. Where to look? Bending over a shelf full of books, holding the candle close, she was examining the titles when Yancy's voice so startled her that her heart jumped and she whirled around.

He stood in the doorway. "Belle? Looking for something to read?"

She slammed her hand to her chest. "You startled me."

"I saw your door was open and came looking for you."

"I couldn't sleep." *Because of you.* "So I thought I'd find a good book."

He came in the library and shut the door. In the dim light of the candle she could see he was still dressed. "You're up late."

"I was playing chess with Richard. And then..." He threw up his hands, as if to admit defeat. "I couldn't sleep, either."

The thin edge of a tremor in his voice told her this was not going to be an ordinary conversation. Nor did she want it to be. The time for meaningless chitchat was over. Maybe the truth came more easily in the middle of the night, in the darkness, when all the pretenses of the day were stripped away. In a clear voice, she asked, "What do you suppose it means when we both can't sleep?"

A moment passed as the meaning of her words sunk in. Swiftly, he crossed the room, took the candleholder from her hand, and set it down. With a deep breath, he cradled her face in his hands and gazed deep into her eyes. "Ah, Belle, you have no idea...."

An overwhelming burn of desire flowed through her. "No idea? Of course I do." She leaned toward him and placed her hands on his shoulders, hearing a little moan that must have come from her. He slid caressing hands beneath the white lace peignoir, pulled her close, and met her lips with a searing kiss that took her breath away. They swayed together, she didn't know how long, until, with a ragged breath he broke away. "Upstairs," he said, and picked up the candle.

* * * *

Exhausted and content, Belle lay in Yancy's bed, her head on his chest, cherishing the steady beat of his heart against her ear. He held her close, stroking her hair. Raising his head, he pressed a kiss on her forehead. "Any regrets?" he asked.

"None whatsoever." She ran her hand through the dark tangle of hair on his chest. "It was bound to happen, and we both knew it."

He laughed aloud, a delighted, carefree kind of laugh she'd never heard from him before. "I came here to say goodbye to my mother. You're the last thing in the world I expected."

She joined in his laughter. "I came here to marry Robert Romano. You're the last thing in the world *I* expected." She'd forgotten passion could feel like this, if she'd ever known in the first place. And, really, she hadn't. The awkward fumblings of her long-ago beaux couldn't begin to compare to Yancy's tenderness and caring. But where would it lead? The words, *what do we do now?* formed on her lips, but she didn't say them. To ask such a question, she'd be breaking this marvelously satisfied mood she was in, and she didn't want it to end.

He wrapped his arms tight around her. "You don't have to go home tomorrow, do you?"

At this point, she wouldn't leave San Francisco if they paid her. She still had her pride, though, and would give him the most honest answer she could. If only her heart were speaking, her answer would be, *Marry me, Yancy McLeish. I want to spend the rest of my life with you.* But he hadn't said he loved her, let alone proposed, and until he did, she wasn't about to make a fool of herself. "I'll stay another day or two. I think the children will be pleased, and I don't believe Bernice would mind, do you?"

He hoisted himself up on one elbow and looked down at her. "Actually I own the house now, so to hell with what Bernice thinks. And, yes, I wouldn't mind in the least if you stay a few extra days." He bent his head and covered her forehead and cheek with kisses. "Not in the least."

"So it's settled then." She pulled away from him and swung her legs from the bed. "It's practically dawn. I'd better get back to my room before the servants get up."

She blew him a kiss. He blew one back. Her heart welling with happiness, she pulled on the white lace peignoir and slipped back to her room. Yancy loved her. He hadn't said so yet, but she knew. When she reached her room, she fell into bed and wrapped her arms around the pillow. Tomorrow she'd write another letter to her family. Better yet, she'd send a telegram to Savannah. She'd confess to hitting a little glitch, but things were working out after all, much better than expected.

* * * *

The next morning, Belle woke up to a whole new world. Was it only yesterday she was dreading the I-told-you-sos she'd receive when she returned to Savannah? What a difference a night made. She'd assumed she was doomed to spinsterhood, paying for her disaster with Robert for the rest of her life, but was she wrong? Could it be she'd found a man she was mad about, and, if she wasn't mistaken last night, a man who was mad about her? *Mrs. Yancy McLeish.* She liked the sound of it, liked everything about him. *Loved* everything about him. They might have to resolve a few minor problems, such as where they would live, but when two people loved each other, all things were possible. She could think of nothing that could ever keep them apart.

She didn't see Yancy until she got to the breakfast table and found him already there with the children, both of them bright eyed and cheerful. It was plain to see that yesterday's outing had done them a world of good.

"Good morning, Belle." Yancy's dark eyes brimmed with such love and tenderness she knew she hadn't been mistaken about last night.

"Good morning to you all." Happiness engulfed her as she slid into her a place. "It's going to be a lovely day."

Richard spoke up. "Uncle Yancy's going to the bank this morning."

"Something about Ronald's affairs," Yancy said quickly. "Shouldn't take long."

Yancy had mentioned the will, and that his brother had left him the house. Such a matter definitely should not be discussed in front of the children, especially when Bernice had to be involved. Belle addressed Richard and Beth. "We'll find something to do while your uncle's gone. Maybe a game?" She grimaced in good humor. "As long as it isn't chess. I used to play with my brothers, but they always beat me, and I finally gave up."

"I've a better idea," Richard said. "While Uncle Yancy's gone, I'll show you some things that belonged to my father."

"I'd love to see them."

After Yancy left, Richard led Belle to the library where he opened a desk drawer and pulled out a strange-looking object that partly looked like a pair of binoculars, but as for the rest, she was mystified. "It's a stereoscope." Richard laid it carefully on the desktop. "There's a lens for each eye. Then this handle sticks out, and you clip a picture at the end of it. It's really two pictures exactly the same, but when you look through the lenses, you see only one, but it's three-dimensional and looks really real."

She picked up the device and examined it curiously. "How clever. Do you have any pictures I could look at?"

"Father had all sorts of them. A lot are of Uncle Yancy when he was in the army."

"Then I'd very much like to see them."

Richard pulled a box filled with pictures from one of the shelves and began to sort through. "Did you know he served under General Sherman? He was on Sherman's march to the sea. That's when they took Atlanta." From the box, he pulled a long, rectangular picture which was actually two identical pictures side by side. He clipped them in place in the stereoscope. "Here he is with General Sherman himself. Take a look."

A sickening knot began to form in Belle's stomach. She didn't want to look, but it would hurt Richard's feelings if she didn't. She took the device and held it to her eyes. She had to focus carefully, but when she did, how remarkable. The two men standing by a horse looked so real she could reach out and touch them. One, obviously the general, wore a long frock coat with fringed epaulets, a gold sash, and two rows of brass buttons down the front. The other—tall, dressed in an officer's uniform but without all the gold—was Yancy McLeish. He was smiling. The general was smiling.

"That was the day the general gave my uncle the Distinguished Service Medal." Pride filled Richard's voice as he continued, "He was a hero, not only in the Battle of Atlanta but the Battle of Savannah, too."

"He fought in the Battle of Savannah?"

"Oh, yes, I'll show you." Richard took another double picture from the box and fitted it into the stereoscope. "Here's Uncle Yancy on the way to Savannah. See the men in the background? They're celebrating because they'd just dug up some railroad tracks, heated 'em up, and wrapped 'em around a tree. Did you know they called them Sherman's Neckties?" He handed the device to her. "Here, Miss Ainsworth, take a look. Uncle Yancy doesn't like to talk about it, so I'd wager you didn't know what a hero he was."

"Thank you, Richard." Shock had caused her words to wedge in her throat, but somehow she'd got them out. She didn't want to look, but this boy had suffered enough and she wouldn't hurt his feelings for the world. She pressed the stereoscope to her eyes. There stood Yancy in his Union Army uniform, and in the blurry background, a group of soldiers were in the midst of wrapping a railing around a tree. That picture could have been taken on the same day Bridger came home on a one-day leave. She'd never seen him cry before, but that day he did. "It's over, Belle," he'd said through choked tears. "The whole countryside is in ruins. People starving. All our food and livestock stolen. They even dug up the railroad tracks...." He could not go on. She'd joined in his tears. Father, Gregory, Jeremy, all of them dead now, and it had all been for nothing.

The next day, Bridger went back to the battle, lost his arm, and sustained the wound from which he'd never recover.

Richard stared at her with concern. "Is something wrong? You look strange."

She forced her lips into a smile. "Nothing's wrong. I'm feeling a little light-headed. I'd like to see all your father's pictures, but right now I'd better go lie down."

She turned, discovering her knees had gone weak. With a determined effort, she managed to walk from the library without gripping the furniture for support. Holding tight to the bannister, she climbed the stairs to her room. With a moan, she collapsed on the bed on her back, an arm flung over her eyes. So Yancy was one of them. She'd known he'd been in the Union Army but had never asked what he did, where he fought. She'd been a coward not to ask, and that was because she'd known in her heart she could never forgive a man who fought against her father and her brothers, who'd helped ruin the land she loved.

But now that she knew...

How could she forgive him? How could she marry him? How could she bring him home to meet her friends and family? The bitter anguish of defeat still lived in the heart of every Southerner. She could only imagine the reaction when she announced, "Meet my new husband, one of those Yankees who fought with General Sherman and brought death and destruction to Savannah."

Belle groaned aloud. No way out. She must have nothing more to do with Yancy McLeish. She must pack her valise and flee, as she'd done with Roberto. Not a good idea, though. For one thing, she had no money, so she'd be penniless on the streets again, a fate worse than death, as far as she was concerned. For another, running away had been a spineless thing to do, even though she'd feared Roberto's wrath, and rightfully so. Yancy wouldn't harm her. He'd been nothing but kind to her and deserved an explanation. So she would not take the coward's way out this time. She still loved Yancy McLeish. That would never change. Facing him, telling him she was leaving and never wanted to see him again would be the hardest thing she ever had to do. She'd do it, though. She had no choice.

Numb from the shock, she waited for Yancy to return home.

Chapter 16

Yancy wasn't fond of banks and dealt with them only when he had to. Today was different. Sitting in Mr. Canfield's office, he'd learned from Ronald's attorney, Mr. Frederick Bartlett, the details of his inheritance. His brother had left him a considerable amount of money, most of it invested in stocks and bonds that Mr. Bartlett claimed would reward him with "top-notch returns" and give him "a more than comfortable living for the rest of his life." Yancy would also receive the house, furnishings, and all the carriages. The children were well provided for with trust funds. "As is Mrs. McLeish," Mr. Bartlett added with a fleeting expression of distaste. "When everything's settled, your brother's investments will be transferred to your name. I understand you'll be leaving San Francisco? In that case, I can deposit the dividends to your bank in Maine, if that's what you prefer. Also, if you decide to sell the house, I can help you with that, too. Just let me know what you want to do."

Only days ago, Yancy would have gone along with the solicitor's suggestions. Deposit the money in his bank. Sell the house. Get out of San Francisco and head for home. Belle had changed all that. How had he been so lucky? He wasn't sure what love was, but if it meant wanting to share his life with her, take care of her, be the father of her children, then love it was. So much remained unsettled, but nothing so difficult that he and Belle couldn't work it out together. That settled it. When he got home, he'd ask her to marry him. "Hold off on that, Mr. Bartlett. My plans have changed."

"Not a problem. I know Leighton Canfield has offered you a position with the bank. Are you interested?"

No, he was not interested in working in a bank nor would he ever be. As for staying in San Francisco, he must talk to Belle. He had no idea where they'd live. All that mattered was they'd be together. "I'll let you know, sir, soon as I know."

With a lift to his step, Yancy left the bank. Funny, he never expected to feel such happiness again. If he'd thought about it at all, the most he'd hoped for was to live in peace in his cabin by the lake until the day he died. It would be a lonely life but free of the inevitable problems that arose when he dealt with his fellow human beings. Except the Indians, of course, and that was because they didn't talk much and left him alone.

But now that he had Belle? He'd never felt like dancing a jig, but if he hadn't been standing in front of the Bank of the Golden Gate for the world to see, he might have done so. He could hardly wait to get home.

* * * *

The first thing Yancy saw when he opened the front door was Belle's valise sitting in the entryway. Why was it there? Before he could think of a reason, she appeared, looking as if she was dressed to go out. He gave her a smile and was about to hold out his arms when something about the expression on her face made him pause. "Is something wrong?"

"We need to talk. Let's go to the library."

This was not the warm and loving woman who'd shared his bed last night. Judging from her grim expression, this was a woman in the throes of some kind of a crisis. Wordlessly he followed.

Once they were inside the library, she shut the door and faced him. Misery filled her eyes. She had to gulp for air before she spoke. "I'm leaving."

It was like she'd punched him in the stomach. For several shocked seconds he stared at her. "What do you mean, you're leaving?"

"Just what I said. I'm leaving today. Now. I only stayed because I wanted to tell you in person and not sneak out like I did Roberto."

The pain hit so hard he had to close his eyes a moment to collect himself. "Well, I'm certainly grateful for that," he said, not suppressing a touch of sarcasm. "And would you mind telling me why?"

"You're angry and I don't blame you, especially after last night. This is hard." A tremor touched her lips. She was pale.

He could see she was struggling, but he needed to know. "Just tell me, Belle. You owe me that much."

"Of course I do." She drew herself up and took in a deep breath. "This morning Richard showed me some pictures. Poor child, he had no way of knowing how shocked I'd be. There you were with General Sherman, the two of you smiling. In the next, you were at the Battle of Savannah twisting railroad tracks around a tree. Seeing those pictures brought back more pain than you can ever imagine. Why didn't you tell me?"

"You knew I fought in the Union Army."

"Yes, I knew, and it's all my fault. I didn't ask what you did in the army because I didn't want to know. But now that I do..." She heaved a despairing sigh. "You're a Yankee. You destroyed Atlanta. At least you spared Savannah, but you starved us, killed us, and broke our hearts all the same. My friends, my family, they'd never accept you. I'd be an outcast if I married you, even though..."

Straight-faced, he'd listened, forcing himself to hear her out without a protest. "Even though what?"

"Even though last night was wonderful, and I'll never forget it."

"I love you, Belle. Today I was going to ask you to marry me."

"Please, stop." Her voice was shaking. "I can't take any more. Just let me go."

He would honor her request. He'd never been one to beg and plead, and he wouldn't start now. "Where will you go?"

"Do you remember Mrs. Hollister from the train?"

"How could I forget?"

"She'll take me in, I think."

"How will you get there?"

"I was hoping Linus would drive me."

"Of course. Do you have any money?" He knew she didn't.

"I don't have a penny."

"We can't have that." He pulled out his wallet and extracted three twenty-dollar notes. "Here, take these, more if you like."

"I can't."

"Take them for God's sake. It's a loan. What if Mrs. Hollister won't take you in? Do you want to be out walking the streets again?"

She carefully plucked one of the notes from his hand. "Twenty dollars is plenty. Put the rest away. I'll pay you back."

"Are you sure you want to leave? Perhaps if we talked—"

"I'm sure."

"Fine, then. If you're ready to leave, I'll go tell Linus."

She lifted her chin. "I'm ready."

"Goodbye, Belle." He turned and walked away, frozen in shock. He'd learned to be hard and tough in the army, and that training had served him well. Otherwise, he couldn't have managed to hide the raw hurt that welled inside him. She would never know how deeply she'd wounded him.

He'd get over it, though. Go back to Maine. Forget Belle Ainsworth ever existed.

* * * *

"Linus, are you sure you have the right address?"

Linus pulled the carriage to a stop. "This is it, the corner of Powell and California. We're on Nob Hill, Miss Ainsworth, where all the rich people live." He nodded toward an elaborate, four-story home up the street. "That's Leland Stanford's house."

Belle had known Mrs. Hollister was well off but never dreamed she lived in a house such as the one before her. Built in Victorian style, it had steep roofs and all sorts of towers and turrets, each decorated with fancy gingerbread trim. At least three stories high, it didn't compare with the fancy mansion up the street, but even so, it must have been built by someone very wealthy indeed. Painted a gloomy dark grey, it looked more forbidding than inviting. Had she made a mistake? Maybe she should have taken more than a mere twenty dollars from Yancy. If she had, she would have had enough for a hotel tonight, and tomorrow she could have bought a ticket for home. But pride had prevented her from making what probably would have been a wiser decision. Now here she was, a stranger come to beg for help from a crotchety old lady she hardly knew, and who could very well not even let her into the house, despite what she'd said. Too late now. "Please wait, Linus. I'm not sure I'll stay."

Belle climbed from the carriage. Her feet dragging, she walked up the steps to the leaded glass front door. She pressed the doorbell and heard a jangling ring inside. The door swung open. A stout, middle-aged woman in a maid's uniform peered out. "Yes? You wanted something?"

"My name is Belle Ainsworth. I'm a friend of Mrs. Hollister, and I'd like to see her."

The maid eyed her suspiciously. "A friend?"

"I met her on the train."

"Wait here."

Belle stood waiting, already wondering where she'd go next.

Time passed. Nothing happened. She was about to leave when a delighted voice called, "Belle? Is that really you?" Mrs. Hollister appeared in the doorway, actually smiling. "How nice to see you. Please, do come in."

Belle glanced toward the street. "I will, but first, I have a carriage and driver waiting, and it's got my trunk and—"

"You've come to stay? Wonderful! Have your driver bring your luggage in." Mrs. Hollister took Belle's hands in hers. "Oh, my dear, it's so good to see you again. You must catch me up on what happened and why you're here."

As might be expected, the inside of Mrs. Hollister's house was beautifully furnished with plush carpets and elaborate French-style furniture. Belle expected to be led to the drawing room, but instead, Mrs. Hollister invited her into what appeared to be the back parlor. The minute they sat down, a little snub-nosed dog with long ears and dark melting eyes jumped on the older woman's lap. "This is Tippet, my toy spaniel." She raised him up and snuggled her face against his silky coat. "Isn't he darling?"

"He certainly is." Was this the same old lady she'd met on the train? Belle could never have imagined she could be this warm and friendly.

Mrs. Hollister settled back in her chair, Tippet snuggled on her lap. "You must tell me what happened. I suspect it's something bad or you wouldn't be here."

Belle told her everything, starting with her dismay that Roberto hadn't met her when she arrived, and how everything got worse from there. When she indignantly remarked, "If I'd married him, he would have had me down at the wharf gutting fish," Mrs. Hollister couldn't hide her smile. Seeing the humor, Belle smiled, too, and before long began to look at the bright side of things, as much as she could, anyway. Losing Yancy had left a giant-sized hole in her heart that would never go away, but she may as well go on with her life and make the best of it. She described her escape from Roberto and how a homeless boy named Luther came to her rescue. Her listener's mouth dropped open when she said, "Then he took me to an opium den where I spent the night." She finished by explaining how Yancy had taken her in but was careful to give the impression they'd been just friends, and she didn't want to impose on him any longer.

"So that's what happened. I want to go home to Savannah but need to earn some money first. So when I remembered you asking me to be your companion, I was hoping...?"

"I'm so glad you came to me." Mrs. Hollister smiled thoughtfully. "As of right now, you're hired. Would twenty dollars a week be satisfactory?"

A vast wave of relief swept through her. In four weeks she'd have earned enough to go home. "That would be fine, as long as you know it's only temporary. What does a companion do?"

"Well, let's see. I hope you like dogs."

"I love dogs."

"Then you will walk Tippet for me, and see that he's fed properly. We have a maid, but she's overworked, to say the least. I also have a son and daughter-in-law, but they don't like Tippet, which is fine with me. I wouldn't trust them anyway. Other than that... I'm so glad you're here, Belle. I do get lonely sometimes. I'd like someone to talk to."

"I'd get lonely, too, living by myself in a place as big as this."

Mrs. Hollister's mouth took on an unpleasant twist. "Unfortunately, I don't live alone. My son, Malcolm, and his wife live here, too. They moved in after my husband died. That was ten years ago, and they've been here ever since."

Belle made no further comment on the subject. It was easy to see her new employer wasn't happy with her son and daughter-in-law, but she wouldn't pry. "When will I meet them?"

"They're both out at the moment. I usually have dinner in my room, but tonight we shall dine with Malcolm and Eugenia."

So why didn't Mrs. Hollister dine with them every night? It seemed a bit strange, but she wasn't about to say so. "I shall look forward to meeting them."

The older woman stood, Tippet wrapped tightly in her arms. "It's time for my nap. I'll have the maid show you around and help you get settled. She complains a lot and is quite the gossip, but pay no attention. Bertha's been with me for years, and we get along fine."

"Will I sleep in the servants' quarters?" Belle asked.

"Certainly not. Bertha will show you the bedrooms. Choose any one you want that's not occupied. You'll like the house. When my husband was alive, he was always making improvements. If he heard of some new modern convenience, he had to have it."

Bertha turned out to be the unfriendly maid who'd opened the front door, and was none too pleased when asked to show Belle around the house. "All right, but I've got more than enough work to do," she complained to Mrs. Hollister. "You know how they are about their room."

Belle soon learned "they" referred to Malcolm and his wife. As Bertha showed Belle around the house, she further revealed her pent-up hostility. "Those two are always asking for extras," she grumbled. "Eugenia likes the sheets changed every day, and the bed made just so. She claims she's a humble servant, doing the work of the Lord. Material things don't matter, she says, but she spends money on herself like it was water. So does he, and it's all his mother's money. Of course, it's not my business. I only work here. You'll soon find out for yourself."

Belle kept her mouth shut. As she followed Bertha on the tour of the house, she marveled at all the modern conveniences. She had always believed her home in Savannah couldn't have been more up to date, but it paled in comparison to Mrs. Hollister's. Hot and cold running water in the kitchen and bathrooms, gas lighting in all the chandeliers and wall sconces. The place had so many bedrooms, two of them for children, that Belle lost count. "Mrs. Hollister keeps the children's rooms exactly like they were," Bertha said. "No one's allowed to change a thing." In one room, she pointed to an elaborate, perfectly preserved dollhouse. "If you look closer, you'll see it's an exact copy of this house, even down to the drapes, linens, and furniture."

"What happened to the little girl who lived here?" Belle asked.

"Little Charlotte died of diphtheria when she was ten. So did Dane, the younger boy, when he was six. Now poor Mrs. Hollister is left with Malcolm, who, in my opinion..." Bertha compressed her lips. "I'll say no more. It's not my place."

Belle didn't urge her to go on. Not her place to gossip either, but she couldn't help feeling sad for a woman who'd gone through so much sorrow in her life. After Bertha had shown her all the available bedrooms, she settled on a large room with a fireplace on the second floor. It overlooked the street and even provided a fine view of the bay. Furnished with a canopied bed, a French-style bureau, and thick carpeting, the room couldn't have been more charming, yet after Bertha left, Belle sank to the side of the bed and stared gloomily at the walls. She'd done all the right things. In a few weeks she'd be back with her family where she'd never have to worry about food, shelter, and worldly comforts again. But her heart ached for Yancy. What was he doing? Was he thinking about her? Had he simply put her out of his mind and forgotten her? But she'd walked out on him, and with good reason. What did it matter whether Yancy thought of her or not? They came from two different worlds and had nothing in common. She'd be crazy to think they could ever be together.

She must get him off her mind. At least, she'd have a distraction tonight when she'd meet Malcolm and his wife at dinner. She wasn't looking forward to it, though. Since she'd stepped through the door of this house, she'd sensed enmity and resentment in the air. Somehow she wasn't expecting a merry evening.

* * * *

That night, dinner was a formal affair, served by the cook in a dining room that could best be described as magnificent with its sparkling crystal chandelier, hand-carved Italian table, and walnut-and-marble sideboard that stood at least eight feet tall. Malcolm Hollister sat at the head of the table. In his late forties, of short stature, he carried an air of preciseness about him, from the meticulous trim of his goatee to his velvet-trimmed tailcoat that fit to perfection. When his mother introduced him to Belle, he gave her a perfunctory, "Delighted to meet you, Miss Ainsworth."

He didn't seem that delighted, but she returned a pleasant, "And I'm delighted to meet *you*."

"I understand you're to be my mother's companion?"

After Belle answered that she was, he proceeded to ignore her and launched into a description of his very important day, wherein he'd had pressing matters to attend to, something about investments and finances that he'd cleverly handled, all of it exceedingly boring.

Malcolm's wife, Eugenia, gave her even less of a friendly greeting, not much more than a nod and a grunt. Short, with a matronly figure, she wore a plain black dress, had a pudgy face, and thin, salt-and-pepper hair pulled straight back from her high, shiny forehead. *Awful*, Belle thought. The woman would look far better if she covered that forehead with bangs or ringlets. Eugenia didn't appear to care much what she looked like. She hardly said a word and seemed utterly absorbed in listening to her husband's description of his fascinating day. Only when he finally stopped talking did she address Belle. "Do you go to church, Miss Ainsworth?"

Surprised by the question, Belle took an extra moment before she replied, "Not lately." She could have explained she'd been a faithful member of Savannah's Trinity Methodist Church for as long as she could remember, but such an abrupt question was a bit off-putting and didn't deserve a detailed answer.

Eugenia pressed her lips together. "There are many churches in our city. Perhaps you'll try one, but if not..." She flicked a glance upward. "Proverbs 15:3: 'The eyes of the Lord are in every place, keeping watch on the evil and the good.'"

Belle had just taken a sip of water and nearly choked. "Well, I'll certainly remember that." After what she'd gone through, she wasn't too concerned about the eyes of the Lord. And finding a church hadn't been of the upmost importance in her mind, not nearly as essential as simply trying to survive.

Eugenia continued on, "I hold a prayer group in the drawing room every Tuesday afternoon. On Thursday, I host the ladies of the Total Temperance Union. You're welcome to attend." Her brows pulled together in an affronted frown. "Of course you'll have to come alone. It appears Mother Hollister is always too busy to come to either one."

Eugenia said no more, and went back to listening to Malcolm as he resumed his tedious discussion of the events of his day. Belle's mind soon wandered. Not until the cook was clearing the dessert plates did she feel Malcolm's sharp eyes upon her, and she focused on where she was again.

"So Miss Ainsworth, you're from Savannah?"

"Yes, I am, Mr. Hollister."

"And what brings you to our fair city?"

Ordinarily, she would have taken Malcolm's question as nothing more than a friendly inquiry, but the cold edge of his voice told her otherwise. "I came for a visit." She wasn't about to describe her disaster with Roberto.

"Hmm. So now you're my mother's companion?"

"That's correct."

"And she's paying you twenty dollars a week?"

"Yes." She was beginning to feel uncomfortable.

"For how long?"

"Malcolm!" Mrs. Hollister glared at her son. "That was a rude question."

A dark, angry expression flitted across his face. "I'm trying to save you some money, *Mother*. You're not helping."

Here came an unpleasant scene, Belle was sure of it. She braced herself for Edith Hollister's wrath. Surely she'd put her son in his place.

The older woman took her time answering. With a tremulous smile, she began, "My goodness, Malcolm, such a big to-do about nothing. You're right, of course, and I mustn't be so extravagant, but Belle is here only temporarily, and I do hope you don't mind."

"If it's only temporary." He gave his mother a condescending smile, as if he were talking to a child. "We shall make Miss Ainsworth welcome, but next time you want a companion, consult me first."

"Of course, dear."

An awkward silence followed, finally broken when Eugenia began to discuss her activities involving the church that day. Apparently, religion was her life, and she seemed to have no other topic of conversation. Belle breathed a sigh of relief when dinner was finally over. Pleading it was a long day and she was tired, she rose from the table and headed straight for the refuge of her room. She needed to be alone for a while, if for no other reason than to adjust her thinking. She didn't care for Eugenia at all. Had the woman even the slightest sense of humor? As for Malcolm, after his insolence and barely concealed hostility, she heartily wished she could tell him how disgusting she found him and march out the door, never to return. But that wouldn't be very practical. What a mess she'd gotten herself into. She would stay, of course. At this point, she had no choice but to put up with Malcolm and his equally obnoxious wife. She would ignore them as best she could, and, more importantly, be as good a companion as she could possibly be.

Poor Mrs. Hollister. Belle shook her head in surprise at discovering the strong, independent, imperious woman on the train had a spine that turned to jelly in the presence of her son.

* * * *

In the morning, Belle arose early and had hardly dressed when Bertha knocked on her door. "Come to make your bed." She wore her usual sour expression.

"I already made it, and will continue to do so. You don't have to bother."

Bertha's face brightened. "I wish they all felt like that. So I'll come in and dust a little." She entered and went to work with a feather duster. "So what do you think of the family?" she asked.

Belle recognized an invitation to gossip, but she wasn't interested. "It's too early to say, and besides, it's not my place to pass judgment on anyone."

"Maybe not, but you'll soon get your fill of Malcolm, if you haven't already. Eugenia, too." Bertha stopped her dusting and sniffed with indignation. "Makes my blood boil, the way he treats his mother. He's stealing her money, you know."

"No, I didn't know."

Bertha bobbed her head firmly. "He's taken over her finances. Wormed his way in, from what I hear. Convinced her she was too old and senile to know what she's doing, and out of the kindness of his heart, he's handling her money for her. She loves him of course, but she's afraid of him, too. He dominates her completely, what with all that talk about what a big, important man he is. Well, he's not. He's crooked as they come. I'd wager that's why she takes all those trips to New York. She wants to get away from him."

"That's terrible." Despite herself, Belle couldn't help but be interested. "You said he's stealing her money?"

"Ha! By the fistful." Bertha put down her feather duster, came close, and spoke softly. "Malcolm plays the part of the successful entrepreneur.

Thinks he's one of the robber barons like Charles Crocker or Mark Hopkins. Well, he isn't. He's a swindler. Cons innocent people with his crooked deals, all of them financed with his mother's money."

Belle had heard enough. Mrs. Hollister wouldn't appreciate her listening to such personal gossip, even if it was true. "I appreciate you telling me all this, Bertha, but it's not my business, and if you don't mind, I don't want to hear any more."

"That's your choice." The maid didn't appear offended. "But if you're smart, you'd better watch out for the both of them. They don't want you here. Eugenia's as bad as he is, what with all that religion she's always spouting. According to her, we're all going to hell if we don't get to church each Sunday. But believe you me, she's no saint herself. She's greedy as they come. If she and Malcolm had their way, they'd keep his poor mother locked in her room. I don't like saying it, but they're just waiting for her to die so they can get their hands on this house and the rest of her fortune. She doesn't have any friends anymore, and they like it that way. I'd wager they weren't too happy when they found out she'd hired a companion. Am I right?"

She was indeed right, but it was definitely time to end this kind of conversation. "It's not my place to say. What time is breakfast?"

The glum maid got the hint. "Eight o'clock. Mrs. Hollister likes to have breakfast alone, before the two of them get up. It'll be nice she has someone to eat with."

* * * *

In the dining room, Belle's new employer greeted her with a smile. "Malcolm and Eugenia sleep late most of the time, so I've taken to eating by myself. Did you sleep well?"

Belle said she had. They chatted pleasantly, and had nearly finished breakfast before her employer sighed and remarked, "About last night. Malcolm can be a bit abrupt sometimes, but you mustn't mind it."

Belle hastened to say she hadn't minded in the least and hardly noticed. Sometimes a small white lie couldn't be avoided.

Mrs. Hollister wasn't finished. "Perhaps I coddle Malcolm too much, but I can't help it. He had a terrible childhood. He was a frail child, and sickly. When he was five, he got whooping cough and nearly died. Then scarlet fever, and again I thought I'd lost him. If that wasn't bad enough, he lost his brother and sister to diphtheria. I admit he's a bit spoiled, and

I know he's helped himself to some of my money, but I truly believe he has my best interests at heart. Perhaps I should be more stern with him, but try as I might, I can't seem to deny him anything."

Belle recognized the earnest plea behind her employer's words: *Please try to put up with my son, even though he's a rude, sarcastic bully and a thief.* "Don't worry, Mrs. Hollister, I'll be here for only a short while, but while I am here, my only concern will be that I can be of service, and in some way brighten your day." She chuckled and added, "I want you to feel I'm worth that twenty dollars a week."

Mrs. Hollister looked relieved and gave her a delighted smile. "I'm sure you will be, Belle. Are you through with breakfast? If you are, I'd like for you to walk the dog. Come to think of it, my rheumatism isn't too bad today, so I'll come along."

During the days that followed, Belle yearned for home, yet she'd resigned herself to the wait and easily fell into the routine of the household. After that first night when they all ate in the dining room, she took her meals with Mrs. Hollister either in the back parlor or her bedroom. During the day, she made herself as inconspicuous as possible, mostly staying by her employer's side, reading to her, or simply chatting. They laughed a lot, played with Tippet, and got along fine. Once, her employer sighed and remarked, "I shall surely miss you when you're gone, my dear. I didn't realize how empty my life had become until you came along."

"But surely you have friends," Belle said.

"When my husband was alive, we had dozens of friends. We went to parties and threw parties of our own all the time. Even though we'd lost two children, after a time we were able to put aside our grief and entertain again. This house was full of fun and laughter, although it's hard to believe now, isn't it? And then, when Gerald died…" Mrs. Hollister heaved a sigh. "That's when Malcolm and Eugenia moved in. He's much too occupied with making money to even think of entertaining. As for her…" Mrs. Hollister's face went grim. "I despise that woman and her self-righteous blather about how we're all doomed if we don't go to church on Sunday. According to her, it's a sin to drink alcohol, dance, and you'd better not laugh too much. The house was bright and sunny until she came along. Now she keeps the drapes drawn so the sun won't ruin the furniture and carpet. *Her* furniture and carpet, mind you, and that's because she thinks of me as dead already and treats me that way. Well, her fondest wish will soon come true. At my age, I face the fact I can go anytime. Many of my friends are dead already. Not all, though. What friends I had, she's driven away with her talk about how we're going to hell unless we do exactly as she says. I avoid her as much as possible, even if it means I'm keeping to my bedroom and the back parlor."

"Maybe your son could speak to her?"

"Ha!" Mrs. Hollister's face grew red. "What does Malcolm care? He's much too busy throwing my money away to concern himself with what his wife does."

Belle couldn't keep the look of surprise off her face.

Her employer shrugged wearily. "I'm sure the servants have already tattled. Told you what a scoundrel he is, and how he's stealing my money. I know Malcolm is not, shall we say, taking as good a care of my investments as he should, but he's my son, and I love him, so what can I do?"

Get a backbone and throw him out, Belle longed to say, but not a good idea. Her employer was waiting for a response, though. She thought a moment. "Mrs. Hollister, nothing in the world is stronger than mother love, and a few words from me won't ever change that. All I can say is there might come a day when you see your way clear to what's to be done, and you'll do it. Or maybe the day will never come. It's as simple as that, and meantime, you shouldn't worry. Malcolm doesn't bother me, and neither does Eugenia. And another thing—I think that's nonsense about how you could die at any moment. You look pretty healthy to me, and I'd wager you won't be leaving this earth anytime soon. So let's simply enjoy our time together and stop fretting about what may or may not happen, what do you say?"

Just then Tippet gave a sharp bark and jumped into his mistress's lap. She shook her head in regret as she gathered the little dog in her arms. "On the train I wasn't very nice to you."

"No, you weren't."

"It was only because my life was miserable, and I shouldn't have—"

"Don't you dare apologize. What's past is past. Let's take Tippet for a walk, shall we?"

"A lovely idea."

Chapter 17

Each day Yancy told himself that tomorrow he would make his train reservation for home, but each day something came up that gave him an excuse to delay. For one thing, he couldn't face leaving the children. Bernice had assured him they'd be well cared for. Yeah, sure. Mrs. O'Brien would be here. The maids. The cook. But who would tuck little Beth in at night and read her a story? Richard had his private school, and that was fine, but who would play chess with him and encourage his sharp mind to grow? The servants did their best, and he couldn't fault them, but the children loved their uncle Yancy, and he loved them. How could he leave when only he could give them the love and encouragement they needed?

And then there was Belle.

He'd told himself to forget her. As yet, that hadn't happened, nor was it likely to. She lived in his head, especially in the middle of the night when she was back in his bed again, in his arms, and nothing in his life had ever been so wonderful. He would see her again. How that would happen, he had no idea, but did he need to know? Linus had told him where she'd gone. Maybe he'd appear at her doorstep and…what? What could he say that hadn't been said? The past was the past. Nothing he could do would change it, nor would he wish to. He'd think of something, though, he was sure of it.

The answer to his dilemma came one evening when he and Richard were playing chess, which they did nearly every night now. Richard was moving his queen when out of the blue, he remarked, "I wonder what Miss Ainsworth is doing. I really miss her."

Yancy's heart skipped a beat at the sound of her name. "Perhaps she's gone home by now. She was only visiting in San Francisco."

"Or maybe she went to look for that boy."

"What boy?"

"The boy named Luther, don't you remember? She told me he helped her once—a whole lot, I guess, and she was very grateful. She said she wished she could thank him properly, but he didn't live any place, just the streets, so she wouldn't be able to find him."

"That's too bad." Yancy continued to play, but from that moment on, he couldn't concentrate, and to Richard's delight he lost the game. Belle had often talked of Luther Allen. What a fine young man he was; what a shame he lived on the streets of the Barbary Coast; how awful that his sister, Susan, who was six, and Helen, who was eight, had to live with a family that wasn't treating them right.

Of course! That's what he'd do. A crazy idea but worth a try.

The next morning, he went to the carriage house and found Linus mending a harness. "What do you know about the Barbary Coast?" he asked.

"God in heaven." Linus looked up in astonishment. "You're not thinking of going there, are you?"

"Maybe. What's it like?"

Linus laid down the harness, consternation in his eyes. "They call the Barbary Coast the wickedest place in the West. Maybe the wickedest place in the world, full of one den of iniquity after another. If you go to a brothel, you'll likely be mugged and robbed. If you go to a saloon and order a whiskey, you could get yourself shanghaied. Those scoundrels will drug a man's drink, and the next thing he knows he's halfway to China in the stinking hold of some ship."

Yancy raised an eyebrow. "Anything else?"

Linus warmed to his task. "It's the haunt of the low and vile of every kind. Murderers, cutthroats, whoremongers, lewd women, cheaters, and scoundrels—you'll find them all there. They drink vile liquor, engage in such vulgar conduct you couldn't imagine, sing obscene songs, and do everything to heap degradation upon themselves. There's drunkenness, debauchery, loathsome diseases—"

"That's enough," Yancy said, laughing. "I get the idea. So if I decide to go, I'd better be careful. Is that what you're saying?"

"That's what I'm saying, and if you don't mind my honest opinion, any man in his right mind would never dream of going to such a place."

"I hear you, and I thank you for your advice."

"Then I hope I've talked you out of it."

"I'll be coming to get my horse around dark, Linus. I'm going out."

"God in heaven," Linus muttered to himself, and said no more.

* * * *

The sun had barely set as Yancy rode along Pacific Street toward the Barbary Coast. So how could he find a fifteen-year-old boy who had no home? As yet, he had no idea, other than to ask around. He had no fear of the numerous "dens of iniquity" Linus was so bothered about. His only concern was that Luther might be impossible to find, what with the scanty information he got from Belle. The boy sometimes slept on the second floor of an opium den. Which opium den? Where could he find one? The boy scavenged for food in the garbage behind the restaurants. Which restaurants? Could he still be found there?

And what if Luther Allen wasn't around anymore? Maybe he'd left the Barbary Coast and gone who knew where?

Keeping his horse to a slow pace, Yancy passed a fruit stand where the vendor, a heavyset man in his forties, was closing down for the night. On an impulse, he stopped and swung from his horse. He didn't expect much, but it wouldn't hurt to ask. "Good evening, sir, can I speak to you a moment?"

The man continued slinging crates of oranges into a wagon. "Talk all you want, but we're closed."

"I'm looking for a boy of fifteen named Luther Allen. Do you know him?"

"Where does he live?"

"The streets."

The man snorted and paused in his labor. "One of the street boys, eh? This city's full of the little varmints. They're nothing but trouble—steal my fruit if I don't watch 'em every second. If you ask me, the police should round 'em all up and throw 'em in jail."

Yancy maintained his patience. "I've never met him myself, but from what I understand this boy is tall, skinny, and has long, sandy-colored hair. He speaks well and has good manners. I can't say for sure, but I don't think he's the kind who would steal your fruit."

"Well, now..." Appeased by Yancy's affable response, the vendor rubbed his jaw in thought. "Maybe I've seen such a boy. Well spoken, you say?"

"Yes, and kindhearted, too. He helped a friend of mine, and I wish to thank him."

"Most of the ones I've talk to don't speak well, and that's because they've never been to school," the man replied in a softer tone. "Most come from broken homes, a lot of 'em just kicked out to fend for themselves. It's a pitiful sight when you see 'em at night, rolled up in a blanket, sleeping in a doorway or out in the open. I've talked to Luther a few times but can't tell you where you could find him. They don't sleep in the same place every night. One thing for sure, he won't be in the dance halls or theaters or brothels. Most likely you'll find him in some alley picking through the garbage."

The vendor had given good advice. Yancy thanked him. As he started on, the vendor called after him, "Watch out for the rowdies on the streets, all of 'em drunk, and they'd just as soon kill you as not."

Heeding the vendor's admonition, Yancy avoided the clogged, unruly streets of the Barbary Coast and confined his search to the alleys. He disliked carrying a gun but was glad he'd brought his revolver along. After four years of war, he thought he'd seen everything but soon realized he hadn't. A drunken woman accosted him, and he had to gently but firmly push her away. Four silent men in seaman's clothes passed him by. Between them, they were carrying an unconscious man by his arms and legs and were no doubt headed for the docks where a ship awaited. Obviously, the poor sod had been either drunk or drugged, maybe both, but no way could Yancy come to the rescue, much as he'd like to.

Once, as he was passing the back of a raucously loud saloon, he encountered a small, lean man with a kindly face, dressed in a plain black suit and the circular, white collar of a clergyman. When they stopped to talk, the man introduced himself as the Reverend Alpheus Madrid of the Franklin Street Church. When Yancy asked the usual question, he replied, "Luther Allen? The name sounds familiar. I may have run across him in my nightly wanderings. I try to know the names of all the children who have no homes."

Surprised, Yancy inquired, "You do this every night?"

"Almost," the reverend earnestly replied. "Countless numbers of homeless and destitute children are adrift in this city, many here in the Barbary Coast. We seek to rescue as many as we can, as quickly as we can. Children are impressionable and susceptible. If they stay too long in a depraved environment such as this, they're beyond all help. Although"—he hastened to correct himself—"we never give up."

"You're doing good work, Reverend," Yancy said. "I admire you. It can't be easy wandering the streets and alleys of the Barbary Coast nearly every night."

The reverend pulled a card from his pocket and handed it to Yancy. "Here's our address. If ever you care to join us in our nightly search, you'll be most welcome. We can take in only a limited number of children now, but we plan to build an orphanage." He chuckled and added, "With God's help, the bank, and a lot of donations."

Yancy took the card, bid the reverend goodbye, and continued on his way. As the hours passed by, he began to see children, some he guessed as young as five, picking through smelly cans of garbage. Like little ghosts, they disappeared into the night when they saw him coming, although a few were brave enough to stay. If they did, he would speak to them in the most reassuring voice he could manage. "Don't run off. I'm not going to hurt you. I want to know if you've heard of a boy named Luther Allen."

They all said no. By the time dawn was about to break, Yancy's shoulders slumped. He was exhausted, and so was his horse. He ached for sleep and had to keep telling himself his search wasn't hopeless, although he was beginning to believe it was. He began to retrace his steps. For the second time, he stopped at a row of garbage cans behind a restaurant and found a skinny, ragged boy of about twelve digging through one of the cans. He would probably run off, but when Yancy rode up, he stood straight and said, "Hello, mister. Can you spare a nickel?"

"I can do better than that." Yancy dug in his pocket and tossed him a quarter. "What's your name?"

"Arthur Sweeney, sir, and yours?"

"My name is Yancy McLeish, and I'm looking for a boy named Luther Allen. Have you seen him?"

"Yes, I have, sir, and if you give me another quarter, I'll lead you right to him."

* * * *

A week had gone by since Belle arrived at the Hollister mansion. In most ways, it had been a good week, and she'd kept busy. She'd written a letter to Victoria, wherein she'd announced her marriage to Robert Romano had fallen through. By way of explanation, she disclosed, "It didn't work out," and that was all. Her sister would be dying to know the details, but she'd have to wait. Belle had added she was staying with friends, having a delightful time, and would be home in a month. She made no mention of Yancy. Why should she? He was gone from her life now, and she'd be much better off pretending he never existed. Not that she was having much luck with that. She'd finally told Mrs. Hollister the truth about her relationship with Yancy McLeish. She hadn't intended to, but the older woman listened with such a sympathetic ear she couldn't resist.

Her employer's response wasn't what she expected. "So let me get this straight, Belle. You love him, but you want nothing to do with him because he's a Yankee?"

"More than that," she'd replied. "He's a Yankee who fought in the Union Army under General Sherman."

"But the war's over."

"According to my family, the war will never be over."

"And according to you?" Mrs. Hollister's faded eyes snapped with challenge. "Do you really want old hurts and resentments to dictate what you do for the rest of your life?"

Not knowing how to answer, Belle said nothing more, but she hadn't forgotten the conversation. Was she wrong? Had leaving Yancy been a mistake? She knew her own mind, didn't she? She certainly knew her own heart, and that was the problem.

That afternoon, she was chatting with Mrs. Hollister in the back parlor, both crocheting as they talked. Eugenia had taken over the drawing room for the weekly meeting of her Total Temperance Union. Ardent in their desire to banish the demon rum from San Francisco, the ladies made a lot of noise. Once, when the sound of enthusiastic applause reached the back parlor, Mrs. Hollister sighed and dropped the scarf she was crocheting to her lap. "It's a worthy cause, of course, but I do so miss a glass of wine with my dinner."

Belle had noticed nothing stronger than water ever being served at the Hollister dining table. Now she knew why. She'd kept her mouth shut on the subject of Eugenia, but for once, she spoke up. "If you don't mind my saying so, it's your house, and if you want wine with your dinner, you should have it."

"I know, I know." Mrs. Hollister sighed. "If it were up to me, I would most certainly indulge in a glass of wine, despite the risk of going straight to hell. But my problem is, I dread unpleasant scenes, and that's what would happen. Eugenia would throw a fit. Malcolm would take her side like he always does. So I drink water, just to keep peace in the family."

By now Belle had developed a deep regard for her employer and hated to see her controlled by her greedy son and his fanatical wife. She longed to say more but bit her tongue. She must keep reminding herself the clashes and conflicts within the Hollister family were not her concern.

The doorbell rang. Belle thought nothing of it, assuming another of Eugenia's guests had arrived. She was wrong. Bertha soon appeared in the back parlor. "There's a gentleman to see you, Miss Ainsworth."

"Did he give a name?"

"It's a Mr. Yancy McLeish, and he's not alone."

Yancy? What on earth is he doing here? For a moment, all rational thought left Belle's head, but Bertha was watching and so was Mrs. Hollister, so she'd better pull herself together. She arose from her chair in what she hoped was a slow and dignified fashion. "Did you show them in?"

"No, I did not. The gentleman appears respectable enough, but there's a boy sitting out in the carriage." Bertha wrinkled her nose. "His clothes are ragged, and he looks like he hasn't had a bath in quite some time."

"Thank you, Bertha. I shall see for myself." Belle smoothed her hair as she walked to the door. Her pulse raced. She paused for a deep breath. Must stay calm and collected, as if a visit from Yancy meant nothing at all. She swung the door open. There he stood, brimming with confidence, his tall, lean figure in its usual casual stance. She'd be casual, too, if it killed her. "My, my, look who's here. Hello, Yancy."

He returned a wide grin. "Good afternoon, Belle. I've brought someone you've been wanting to see. Come with me."

She looked toward the street where Ronald's brougham sat at the curb. A boy was climbing down. Tall, gangly, sandy hair…

"Luther, it's you!" Gathering her skirts, she rushed down the walkway to the curb. Ignoring Luther's ragged clothes that were none too clean, she threw her arms around him and hugged him tight. "It's so good to see you. I wanted to thank you properly, but you ran off before I could." She drew back and clasped both his arms. "Let me look at you. Where have you been? What have you been doing?"

"Not much." Luther dipped his head modestly. "It's good to see you again, Miss Ainsworth. Looks like you're doing all right."

Belle looked toward Yancy who had followed her back. "Where on earth did you find him?"

"I found him early this morning in an opium den," Yancy offhandedly replied. "I believe the same one where you spent the night."

"But how did you—?" Something clicked in her mind. "You deliberately went looking for him?"

"It's a long story. Let's say I had a hunch you'd like to see him again, so here he is." He looked toward Mrs. Hollister's mansion. "I don't expect to be invited in. Let's sit in the carriage, shall we?"

Belle reluctantly agreed. Up to that moment, she hadn't thought beyond her delight at seeing the boy who'd saved her life. At the least, she wanted to invite him in, but how could she? If this were her own home, she wouldn't have hesitated, but Mrs. Hollister would, at the least, disapprove of his unkempt and ragged condition, and no doubt Eugenia would be appalled.

She was about to climb in the carriage when she heard, "Mr. McLeish! How nice to see you again."

Here came Mrs. Hollister down the walkway. When she arrived, she gave Yancy an embrace and looked toward Luther. "And who is this young man?"

"This is the boy who saved my life," Belle said.

"Well, why are you standing on the street? Come in, everyone. I'll have Bertha serve us some tea. It'll have to be in the back parlor, though. It seems we're battling the wages of sin in the drawing room."

Belle laughed to herself. Mrs. Hollister had begun to reveal a subtle sense of humor she'd kept hidden before. She seemed smarter and kinder, too. Belle wouldn't have guessed a lady so rich and genteel would invite a child of the streets into her home, but she'd been wrong.

In the back parlor, a harried Bertha not only served them tea, she'd added delicate cucumber sandwiches. "Meant for the temperance ladies," she grumbled. "Had to sneak 'em out or they'd have gobbled them all up and looked around for more."

Yancy and Luther sat on the settee, Yancy looking as cool and self-possessed as always. How had he managed to find Luther in the midst of the Barbary Coast? There had to be quite a story there, and Belle was dying to know. Watching Luther, her heart welled with sympathy. Obviously he'd been taught good manners, but plain to see he was hungry, had to force himself to eat slowly and not wolf down the tiny cucumber sandwiches. At Mrs. Hollister's insistence, he retold his story of how his parents had died, how the neighbors took him and his sisters in, and how eventually he had to run away.

Mrs. Hollister listened intently, eyes brimming with sympathy. "That's terrible. I can't imagine how you can live on the streets that way."

"I do fine," Luther answered with a shrug. "It's my sisters I worry about. Mr. Shelton's a mean man, and they're afraid of him. I worry about what he'll do to two little girls who can't defend themselves. Like I was telling Miss Ainsworth, soon as I get a job and save some money, I'll get my sisters out of there. I'm aiming for a home of our own."

Mrs. Hollister scanned Luther with a critical eye. "It looks as if you could use a good meal. I want you to stay for dinner with my family tonight."

The boy vehemently shook his head. "I couldn't do that. Look at me. I don't belong in a nice place like this."

"You let me worry about that. My husband was about your size, and I've kept all his clothes. I'm sure we'll find something to fit. After a nice hot bath, you'll look fine. I think you should spend the night and Mr. McLeish can pick you up in the morning."

"Why, that's...that's..." Luther clearly couldn't find words to express his gratitude.

"It's only for tonight, understand," Mrs. Hollister said briskly. "And what about you, Mr. McLeish? Can you stay for dinner?"

"Sorry. My niece and nephew are expecting me, and I don't want to disappoint them." Yancy rose to leave. "You're very kind to do this. Is it settled then? I'll pick Luther up in the morning."

Mrs. Hollister beamed from the praise. "That would be splendid."

"I'll see you out." Belle walked with Yancy to the door, past the loud ladies in the drawing room who were still diligently plotting to save the city from the demon rum. Once outside, she accompanied him to the carriage. "How are Richard and Beth?" she asked.

"They're fine. They miss you."

His answer stabbed at her heart. "And I miss them. I can't thank you enough for finding Luther."

"My pleasure."

"It couldn't have been easy."

"No, it wasn't."

Damn. He could be infuriating sometimes with his short, curt answers. "So why did you do it?"

He gazed at her, a faint light twinkling in the depths of his brown eyes. "You wanted to properly thank him, didn't you?"

Before she could think of a reply, he spoke again. "Don't worry, I'm not going to hound you. Have dinner with me tomorrow night."

Her mind went spinning. She needed time to think. "I'm surprised you're still in San Francisco. I thought you would have returned to Maine by now."

"So did I, but I've been delayed." With a self-deprecating little grin, he added, "For several reasons, including you."

"But I've already said goodbye." *And will never forget the pain of it.*

"I know. It's up to you."

Her memory of the night they made love hadn't dimmed. That was the night she knew he was everything she could ever want in a man. She would love him forever, for his strength, kindness, humor—and the rapturous way he'd made her feel. So yes, indeed, with all her heart she wished she could accept his invitation, but she couldn't. He was still one of the hated Yankees who marched with General Sherman through Georgia, and her family would never approve. She must use her common sense and decline. "Thank you for asking, but I must say no. Nothing has changed, really, although I much appreciate you finding Luther for me."

He shrugged, as if not the least disappointed. "He's a fine boy. I plan to give him some money, but it won't be enough to get him off the streets. I'd give him a job—put him to work with Linus, but I'll probably be leaving soon." He climbed to the carriage seat, picked up the reins, and nodded goodbye. "See you tomorrow."

She bit her lip in frustration as she stood at the curb and watched him drive away.

Chapter 18

Thanks to Mrs. Hollister, Luther appeared at the dining table freshly bathed and properly attired in a dark wool suit and white shirt that had belonged to the late Gerald Hollister. They must have been about the same size, Belle thought, because they fit perfectly. Not only did Luther look presentable, he knew his manners. He didn't slurp his soup, knew which fork to use, and didn't blow his nose on his napkin. All things considered, with decent clothes and his hair combed, Luther would be acceptable at any fine dining table.

Eugenia had been taken by surprise. Busy with her temperance ladies, she hadn't known about the guest until she sat down to dinner and her mother-in-law announced in her most cordial voice, "I want you to meet Luther Allen. He's originally from Nebraska but now dwells in San Francisco."

Eugenia returned her most cordial greeting. "And what part of the city do you live in, Luther?"

"The Barbary Coast, ma'am."

"The Barbary Coast? But where…?"

"I live on the street, ma'am. Sometimes there's an opium den where I sleep at night, or sometimes, if it's warm enough, I wrap myself in a blanket and sleep in an alley."

"Oh." Momentarily silenced, Eugenia sat back in her chair, her mouth set in a tight, grim line.

Mrs. Hollister hastened to explain. "In case you're wondering, he'll be staying just the night. I've put him in Dane's old room."

"How nice," Eugenia replied in an icy tone.

Malcolm smirked and remarked to no one in particular, "That's my dear mother for you. One wonders what she'll do next."

Little more was said, but a prickly atmosphere hung over the rest of the meal. Malcolm's wife sat with lips compressed, nose twitching, and a contemptuous glare that made Belle distinctly uncomfortable. At least Eugenia's wrath wasn't aimed at her. It was aimed at Luther, who didn't seem to notice and was enjoying every mouthful of his Veal Marsala and French apple tart for dessert. When the meal was over and they were getting up from the table, Malcolm beckoned to his mother. "Let's step into the drawing room, shall we? We need to talk."

Belle spent the rest of the evening having an enjoyable conversation with Luther in the back parlor. He'd gone to bed by the time Mrs. Hollister returned from her chat with her son and daughter-in-law. "Oh, dear," she said as she sank into her chair. She picked up her crocheting and threw it down again. "I'm so disappointed."

"And why is that?"

"I like the boy. He doesn't deserve all the misfortune that's come his way. I had thought that perhaps he could stay. Maybe not upstairs, but there's a small room over the stable that's not being used. I could have hired him to help my stableman. He's been claiming for years he's overworked. I even thought we could give Luther time enough to go back to school. I can see how smart he is, and with a good education he could make something of himself, but..." She heaved another sigh. "Malcolm disapproves."

"He does?" Belle wasn't the least surprised.

"He went on a rant about how unsafe it is to let a boy of such low status into our home. We'd no doubt all be murdered in our sleep, he said, and of course Eugenia agrees. They were both quite horrified, actually. Malcolm accused me of trying to replace the son I lost with a worthless boy from the streets. As if anyone could replace Dane! But I thought..." She bit her lip in chagrin. "They wanted me to get rid of Luther tonight, but I talked them into waiting till Yancy comes for him in the morning."

Anger welled within her. "Mrs. Hollister—" *Careful.* Belle clamped her lips shut. People said unwise things when they were angry, and she didn't want to make this poor woman feel worse than she already did.

Her employer slumped back in defeat. "I suppose you think I have no backbone, the way I let Malcolm order me around."

"You don't want my opinion."

"Yes, I do. Please go ahead."

Belle gathered her thoughts. She wouldn't hurt Mrs. Hollister's feelings for the world, but the truth was best. "You told me your age once. Seventy-five, as I recall. That's an age when a person is supposed to know all the answers and not need advice from anyone on how to run her life."

Mrs. Hollister laughed wryly. "One would think. But of course, Malcolm means well. He's handled my affairs for so long I don't know what I'd do without him."

Belle chose her words carefully. "You need a financial adviser, but does it have to be your son? I don't want to speak out of turn, but you might consider replacing him with someone else. I can think of one person already—Mr. Leighton Canfield, vice president of the Bank of the Golden Gate. I'm sure he'd be glad to handle your finances for you, or point to someone who can. He's a man of integrity, and he also has a heart, unlike…" *Your son Malcolm*. She'd caught herself just in time.

In deep thought, Mrs. Hollister gazed toward the ceiling. When she looked back, she let out a sigh. "I thank you for your advice, Belle, but it's too late for me. They say you can't teach an old dog new tricks, and I'm afraid that's true. I'm too old to stand up for myself. Too old to change. Maybe too weak willed to change."

Belle gave her a sympathetic pat on her arm. "You're not weak willed. You're one of the strongest women I know. Choices are hard to make sometimes. Not long ago, I, too, had to make a tough decision. I could remain in my comfortable little world in Savannah, or I could say goodbye to everything I held dear and start a new life."

"How sad your decision didn't work out as you'd hoped."

"No it didn't, but…" Mrs. Hollister's remark set Belle to thinking. Until this moment, she hadn't realized, but since the day she left Savannah, she'd never regretted it—never once thought she'd made a terrible mistake. Had she stayed home, she would never have experienced her trip on the transcontinental railroad where each day was an adventure and she'd seen some of the most gorgeous scenery in the world. She would never have crossed San Francisco Bay in a ferryboat on a sparkling, sunshiny day. Never have seen the sea lions sleeping on the rocks, never sat on a beach where she could almost see China across the azure blue of the Pacific. And never met Yancy McLeish, even if it didn't work out. "I know this sounds crazy, but despite nearly getting my head blown off, and Roberto Romano, the Barbary Coast and all the bad things that happened, if I had to do it over, I wouldn't change a thing." She hastened to add, "But that's just me. You're the best judge of what's best for you."

"How very true," Mrs. Hollister replied without much conviction. "I appreciate your trying to help, but I'm too set in my ways ever to change." Wearily, she arose from her chair and said good night.

Belle got an ache in her throat as she watched her employer leave the room, a defeated sag to her shoulders. How awful to be old, dependent, and too afraid to stand up for yourself. *But where will I be when I'm seventy-five?* She hoped better off than Mrs. Hollister, but who knew what the future would bring? As things stood now, her fate could be even worse. At least her employer had plenty of money, whereas when she, Belle, got old, she wouldn't have a penny. Was she destined to become just another old maid completely dependent on her family? What a horrible thought, yet judging from the way her life was going, not all that far fetched.

The next morning, Belle and her employer were having breakfast in the dining room when Luther appeared, still wearing his borrowed clothes. "Good morning," he said and sheepishly added, "I looked for my own clothes but couldn't find them."

"That's because I had them burned," Mrs. Hollister replied. "The clothes you're wearing are yours to keep. My husband is long since dead, so I'm sure he won't mind." She pointed to the marble sideboard where the cook had laid out breakfast. "Help yourself."

"Thank you, ma'am." Luther eagerly filled his plate and joined them. "I can't tell you how much I've enjoyed my stay with you two ladies. I'll never forget how kind you've been."

Mrs. Hollister frowned with concern. "I hate to see you go back to that awful place."

"I'll do fine." Luther squared his shoulders and regarded them earnestly with his clear blue eyes. "You shouldn't worry. There are lots of people in this world a whole lot worse off than I am."

Belle felt bad before, but hearing Luther's brave declaration, she felt even worse. What a shame such a bright, talented boy must return to the streets. She'd heard homeless children didn't last long, what with diseases, poor food, and the ever-present danger of sharing the streets with cutthroats, robbers, and the lowest dregs of humanity.

Mrs. Hollister must have been thinking the same thing. She hardly touched her breakfast. Belle had never seen her looking so dejected.

Yancy arrived not long after breakfast. Bertha led him into the back parlor where they sat waiting. "Good morning, I've come to get Luther," he said.

Luther greeted him with a smile. "I'm ready, Mr. McLeish." He said his goodbyes to Belle and Mrs. Hollister, who wore an expression of dismay on her face.

Belle said, "I'll see you off." With a heavy heart, she followed Yancy and Luther to the street. While Luther climbed into the carriage, she thanked Yancy again. "What a kind, thoughtful thing for you to do. I won't soon forget it."

Yancy smiled wryly. "So have dinner with me."

Belle opened her mouth to say no, but before she could, Mrs. Hollister burst through the front door and headed down the walkway. "Wait!" she called. When she got close, she looked up at Luther, who sat on the high seat of the carriage. "I have a job for you if you care to accept it. My stableman needs someone to help him in the carriage house. You could work and still have time to go to school. Are you interested?"

Luther squeezed his eyes shut a moment, as if giving a thankful prayer. "Yes, very interested, Mrs. Hollister." Tears glistened in his eyes. He quickly wiped them away.

Belle and Yancy shared a smile as she wondered what on earth had caused Mrs. Hollister's sudden change of heart. She remained at the curb as Luther followed his new employer back into the house. Looking after them, Belle said, "That dear old lady never ceases to amaze me. Her son didn't want Luther to spend the night. It took a lot of courage to defy him. He's a hateful, overbearing kind of man, and I'm not sure she'll be able to hold her own against him."

"I admire her no end," Yancy replied. "And I'll help any way I can. And so?" He raised his eyebrows and regarded her intently. "I won't let you off so easily. As I was saying, have dinner with me. How about this Friday night? Say yes, and you'll have several days to decide if you'd rather not."

She would love to accept. Well, why not? Maybe just once. What would it hurt? "If I have dinner with you, nothing will change."

"Of course."

"It'll be a 'friends only' kind of thing."

"Of course."

"Then I accept. I'll have dinner with you Friday night."

She'd halfway expected his face would light with pleasure at her reply, but his nonchalant expression didn't change. "I'll pick you up at eight." He climbed in the carriage, gave her a casual wave, and drove away.

Belle hastened to find Mrs. Hollister. "I'm so glad you changed your mind," she declared. "What did it?"

Contrary to her recent miserable indecision, the older woman brimmed with confidence. "It was you, Belle, and what you said about making difficult choices. I was moping around, hating the thought of that fine young man living on the streets, eating out of garbage cans. Then when I saw that poor boy walking out the door, going back to that awful Barbary Coast, I suddenly knew I needed to make that difficult choice you talked about. I could either let Luther stay and risk Malcolm's anger, which you know I dread, or I could let my dear son and his wife bully me yet again. I hadn't realized till now how much they've taken over my life."

"I'm still curious. As I pointed out, my choice didn't work out very well."

"Makes no difference." Mrs. Hollister set her chin in a stubborn line. "I did what I had do. Just like you did, and damn the consequences."

Belle silently applauded and could only hope she meant what she said.

* * * *

Malcolm was gone all day and didn't return until dinner. Belle and Mrs. Hollister were sitting in the back parlor when he came in. She could tell from the tight expression on his face that someone, probably Eugenia, had informed him Luther was staying.

"Good evening, Mother. I want to talk to you." Malcolm threw a frosty glance in Belle's direction. "Alone."

Mrs. Hollister coolly tipped her head and inquired, "Is this about Luther? Anything you have to say to me, you can say in front of Miss Ainsworth."

"Yes, it's about Luther." Malcolm's face began to turn red. He appeared to be talking through gritted teeth. "It is beyond my comprehension why you would go against me this way and take a no-good street urchin—a worthless ragamuffin—into our home."

"*Our* home?" Mrs. Hollister calmly inquired. "Last I heard, it was *my* home, which I graciously allow you and Eugenia to share."

Malcolm's head jerked back. He seemed to need a moment to recover, and when he did, his face became a glowering mask of rage. "Do you realize I could have you declared incompetent? Those endless trips to New York. Throwing away your fortune on fancy jewelry. And now this? What next? Do you plan to turn your home into a haven for wayward boys?"

"Not a bad idea." Mrs. Hollister picked up the scarf she'd been crocheting and started working the needles again. "Now, will you please leave, Malcolm? I swear, you're giving me a headache."

Belle watched as Malcolm, his lips working, sought to find a cutting reply, but his shock was so great he could only sputter, "You're going to regret this." He spun on his heel and left without another word.

Belle raised her hands and applauded softly. "You did it! That was magnificent."

Mrs. Hollister looked doubtful. "Magnificent or not, he's set me to worrying."

"That he might have you declared incompetent?"

"He could, you know. My son has a lot of power in this town. He's very angry. I wouldn't be surprised if he meant what he said. Claims I'm crazy and should be put away."

"I'm sure he didn't mean it."

"What if he did? I must be careful. I'm not about to change my mind about Luther, but I'd best keep him out of Malcolm's and Eugenia's way as much as possible. Tonight we'll still have dinner in my room."

How disappointing. Belle had applauded when she thought Mrs. Hollister had at last found her courage. Obviously, she hadn't found all of it.

* * * *

Yancy had always scorned indecision. Hesitation was weakness, as far as he was concerned. He'd lived his life never dithering, and that included everything from what to eat for breakfast to the darkest days of the war when he, Captain Yancy McLeish, the fate of dozens of men resting on his shoulders, must decide whether to draw his sword and yell "Charge!" or withdraw from the battle to fight another day. So what was the matter with him? Time was flying by, and here he was, still in San Francisco long after he'd planned to return home. Other than his upcoming dinner with Belle, nothing of importance kept him here. That's what he kept telling himself, but deep down, he recognized his feelings for Belle Ainsworth were enough to influence any decision he might make.

Not one to remain idle, he decided to pay a visit to the Franklin Street Church and find the kindly clergyman he'd met when he was scouring the Barbary Coast to find Luther. The Reverend Alpheus Madrid greeted him warmly. Although Yancy had planned nothing more than a brief call, he soon found himself on a tour of the church's makeshift orphanage. "We'd like to start a kindergarten if we can get teachers to volunteer," said the reverend. "The older children go to the neighborhood school."

No girls were present, only boys when he arrived. They were eating lunch, and Yancy and the reverend joined them. When the boys discovered Yancy lived in the Maine woods, they besieged him with questions and listened attentively as he described his solitary life, everything from his friendly Indian neighbors to being chased by an angry grizzly bear.

When he was about to leave, the reverend remarked, "I don't wish to pry, but were you in the military?"

"Four years in the Union Army."

"You were an officer." It was a statement, not a question.

"I was a captain."

"I knew it," said Reverend Madrid. "You're a natural leader of men. I could tell by the way those boys hung on your every word. Come with me tonight."

"To the Barbary Coast?"

The reverend could hardly contain his enthusiasm. "You'll be saving lives, Yancy. It's hard to believe, but I've come across many a boy who doesn't want to be rescued. On the streets they're free to do what they please, and some like it that way. Today I saw how those boys looked up to you. If anyone could persuade them to come with us, it'd be you. If you could save one child from a life of misery and a probable early death, wouldn't you wish to do so?"

Of course he would. So that night he accompanied Alpheus Madrid to the Barbary Coast to "do the work of the Lord," as the reverend put it. He'd gone again the next night, and would be the first to admit he got an immense amount of satisfaction each time he successfully persuaded a homeless child to leave the streets and come with him.

With every passing day, he'd become more attached to Ronald's children, and they to him. So far, they'd received one short letter from Bernice, in which she raved about what a wonderful time she was having, no mention of when she'd return. Both Beth and Richard were hurt. So was he, just seeing the wounded look on their faces. How much worse would they feel if he left, too? No, wait. He had to correct himself. *When* he left, not *if* he left. Of course he was going home.

But whatever he did, his thoughts always returned to Belle.

Thank God, she couldn't see the way his heart leaped when she accepted his dinner invitation. But why had he asked her? How could they possibly ever have a life together? Her family would never accept him. She made herself abundantly clear concerning the kind of welcome he'd receive, should he be fool enough to present himself at the family doorstep in Savannah. And what if he took her home with him to Maine? He could not begin to imagine how well Miss Belle Ainsworth, delicate, privileged Southern belle, would adjust to life in a rustic cabin in the wilderness. Gutting the fish—she'd already made herself clear on that subject. A moose hunt perhaps? He set himself to laughing, picturing the elegant Miss Ainsworth slogging along beside him, musket at the ready, heart set on bagging her first moose.

Actually he liked San Francisco far better than he thought he would. It was a city like no other, with its crisp fresh air, sudden thick fogs, and houses defying gravity on impossibly steep hills, all of it overlooking the beautiful bay. No wonder his brother chose to live here. Fortunes could be made, and Ronald had done well. Lately, even Yancy felt a tug of challenge. Not to make a fortune. Money meant little to him, especially now that he'd inherited a veritable fortune, but for the first time in years, he found himself wondering if he might not need some sort of purpose in his life. In his cabin by the lake, he'd been content to arise in the morning with no other goal than to get through the day with as little aggravation as possible, maybe do a bit of hunting or fishing, then go to bed at night, get up next morning, and do the same thing all over again. Was that really how he wanted to spend the rest of his life? Lately he'd been wondering.

Belle didn't change her mind. Tonight they occupied a booth at the Tadich Grill, one of the finest restaurants in the city. "You look nice," he said, finding his words barely adequate, but being a quiet man who never talked much, that was the best he could do. "Nice" was hardly the word. Sitting across, she nearly took his breath away in the blue velvet dress she was wearing, the bodice cut low to reveal the soft curve of her breasts. She smelled of that sweet perfume Queen Victoria wore, which he liked very much. A jeweled comb sat amidst the shiny dark curls piled atop her head.

Seeming pleased, she thanked him for the compliment and looked around the restaurant. Dark wood paneling with large mirrors covered the walls. Art deco brass and milk-glass fixtures hung from the fifteen-foot ceiling. "So this was Ronald's favorite place to dine?" she asked.

"He told me you can't get fresher fish than here. It's always last night's catch."

She smiled appreciatively. "Sometimes Mrs. Hollister sends Bertha, her maid, to Meiggs Wharf where you can buy fish straight off the boat. I'd love to go with her sometime, but I don't dare."

"Roberto?"

"What if he saw me? At the very least I'd get tossed off the pier, and maybe even worse." She'd spoken lightly, but Yancy took her seriously. He'd never met Roberto Romano, but from what he'd heard of the man's arrogance and dominating nature, Belle should indeed be careful.

Easy conversation flowed between them as they dined. Once, when she asked if he was planning on returning home soon, he had to answer vaguely, "I'm not sure. There are still matters to attend to." Matters such as he wanted her back, couldn't bring himself to leave her. But wait, he was going around in circles again. Why would he want her back if he was going home?

And meantime, he could tell she cared for him. Little things, like the extra-long clasp of her hand when he helped her from the carriage.

Like the tenderness shining in her warm grey eyes when she listened to him talk. Like... Hard to explain. He could only describe it as a kind of hot undercurrent that kept passing back and forth between them, and he knew she was thinking of that night they spent in his bed making love, just as he was.

Toward the end of the meal, she talked about Luther, and how happy he was that Mrs. Hollister had taken him in. "He worries about his sisters, though. He doesn't get to visit them often, and that bothers him. Apparently they're not treated well."

"Then we'll take him for a visit," Yancy replied. "How about tomorrow? Will you come along?"

"How kind of you. Of course I'd like to come."

Fine. He would see her tomorrow. The rest could wait.

Later, when he took her home, he escorted her to her door. Before she could protest, he firmly clasped her upper arms and planted a light kiss on her forehead. He could tell from the slight lean of her body toward him that he needn't stop. He did, though, and instead pulled away. "Good night, Belle. See you tomorrow."

Like the perfect gentleman, he waited till she'd gone inside and shut the door before he returned to his carriage. With a muffled curse, he climbed to the seat and drove home. If there was anything worse than being in a state of indecision, he didn't know what it was.

Chapter 19

The next afternoon, Yancy pulled the carriage to a stop in front of the address on Vermont Street and turned to Luther. "Is this the place?"

"Yes, sir, this is where the Sheltons live." Luther climbed eagerly to the ground. "I hope you and Miss Ainsworth will come in and meet my sisters."

Up to now, Belle had every intention of going in, but one look at the dilapidated house gave her pause. The yard was a muddy mess, strewn with trash. A few scraggly weeds, the only signs of greenery, struggled to survive. The house had once been painted white, but most of the paint had long since worn away leaving a weathered, dreary grey. But of course she'd go in. She wouldn't hurt Luther's feelings, and besides, she wanted to meet his sisters.

Belle carefully lifted her skirts as they followed a muddy walkway to the door. When it opened, a thin little girl peered out. "Luther!" She squealed with delight, swung the door wide, and threw her arms around him. Another little girl, slightly older, appeared, and he hugged them both. "Meet Susan and Helen," he said.

Belle gave them both a cordial greeting. How unkempt they looked, both of them barefooted, wearing faded, frayed dresses. Susan's brown hair hung limp and full of snarls around her shoulders. Helen's fine, blond hair looked as if it had never seen a comb.

When they stepped inside, Belle had to adjust her eyes to the dim light in the dingy front parlor. When she did, she made out an immensely obese woman sitting with her legs spread—most unladylike—on a sagging sofa. The woman was gnawing on a chicken leg and made no effort to get up to greet them.

"This is Mrs. Shelton," Luther said. "She and Mr. Shelton are the ones who took in my sisters."

"Out of the kindness of our hearts," Mrs. Shelton remarked, her many chins jiggling. She waved her chicken leg toward some shabby, greasy-looking chairs. "You wanna sit down?"

Not really, Belle thought. The visitors remained standing as a burly, unshaven man in drooping pants and a sweat-stained undershirt appeared, looking none too pleased to see them. "Back again, Luther?" he asked. "Who are your friends?"

Yancy spoke up. "You're Mr. Shelton? We're friends of Luther. He wanted to visit his sisters and see how they're doing. We're here to oblige."

Shelton scowled. "I pay good money to feed 'em, give 'em a roof over their heads, and they're doing fine." He glared at Luther. "See that you don't stay too long. The girls have their work to do." Without another word, he turned and left.

His wife waved her chicken leg around. "Jake's right. There ain't nothing wrong with these girls except they're lazy. They like it here." She looked to where Luther's sisters still clung to him. "Ain't that right, girls?"

Belle had to bite her tongue. Obviously the sisters did not like it here. Aside from their bedraggled appearance, their arms and legs were like sticks, a sure sign they weren't getting enough to eat. Not only that, she'd seen their look of fear when Shelton appeared. What a loathsome man he was, and his wife, too. What a disgusting place this was. Good manners weren't necessary in a place like this, and she'd had quite enough. "I'll wait in the carriage," she said abruptly and headed for the door. Once outside, she took a deep breath of crisp, clean air. Those poor little girls. Something had to be done.

Yancy and Luther soon joined her. For a time, as Yancy drove back to Mrs. Hollister's, they sat in silence, Luther with a pained expression on his face, Yancy with his jaw clenched. Belle couldn't find words for her anger.

Luther finally spoke up. "I'm sorry. I should never have taken you to see them."

"Yes, you should have," said Yancy. "We're going to get your sisters out of there."

"But how?"

"You let me worry about that."

Luther said no more, and neither did Belle. She didn't need to. If Yancy said he was going to do something, she could count on him to do it.

* * * *

Only a few days had passed since Luther's arrival, but no longer was Mrs. Edith Hollister the glum, brittle old lady Belle met on the train. She'd acquired a smile on her face and a spring in her step. Now, having served tea to Belle, Yancy, and Luther in the drawing room, she sat back and inquired, "Was there something you wanted to ask me? I have the feeling there is."

Belle spoke up. "As you know, we took Luther to visit his sisters today...."

She went on to describe the deplorable conditions in which the two little girls were living, and how they must be rescued. "So I was thinking…"

"That you'd like to bring them here?" Mrs. Hollister asked.

"It would be only temporary," Luther said. "Only until I can save a little money and find a decent place for them to live."

Belle addressed Mrs. Hollister. "You don't have to say yes. What with taking Luther in, you've done far more than enough already. Besides, I suspect you'd have even more trouble with Malcolm and his wife."

With a wry smile, Mrs. Hollister replied, "Oh, I'm sure I would." She paused to reflect. "Lately I've been taking a good look at myself and asking, why should I tolerate Malcolm and his threats? How dare he tell me what to do?" She firmly nodded her chin. "This is my house, and I'll do what I please. I have plenty of room. Yancy, go get those girls. I want them here."

* * * *

What a transformation! When the two little sisters arrived at the house on Nob Hill, grimy looking in their ragged clothes, they'd clung fearfully together, not knowing what was to become of them. Belle and Bertha pitched in and gave them baths while Mrs. Hollister bustled about in the bedroom that had belonged to the daughter who'd died of diphtheria all those years ago. She'd kept the room just as it was, including the little girl's clothing piled neatly in the drawers of the fruitwood bureau or left hanging in the walnut-carved armoire.

Now, only hours later, Susan and Helen couldn't contain their excitement. "Look at us," Helen exclaimed. Both she and her sister were twirling around, admiring themselves in the full-length mirror. Each had a big bow in their hair that now shone and hung prettily around their shoulders. Each wore a ruffled dress—Susan's pink, Helen's blue—with a matching satin sash tied in a big bow in the back. Each wore pantalets.

Mrs. Hollister stood watching, a gleam of pride in her eyes. "How do you think they look? It's been forty years since Charlotte died, yet except for the pantalets, styles for little girls haven't changed all that much. I shall buy them the proper undergarments tomorrow."

"They look marvelous." Deeply moved by the older woman's joy, Belle added, "It's so kind of you to do this."

"I haven't felt this good in years." Mrs. Hollister looked toward the dollhouse which the two little girls had quickly spotted. Both now knelt on their knees in front of it, gazing in awe.

Susan clasped her hands together. "Look at the teeny furniture."

"And the little pots and pans and dishes in the kitchen," cried Helen.

With a couple of grunts caused by her rheumatism, Mrs. Hollister knelt beside them and reached into the dollhouse, into what looked like the library. "See what's on the bookshelves?" She pulled out a tiny, but real-looking book.

The girls laughed with delight. Helen asked, "Can we play with the dollhouse, Mrs. Hollister?"

"Indeed you can, and you can call me Aunt Edith from now on." Mrs. Hollister gazed up at Belle. "In celebration of our new arrivals, we shall dine in the dining room tonight."

Malcolm and Eugenia. Instantly wary, Belle dreaded the thought of another scene in the dining room like the one on the night Luther arrived. "You don't think—?"

"Don't worry about it. I'll handle it."

This time, Mrs. Hollister had a glint of determination in her eye that Belle hadn't seen before.

* * * *

That night, Belle enjoyed the sight of Luther and his sisters at the dinner table. The two little girls gazed in growing amazement at the food being served. "We mostly ate porridge at the Sheltons'," said Susan as she finished the first course of mock turtle soup. When Bertha set a plate of scalloped oysters in front of her, Susan's eyes went wide. "You mean there's more?"

The sisters' wonderment grew as Bertha served course after course: glazed salmon, prime rib roast accompanied by mashed potatoes, scalloped Brussels sprouts, green peas, followed by a salad, ending with a delicious *mousse au chocolat* for dessert.

At the end of the meal, both girls sat back, blissfully content. Helen asked, "Do you always eat this way?"

"Indeed, we do," a smiling Mrs. Hollister replied. "You'll never go hungry in this house." Belle had never seen her so happy. It was as if she'd finally found the real purpose of her life.

As far as Belle was concerned, the evening was perfect with only one exception. Malcolm and Eugenia sat through dinner hardly saying a word. They didn't have to. Their compressed lips and withering glances clearly indicated their intense disapproval of the three orphans' presence at their dinner table. Knowing Malcolm, Belle was sure he'd soon be speaking his mind. Poor Mrs. Hollister was in for another lecture, and probably another threat to have her declared incompetent. She had stated she'd stand up to her son this time, but would she? Belle could only hope her kindhearted employer wouldn't let herself be intimidated yet again by her greedy son.

Belle was right. After the girls had been put to bed, Malcolm summoned his mother to the drawing room. She was gone a long time and had a strange expression on her face when she returned to the back parlor. "Is everything all right?" Belle asked.

"Everything is fine. I gave Malcolm and Eugenia their notice. They'll be leaving in two weeks or less."

"How...how...?" Belle sputtered.

"How did I get up the courage to do it? Well, for one thing, I know I'm not crazy. How could Malcolm even hint that I was? Also, I took your advice and went to see that nice Mr. Canfield at the Bank of the Golden Gate. He informed me that my son has no business controlling my money unless I want him to. It's mine to do with what I please. I've already signed the papers to transfer my accounts. From now on, Mr. Canfield will be in charge of my investments."

"And what of Malcolm?"

"He is my son after all, and I won't put him out on the streets. He'll be receiving a small stipend, enough to live on comfortably." She shook her head regretfully. "He didn't take it well, I'm afraid, but you would have been proud of me. He's been robbing me blind for years. Up to now, I was weak and let him get away with it, but no more. Tonight I stood my ground and will continue to do so."

"I'm so happy to hear it." Belle gave her employer a hug. "If anyone deserves some happiness, it's you."

Mrs. Hollister looked absolutely radiant. "Ah, Belle, if you hadn't sat next to me on the train, this would never have happened. You're the one who gave me the strength to stand up to him. Now look what's happened. Luther and those two little girls have given me a new lease on life."

Belle gave a modest shrug. "You did it yourself."

"No, it was you, Belle, and I can only hope"—Mrs. Hollister made a little moue—"it's not my business, and I don't know all your reasons, but in my humble opinion you're a fool to let Yancy go. He's a fine man, and if you're thinking you can find anyone finer, then I wish you luck because you'll need it."

Belle let out a sigh. "You could be right."

"I know I'm right. Now let's go upstairs and check on the girls, shall we? If there's anything more endearing than watching little children as they sleep, I don't know what it is."

* * * *

Retiring to her room that night, Belle breathed a sigh of satisfaction. Today everything had gone right. Luther's little sisters had been rescued. Mrs. Hollister had got her spine back, and the horrible Malcolm and Eugenia would soon be gone. This was a day far different from the one when she'd run away from Roberto and ended up lost and desperate on the streets of San Francisco. Today only thoughts of Yancy McLeish cast a shadow over her heart. That he loved her, there could be no doubt. That she loved him? No doubt about that, either. But the problem was, everything had changed, yet nothing had changed. Marry the Yankee soldier? If she did, she knew herself too well to believe she'd never regret cutting herself off from her family for the rest of her life.

So far, she'd managed to save most of the money she'd earned. She didn't have enough to get home on yet, but she would soon. And meanwhile...

The more she saw Yancy, the worse would be the pain when she finally left. If she had any sense, she'd tell him she didn't want to see him again. If she had any sense, but when it came to Yancy McLeish, she was beginning to realize, she had no sense at all.

Chapter 20

In the days that followed, Belle found herself busier than ever. Luther hadn't been to school since he was twelve. Realizing how far he lagged behind, she, with help from Mrs. Hollister, acquired the books he needed to catch up, and tutored him every afternoon after he'd finished his work in the stables. She could hardly keep up with him. He absorbed information like a sponge, always eager for more

Impressed by Luther's swift progress, Belle told her employer, "He's very bright and should aim for that new university that just opened in Berkeley across the bay."

She saw Yancy a lot, more than she planned to, but he was always suggesting delightful outings with the children, and she could hardly refuse. Those were the happiest of days, when she and Yancy, along with Susan, Helen, Beth, Richard, and sometimes Luther, if he wasn't busy in the stable, took in the many delightful sights San Francisco had to offer. Sometimes Mrs. Hollister came along if her rheumatism didn't bother her too much. They went to the zoo at Woodward's Gardens again, this time visiting the aviary and snake house. They went on a picnic in Golden Gate Park and spent another enjoyable afternoon on the beach beneath the Cliff House. The children got along well, and so did she and Yancy. Sometimes when she looked at him, her heart ached with longing, but they were "just friends" now. She wouldn't dream of acting otherwise, and apparently neither would he.

Lately, Yancy had been spending much of his time with Reverend Madrid. Two or three nights a week, they searched for homeless children along the wicked streets of the Barbary Coast. On one such night, Yancy found Arthur Sweeney, the boy who'd led him to Luther. Now off the streets, living in the orphanage, Arthur faced a much brighter future. Yancy didn't say much, but Belle suspected he'd become deeply involved in the reverend's plan to replace the makeshift orphanage with a much-needed home for boys and girls, befitting a city the size of San Francisco. One day Yancy took Belle for a visit. The instant she saw those homeless little children, her heart went out to them, and before long she was reading *Jack and the Beanstalk* to a group of little ones gathered around. Afterward, the reverend drew her aside. "I see you have a way with the little ones," he said. "We need volunteers, and if you could give us a bit of your time, we'd be delighted to have you."

Belle thought that was a fine idea, and after checking with Mrs. Hollister, who also thought that was a fine idea, she started spending time at the orphanage. At first she did nothing more than play games with the little ones and read them stories. Before long, her natural teaching skills emerged, and she was helping children who'd never been to school to read, write, and know their numbers.

"Do you enjoy it?" Yancy asked her one day.

"I love it." What a joy to work with the lost little children of this world. Never had she felt so useful, so needed.

Yancy appeared to feel the same. "As you know, Ronald left me a lot of money, and I've been thinking I might put it to good use."

"You mean like building a new orphanage?"

"That's what I mean."

She said no more on the subject but his reply set her to wondering. If Yancy got involved in building an orphanage, how could he possibly be going home to his cabin by the lake anytime soon, if ever?

* * * *

One bright, sunny Sunday, Belle, Yancy, and the children were leaving the house for a picnic when Richard spoke up. "Father used to take us to Meiggs Wharf. It was fun. Can we go again?"

Meiggs Wharf, where Roberto kept his fishing boat. Belle had been so busy she hardly thought about Roberto Romano anymore, but the mere mention of Meiggs Wharf brought back painful memories and more than a little anxiety. What if Roberto saw her? Who knew what he would do? He probably thought she was back in Savannah by now, and she'd very much like to keep it that way.

Yancy must have sensed her unease. After a quick glance at Belle, he replied, "Sorry, Richard, we won't have time."

With an eight-year-old's enthusiasm, Richard replied, "Oh, yes, we would!"

"It would be fun to see all the ships," said Luther. "The girls would like it, too."

Above all else, Belle hated to disappoint the children. She dreaded the thought of running into Roberto Romano, but this was Sunday, wasn't it? The so-called day of rest when the Romanos would all go to church and not do anything resembling work. Meiggs Wharf was the last place on earth they'd be. She pulled Yancy aside. "The boats don't go out on Sunday. Roberto won't be there. I think it would be all right."

Yancy frowned with concern. "Not a good idea, Belle. Why take a chance?"

"I hate to disappoint the children. Even if I saw Roberto, which is highly unlikely, what could he do?"

Yancy pondered a moment. "I'm against it, but if you insist—"

"I insist," she said, laughing. She turned to the children. "You win. We're going to Meiggs Wharf."

Seeing the smiles on their faces was all the reward she needed. Besides, she'd be silly to worry. Life was good now. That whole episode with Roberto and his family was nothing but a fading memory.

When they arrived at Meiggs Wharf, they found a festive atmosphere where couples, whole families, and lots of children mingled, everyone looking happy, expecting a good time. As Yancy, Belle, and all five children began their stroll along the wharf, they sniffed the crisp, clean smell of the bay mixed with the aromas from fish of all kinds, freshly baked bread, spices from ships newly arrived from the Orient. They strolled past shops and food booths, listened to an organ grinder, stopped at a shooting gallery where the boys tried their skills, and Yancy showed them how. The crowds thinned as they passed the last of the shops and came upon the fishing fleet, all boats tied to their stanchions in observance of Sunday. Up to now, Belle hadn't a care, and had simply been enjoying herself, but now? She halted in her tracks. Perhaps she'd be foolish to go any farther.

"What are we stopping for?" Richard asked. "Aren't we going to see the fishing boats?"

"Just resting a moment."

Yancy regarded her with concern. "You don't have to go any farther. In fact, I wish you wouldn't."

Belle truly wanted to stop, but the children would be disappointed, especially Richard, who had an avid interest in all modes of transportation, and that included trains, the under-construction cable car system, and, of course, boats of all kinds. She started to walk again. "I want to see the boats, too," she breezily called. They continued along the wharf and began to pass the sailboats of the fishing fleet, all of them deserted this Sunday afternoon. Most were painted green, just as Tony had said, with the names of patron saints painted on the hulls. As they passed, Richard read the names aloud. "*Rose of Lima, Thomas Aquinas, Florian—*"

Belle stopped short. "*Florian?* That's Roberto's boat." It looked deserted like all the rest, but even so, her stomach clenched tight.

"We're going back right now," Yancy said. He called to the children, "We've gone far enough."

Just as Belle was turning around, a man appeared on the deck of the *Florian*. Tall and muscular...full head of hair...handsome face...Tony Romano! Thank God it was him, not Roberto.

He was looking straight at her with a puzzled expression. His face lit with recognition. "Miss Ainsworth, is that you?"

She could hardly get the words out. "Yes, Tony, it's me."

"Well, I'll be damned." With one easy leap, Tony was off the boat, standing in front of her. "What happened? We thought you'd be back in Savannah by now, but you're still here?" A sudden frown creased his forehead. "Look, I don't want to sound rude, but I think you'd better go. Roberto's here, down in the cabin. If he sees you here, he's not going to like it. He was pretty mad when you ran off like you did, and I don't think you'd want to—" He gazed back at the boat. Here came Roberto, climbing to the deck. "Uh-oh, he's coming. Better get out of here."

Belle had every intention of leaving, but her body wouldn't cooperate. She stood frozen, her gaze fastened on the man she nearly married as he emerged from the cabin, crossed the deck, clasped the railing, and gazed at her with an expression that slowly changed from mild curiosity to... He'd recognized her! She could tell by the slight lift of his eyebrows. Other than that, his expression didn't change. He simply stood staring at her, his face unreadable. Even so, although she couldn't define it, something in his expression sent a chill through her. Clearly he hadn't forgotten.

Yancy took her arm and spoke softly in her ear. "Let's get out of here."

She allowed herself to be led away. They were nearly off the wharf before she got her voice back. "Did you see him?" she asked Yancy. "That was Roberto Romano."

"I gathered that."

"He hates me."

"I gathered that, too."

"I owe you an apology. You told me not to go to Meiggs Wharf, but I went anyway."

Yancy smiled generously. "You're forgiven. Are you all right? Your face is pale."

Belle's pulse still raced. She needed to calm herself. If she didn't, she'd upset the children. "I'm fine now. I didn't like the way he looked at me, but why worry? He has no idea where I live, and in a city this size, how could he ever find me?"

Yancy remained oddly silent.

"You don't think he could, could he?"

"I think you'd better be careful. Come on, let's go home."

Chapter 21

By the third day after her visit to Meiggs Wharf, Belle was back to her sunny mood. Seeing Roberto had been a shock, but why worry? Even if he could find her, why would he want to? She must have been mistaken about the malice she thought she'd seen on his face. He was merely surprised when he saw her on the wharf, just as she was surprised to see him. She doubted he'd entirely forgotten, but being the busy man that he was, by now he would have accepted his loss and moved on. She certainly had. With her duties as Mrs. Hollister's companion and her work at the orphanage, her life had become so full she had no time to worry over what Roberto Romano might do. She still spent time with Yancy, too. He was always coming up with new ideas for fun with the children, and she gladly went along. Being "just friends" was hard as ever, but she'd made up her mind. She would return to Savannah as soon as she'd saved enough money, and that wouldn't take much longer.

Lately, she had more reason to go back than ever. She'd finally received two letters from home, one from Bridger, the other from Victoria. She opened Bridger's first. In it, he told her how well he was feeling, and how she'd done the right thing when she'd run out on her marriage to "that lying scoundrel, Roberto." Victoria's letter warmed Belle's heart. "We all make mistakes," she wrote. "Come home as soon as you can, back to the loving arms of your family." At the end of her letter, she wrote, "Bridger is not doing well. He stays in his room all the time now and tries to conceal his pain, but I know he's suffering more than ever."

That settled it. She must get home to Savannah as soon as possible.

Early one afternoon, when Belle and Mrs. Hollister were chatting in the drawing room, the doorbell rang. Bertha answered and soon came in to announce, "Miss Ainsworth, there's a man wants to see you. He says he has a message for you but won't come in."

Curious, Belle hastened to the door and found Tony Romano standing on the doorstep, a tentative smile on his face. "Hello, Miss Ainsworth, I'll bet you're surprised to see me."

Flabbergasted would be more like it. She liked Roberto's younger brother. He'd always been friendly, and she'd never considered him a threat. "What a surprise, Tony. To be honest, you're about the last person I expected to see. How did you find me?"

"Well, uh..." Tony looked uneasy. "I don't know exactly. Roberto found you, but I don't know how."

Belle remembered her manners. "Won't you come in?"

"No, thank you, I won't. I just needed to deliver this message."

"Then go ahead, Tony, if you're sure." She couldn't imagine what he had to say.

"There's a big family dinner tonight at Romano's Fish Grotto, and you're invited."

She stared at him, tongue-tied. "*I'm* invited?"

"Yes, you."

"But why? Roberto must still be angry at me. I can't say that I blame him, considering how I ran away like I did."

Tony nodded in agreement. "He was fit to be tied, and with good reason. I know it sounds crazy, but he's beyond all that now. He's not mad anymore. He's forgiven you, and when he saw you at Meiggs Wharf the other day, he got to thinking what a nice idea it would be if we all got together for dinner at his restaurant. He talked to the family, and they all agreed. They were happy when they found out you hadn't left the city yet, and really want to see you again. That means everyone, including the kids."

What should she do? She would love to see Mama and Rosa again, even Gianna, but she hadn't forgotten Roberto's arrogance and conceit, and found it hard to believe he'd actually forgiven her. "I'm not sure." She remembered the other day, and how Tony had acted on the wharf. "If Roberto has forgiven me, why were you so anxious for me to leave the other day?"

"I was mistaken. He was happy to see you, and you don't have to worry about a thing. And besides, it's not like Roberto wants to get you off to some dark, secret place by himself. We'll all be in his restaurant, surrounded by people. What could be safer?"

He had a point. She had nothing to worry about, so why not go? She'd be leaving the city soon, probably forever, and would feel a lot better knowing she'd made amends with the family that had treated her so well. Bruno excepted, of course. "What time?"

"I'll come get you at seven."

Back in the drawing room, Belle told Mrs. Hollister about her surprising invitation.

The older woman arched a skeptical eyebrow. "You're not actually thinking of going, are you?"

"I wouldn't if I didn't think it was safe, but Tony assured me Roberto isn't angry anymore. I couldn't care less about seeing him, but Mama and Rosa were especially kind. I'd like to tell them so and say the proper goodbyes."

Mrs. Hollister gave one of her disdainful sniffs, the kind Belle well remembered from the train. "If you want my opinion, you're making a mistake."

"Why do you think so?"

The older woman frowned in thought. "I'm simply going by what you've told me about Roberto. He's a vain, arrogant man, and those kind never forgive."

"I'll be careful."

"Maybe you should bring Yancy with you."

What a bad idea. Belle would have laughed aloud if Mrs. Hollister hadn't been so serious. "Yancy wouldn't be interested. And besides, like you, he'd think I was making a mistake."

"That's because maybe you are."

Was she? For a moment, a chill crossed her heart. Even so, a few second thoughts weren't enough to change her mind.

* * * *

Belle gave careful thought to what she would wear for her dinner with the Romanos and decided upon the royal-blue gown that was becoming but not too fancy. Tony picked her up at seven. As usual, he was easy to talk to, and by the time they reached Romano's Fish Grotto, she was chatting away, the last of her uneasiness forgotten. "Big crowd tonight," Tony remarked as he found a free space among the many horses and carriages parked around the building.

Belle stepped eagerly from the carriage. "I'm so looking forward to seeing your family again."

A steady murmur of voices greeted her as she stepped inside the large room filled with tables, all of them full. She looked for the Romanos but didn't see them. "Where—?"

"We're dining privately." Tony led the way to the other side of the restaurant to a heavy oak door marked Banquet Room. He opened it and stepped back. "You first, Miss Ainsworth."

Belle stepped into a dimly lit room almost cavernous in its proportions. At first she couldn't see much. Squinting, she took a step forward. The room seemed empty. Where was everyone? She heard a clicking noise behind her. Was that a door shutting? She turned to ask Tony, but he wasn't there, and the door was shut. "Tony!" She grasped the doorknob and tried to turn it, but it wouldn't move. "Tony!" she called louder this time.

"Good evening, Belle. I'm so happy you could join me."

Roberto's voice, coming from deep within the room. She turned to look at him, her back pressed defensively against the door. She could see him now—seated at the head of a long banquet table that ran down the center of the room. Her eyes gradually adjusted to the dim light, and she could see several long tables, all of them empty. "Where is everyone?"

"I'll explain everything," Roberto replied in a reasonable voice. "No cause for alarm. Come and sit down, Belle."

What was going on? Where were Mama, Rosa, and all the rest? Hadn't they arrived yet? She moved closer. At first she hadn't noticed, but the room seemed to be decorated for a special occasion—a wedding, she guessed, judging from the white crepe paper streamers and wedding bells that hung from the ceiling. Rows of complete settings—plates, silverware, napkins, water and wineglasses—lined each side of the tables, along with large flower arrangements placed in the center.

But wait. Something wasn't right, and she couldn't quite figure out what it was.

While she moved toward the table where Roberto was sitting, she took a closer look. Apparently dinner had already been served because the plates were full of food. She looked closer still and nearly gasped aloud. Not fresh food, but withered, dried-looking food that had been sitting on the plates for who knew how long. Some of the water glasses were full, some half full, some empty. Same with the wineglasses. Napkins had been tossed every which way. The haphazard position of some of the knives and forks indicated they'd been thrown down in a hurry. "Roberto, what is this?"

"Come sit down and I'll explain," he replied, his tone friendly and reasonable.

She didn't want to sit next to him. She wanted to leave, but the door was locked, and he wasn't going to open it. *Stay calm.* At least he didn't sound angry. She would listen to whatever he had to say and then demand he unlock the door so she could get out of here. She walked to the head of the table. There he sat, a slight smile on his face, dressed in a black formal tailcoat and white bow tie—exactly what he would have worn at their wedding. He rose from his seat. "Before you sit down, I want to show you something." He led her to a long table that stood against the back wall. A beautifully decorated four-tiered wedding cake sat in the middle, complete with black-and-white figures of a bride and groom on the top. A large punch bowl sat on either side of the cake, surrounded by rows of crystal punch cups. A knife decorated with a big white bow lay next to the cake.

Roberto placed a hand on her shoulder. "Can you see what's written on the bottom layer?"

Belle bent to look closer. *Oh, my God.* She could hardly believe it, but there it was: "Roberto & Belle" written in pink icing, surrounded by tiny pink and white rosebuds. She raised up and stared at him in astonishment. "This is our wedding dinner?"

"How did you guess?" A small measure of sarcasm had slipped into his voice.

"But this is insane."

"You think so?" He led her back to the head of the table where two place settings, one of them unused, had been arranged. He pointed to the unused one. "Let me tell you about that night, Belle. This is where you were going to sit. I sat here waiting…and waiting. The guests were getting hungry, so I decided we'd start the dinner. So everyone sat down at the tables, but they kept looking around. 'Where's the bride?' They kept saying it. 'Where's the bride?' Then gradually I saw it on their faces. 'She's not coming. Roberto has been jilted. Roberto has been made a fool of.'"

His voice had been low when he started, but it kept rising until now he was almost shouting. She could try to explain, but what could she say? If she told the truth, she'd have to admit she had disliked him on sight and loathed and despised him by the time she left. "Roberto, I'm truly sorry I caused you any pain. It was not my intention. I simply realized the marriage wasn't going to work, and it would be best for me to leave as quickly as possible."

"Do you realize…?" He drew in a deep, uneven breath that revealed the fury raging beneath his calm façade. "Here I sat with a roomful of guests. Friends, family, neighbors, my employees, Belle, *my employees*! Can you understand my humiliation when you didn't show up?"

Her knees were going weak. "Well, I…"

"Not to mention the money I spent. The band. The flowers. The food. Look around you." In a wild, uncontrolled gesture, he waved his arm. "'Spare no expense,' I said. 'This is my wedding day." Shouting, he repeated, "MY WEDDING DAY!"

The last of Roberto's friendly pretense had dropped away. Looking into his cold, hard eyes, Belle could hardly breathe. Here was a man in a black rage with hatred in his heart. She thought she could control the situation but how foolish. She was helpless, at his mercy. She wouldn't give up, though, and would try to calm him down. "Let's sit and talk, shall we?" she suggested in a pleasant tone. "I'll try to explain." Although what she could possibly say she had no idea.

His breath coming hard, he replied, "Of course, Belle." He pulled out the chair from her unused place at the table. "Have a seat." He sat and faced her. "Better late than never."

She sank into the chair, ignoring the heavy sarcasm in his last remark. She would try to distract him. "How did you find me?"

He laughed and replied, "That was easy. Remember the day your friend came to get your trunk? My fine nephew, Bruno, hitched a ride on the back of his carriage when he returned home, so I knew where you were staying."

"But I didn't stay there long."

"You think your friend wasn't easy to follow?" Roberto's eyes narrowed. "So you live on Nob Hill now? Cavorting with the millionaires? Nice work, Belle."

Any explanation concerning why she was living on Nob Hill would be worthless, and she wouldn't even try. In desperation, she slanted a quick glance toward the door.

"Don't bother," he said. "You're not going anywhere."

"What about Tony?"

"He does what I tell him to do."

So Tony not only knew, his lies were what brought her here. "I can't believe this." She looked around the room again. The white crepe streamers were beginning to sag. The flowers had long since wilted and turned brown. The pathetic sight jogged her memory. This was a scene straight from Charles Dickens's *Great Expectations*. She'd read the book ages ago but still remembered poor Miss Havisham, the crazy old woman who'd been jilted at the altar. Decades later, she still wore her wedding dress and had left everything the same as on her wedding day, cake and all. But Miss Havisham was a figment of the author's imagination. Nobody in real life could be that crazy. "Roberto, why haven't you had this room cleaned up? There must be a reason."

He smiled and didn't answer. He picked up an unopened bottle of champagne and gazed at the label. "*Veuve Clicquot.* Special for our wedding dinner." His dark eyes narrowed and hardened. "I paid over two hundred dollars for just one bottle."

Fear gripped her heart. She didn't know what he was planning, but he did not wish her well. "I'm truly sorry I cost you money and caused all this grief, Roberto."

"Let's drink a toast anyway, shall we? For old time's sake." Without waiting for an answer, he popped the cork from the *Veuve Clicquot*, pulled two champagne glasses close, and started pouring. "Oh, don't worry," he said. "The glasses are clean and straight from the kitchen." When he finished pouring, he handed her a glass. "Drink up. Let's not waste my two hundred dollars."

"Thank you." She took the glass and set it on the table.

Her action seemed to amuse him. He lifted his own glass and took a sip. "It's not poisoned."

The last thing she wanted was a glass of champagne, but she'd better go along with whatever he said. "I didn't think it was." She lifted the glass and took a sip. The bubbling liquid tickled her palate. It was all she could do to keep from wrinkling her nose.

"Fine then." He leaned back in his chair, as if he were all relaxed, but she knew he wasn't. "This is an interesting room," he said. "Do you know its history?"

She shook her head.

"The restaurant is new, but the banquet room is part of an old saloon called the Golden Spike. It was built back in the gold rush days. From what they tell me, it had a bad reputation. Did you know we're sitting over the bay?"

"I had no idea." She was trying to sound relaxed, as if they were having an ordinary conversation, but she couldn't keep a slight tremor from her voice.

"Seems the Golden Spike was best known for drugging sailors, dropping them through a trapdoor to a waiting boat, and hauling them out to some ship where the captain would pay well for another crewman." He nodded toward her nearly full glass. "You don't like the champagne?"

"Of course I do." She took another sip, a bigger one this time to keep him happy. "Drugging someone is a cruel thing to do," she said.

"They used a drug called chloral hydrate. A few drops in a glass of beer was all it took. 'Shanghaied' they called it. That's because the poor sod who got drugged often ended up in Shanghai, China. He'd be gone for years, sometimes forever. The original trapdoor still exists. It's over in the corner. Would you like to see it? I've left it just as it was."

No! She definitely did not want to see the trapdoor, nor even get close. She took another sip of champagne. "I trust you don't use it anymore." She'd tried to sound funny and relaxed but heard the fear in her voice.

He chuckled with a dry, cynical sound. "Men still get shanghaied. Not here, of course. I haven't used the trapdoor yet, but you never know when I might have good reason to get rid of someone."

The truth dawned. She could threaten, beg, plead, and present every rational argument she could think of, but nothing she tried would do any good. She'd committed the unforgivable sin of embarrassing and humiliating Roberto Romano, damaged his huge ego, and he would never forgive her. All her own fault. What a fool she'd been to believe Tony's lies. Why hadn't she listened to Mrs. Hollister? Why hadn't she told Yancy? She fastened her gaze on Roberto. "So what are you planning to do? Drop me through that trapdoor?"

"Yes, I am, Belle. Nobody gets the best of Roberto Romano." He leaned back, sipping his champagne contentedly. "Can't be helped. You will simply go missing and never be found."

She couldn't run, he'd catch her. The walls and door were so thick nobody would hear her if she screamed. *The cake knife.* At least she could defend herself and go down fighting. On the table, next to the cake. She must get her hands on it. She arose halfway from her chair. Something was wrong. Sweat breaking out on her forehead. Funny feeling in her head. Everything spinning around, light-headed, dizzy. She grabbed the table with both hands. "Roberto…you didn't…"

"I did."

The smiling face of Roberto Romano was the last thing she saw before she felt herself falling to the floor and darkness enveloped her.

Chapter 22

Yancy was having dinner with the children when Mrs. O'Brien announced he had a visitor. Mrs. Edith Hollister, who appeared to be quite anxious about something, awaited him in the drawing room. Yancy immediately arose from the table. He couldn't imagine why that formidable lady had come to see him, but whatever the reason, it couldn't be good.

Entering the drawing room, he found Mrs. Hollister pacing the floor. Not bothering with a greeting, she exclaimed, "Oh, Mr. McLeish, I think Belle's in trouble." She started to explain, but when he heard "Robert Romano" and "Romano's Fish Grotto," he held up his hand.

"Let's go," he said. "You can tell me the rest on the way."

Luther waited in the buggy. Yancy took over the reins and headed for Meiggs Wharf, Mrs. Hollister wringing her hands as she explained why she "just had a feeling" Belle was in danger even though she claimed she'd be perfectly safe.

"You were right to come to me," Yancy said. He "just had a feeling," too, and urged the horses to pick up their pace. When they arrived at the restaurant, Yancy spied a young man hurriedly climbing into a buggy. Tall and dark, full head of black, curly hair—that had to be Tony, the younger brother he'd mistaken for Roberto the day he arrived in San Francisco. "Wait up!" he called. Tony didn't stop. Yancy leaped to the ground and grabbed his arm. "Where's Belle?"

Tony got a funny look on his face. "I don't know what you're talking about."

"Yes, you do. You're going back inside."

"No, I'm not."

"Yes, you are. Let's go."

Yancy hadn't raised his voice, but it carried such a ring of command that Tony shrugged in defeat. "All right," he replied in a docile tone. "No need to get mad about it."

Tony returned to the restaurant, Yancy, Luther, and Mrs. Hollister following close behind. Once inside, Yancy demanded, "Show me where she is."

Tony started stammering. His eyes kept shifting, as if he was looking for a chance to run away. Yancy gripped his arm. "Tell me!"

Tony cringed and cried, "All right, I'll show you."

"Lead the way."

Tony led them across the large dining room to the door of the banquet room. He stepped aside. "She's in there."

Yancy tried the door and found it locked. "Where's the key?"

"I don't have it."

Yancy reached beneath his coat and pulled out his revolver. Thank God he'd thought to carry it. He aimed at the lock on the door. "Give me the key or I'll blast the lock open." He glanced around. Already some of the diners were curiously looking their way. "We can do this quietly, or do you want the whole restaurant in a panic? One shot should do it."

Wordlessly, Tony reached in his pocket, handed Yancy the key, and bolted away.

Yancy unlocked the door, and the three stepped inside. "My goodness, it's so dim here," Mrs. Hollister said. Yancy could see well enough to make out a lone figure standing at the far end of the room. He started toward it, able to see the figure was a man holding something in his arms. He drew closer. That must be Roberto Romano, and he was carrying someone. Was it Belle? "What are you doing?" he shouted, not slowing down.

Romano dropped his burden to the floor. With a snarl, he rushed at Yancy and threw a punch aimed at his head. Yancy easily blocked it and returned a blow that knocked his attacker back against the far wall, next to what looked like an open trapdoor. He staggered to his feet. Yancy headed toward him. For a brief moment Romano hesitated, as if not sure what he'd do. And then he was gone. Yancy stopped in his tracks. A splash came from below. He walked to the trapdoor and peered down into the darkness. Although he couldn't see a thing, the sound of water lapping against the wooden pilings told him this part of the building stood well over the bay. Luther joined him, shaking his head in astonishment. "Was that Mr. Romano? Why would he do such a thing?"

"Because he was afraid to face me." Yancy got to his feet and hurried to where Belle lay unmoving on the floor, Mrs. Hollister kneeling beside her. "Is she all right?"

"She's breathing just fine. There's no blood anyplace, and I don't see any injuries."

Relief swept through him. He knelt by Belle's side and examined her closely. Yes, she seemed to be all right. Most likely Romano had slipped her some kind of knock-out drug.

"What do you think happened to that awful man?"

"It's hard to tell, Mrs. Hollister. He either drowned, swam to shore, or he's still down there hanging on to one of the pilings."

"But if he's alive, won't he still try to hurt her?"

"Romano's a coward. It's highly unlikely he'd ever want to tangle with me again." Belle moaned softly. "Let's get her home and call the doctor."

* * * *

In the darkest recesses of her mind, Belle slowly become aware she'd been in a faraway place she'd never been before. Simple awareness sufficed. Only gradually did questions begin to form. Why am I lying down? Where am I? Why do I feel so peculiar? She opened her eyes and found herself lying in her own bed. Mrs. Hollister sat beside her, Tippet curled on her lap. Seeing Belle had opened her eyes, she remarked, "So you're finally awake. It's about time."

"Where...where have I been?" Hard putting the words together.

"What do you remember?"

She could barely think straight. The ride to the restaurant with Tony. Stepping into the banquet room. The locked door. The sagging white streamers... "Roberto! He was going to kill me."

"And just about did. You're a lucky girl. We almost lost you. If it hadn't been for Yancy, you'd be gone forever, and we'd never know what happened to you." Mrs. Hollister went on to describe the horrifying scene in the banquet room and how Yancy had come to her rescue. When she finished, she placed Tippet on the floor and handed Belle a full glass of water. "Here, drink this. The doctor said you should drink lots of liquids. To flush your system out, he said."

Belle struggled to sit up. She welcomed the water and drank the whole glass at once. "What time is it?"

"Four o'clock in the afternoon. You slept the day away."

"How did I get home?"

"Yancy carried you to the buggy and got you back here in a hurry. We sent for the doctor. He said you'd been drugged, probably with chloral hydrate, the same thing they use to shanghai those poor sailors."

"But how could Roberto have drugged me? He made me drink some champagne, but he drank some, too, from the same bottle."

"What about your glass, Belle? Could he have put the chloral hydrate in the glass before he poured the champagne?"

Belle pictured the scene in her mind. "He said he'd brought fresh glasses from the kitchen, so of course that's what he did." With a groan, she declared, "It's all clear now. What a fool I was."

Mrs. Hollister vigorously nodded her head. "Yes, you were, but at least you're alive, and the doctor said you'd be all right. Yancy stayed for a while, but you slept so long he finally went home."

"It looks like I owe him my life, and you, too."

"Thanks, but it was mostly Yancy. If ever there was a hero, it's him, and why you refuse to marry the man is beyond me. I'll leave you now, so you can get some more rest." She picked up two letters from the bedside table and handed them to Belle. "These came today."

After she left, Tippet following behind, Belle laid the unopened letters on the bed beside her and stared into space. Hard to get it through her head that Roberto had nearly killed her. If not for Yancy, she could be deep in her watery grave by now. Once again, he'd come to her rescue. That made twice he'd risked his life for her, yet she'd rejected him even though she loved him. *Why?* Because he was a Yankee and her family wouldn't approve? How foolish could she get?

And yet...

Soon she'd be leaving San Francisco, headed for home. But was that what she really wanted? Why must life be so confusing? She picked up the letters. Both came from Savannah, one from Bridger, the other from Victoria. Strange, how the letter from Bridger was in Victoria's handwriting, yet his name appeared in the corner. She opened it first and read:

Dearest Belle,

In case you're wondering why Victoria is writing this for me, it seems I've "taken a turn for the worse," or so the doctor says, and now find myself a prisoner of my bed, too weak to lift a pen.

You wrote to me about Yancy McLeish, the man you met on the train and fell in love with. You say you can't marry him because he's a Yankee

*and friends and family would disapprove. My dear little sister, are you
out of your mind? Are you still worried about what people think? Are
the opinions of your family so important you'd throw your happiness
away? Do you really care what Mrs. Beauregard Bedford Stuart and
the Georgia Ladies of the Confederacy might say?*

*Remember what I told you once: All we really have is not yesterday,
not tomorrow, but <u>now</u>. You can't look back. The war is over. Who
fought whom doesn't matter anymore, even though there's many a
stubborn Southerner who'd argue otherwise. You can't look ahead,
either. Nobody can. Unless you've completely lost your mind, for
God's sake, just marry the man and let the future take care of itself.*

*This may be my last letter to you. I won't lie and say I don't mind
that my life has been cut short, but I shall leave this world knowing
I did my duty as God saw fit. My deepest wish is for your happiness,
and on the day of your wedding to Yancy McLeish, kindly raise a glass
to the brother who loved you more than words can ever say.*

Bridger

For a long time, Belle sat on the edge of the bed, numb with grief.
After a time, she walked to the window, a bit wobbly at first, but the drug
had completely worn off and she was fine. She stared out the window for
she didn't know how long, not wanting to return, not wanting to open
that second letter.

But she couldn't stand here forever. She left the window and sat on
the edge of the bed again. With a deep sigh of acceptance, she opened the
letter from Victoria.

My Dear Sister,

*It is with great sorrow that I must tell you our beloved brother left
us last night. Bridger was cheerful to the end. He had accepted his fate
and firmly believed he was going to a better place, and I'm sure he has.*

*Before he died, he told me about you and that Yankee, Yancy McLeish.
He said you loved him but would never marry him because of what
your family might say. I admit there was a time when my hatred of
the Yankees knew no bounds. At the least, I wished them all dead,
and if I never saw another Yankee soldier, it would be way too soon.
But time has erased those awful memories and softened my heart.
With Bridger's help, I have learned forgiveness. If he, who had gone
through so much suffering, could forgive and forget, then so can I.*

I weep as I write this and can only hope Bridger's death will mark the last of our family's tragedies. Marry your Yankee, Belle. Bring him home to meet us, and he will be welcomed with open arms.

Your grieving sister, Victoria

Despite the deep, wrenching sorrow that overcame her, at long last Belle found the peace of mind she'd long been seeking and knew what she had to do.

* * * *

Yancy was having a busy day. In the morning, he'd met with Ronald's attorney, Mr. Frederick Bartlett, to discuss his adoption of Beth and Richard. Assured she'd still receive her share of Ronald's estate, Bernice had readily agreed to sign the papers. In the afternoon, Yancy met with Reverend Madrid to discuss plans for the building of a new orphanage. Yancy had become deeply involved, both personally and financially. He liked to think his brother would be pleased knowing a sizable portion of his hard-earned money would be put to good use. What more noble cause than bettering the lives of underprivileged children?

Looking back, Yancy couldn't pinpoint the exact moment he decided to stay in San Francisco and make it his home. Although he would miss his hermit life in the Maine woods, he'd gradually come to realize he wasn't a stranger in a strange land anymore. He belonged in this bustling, beautiful city where each and every morning he awoke with a purpose in his life, eager to begin his day.

And then there was Belle.

Thanks to Roberto Romano, he'd come close to losing her. That made twice now. How many times must he show her his love before she realized they belonged together? She might be flighty sometimes. She might be prone to making bad decisions, but no man could love a woman more than he loved Belle Ainsworth. How could she not know that? He would wait forever if he had to, even if she returned to Savannah, which he highly doubted she would. One of these days she'd come to her senses. He just had to be patient enough.

He was in the drawing room when he heard the doorbell ring. Soon Mrs. O'Brien appeared. "Miss Ainsworth is here to see you."

"Show her in."

Here she came, dressed in her brown wool suit, another one of those silly ostrich-plumed hats upon her head.

"Hello, Yancy." She had a sort of tentative smile on her face, as if she wasn't sure if she'd be welcome or not.

He nodded briefly. "I see you got a new hat."

"Yes, I did, but that's not why I'm here. For one thing, I came to thank you for saving my life last night."

"Think nothing of it." He waved toward the settee. "Care to sit down?"

"I'll stand, thank you. I have something else to say."

He caught his breath. It was all he could do to return a careless, "Is that so?"

She gazed at the ceiling and back again. "Bridger is dead."

"Oh, Belle, I'm so sorry." He took a step toward her.

She held up her hand. "Wait. Hear me out. Before he died, he wrote me a letter. He asked if I was out of my mind because I wouldn't marry you. He was right. Bridger was always right." She choked up and for a moment couldn't speak. He waited patiently until she could go on. "So the reason I'm here is to tell you that I love you, Yancy McLeish. I love you with all my heart, and if you still want me, I'm yours."

"Ah, Belle..." He took her into his arms. "Of course I still want you. I've loved you since that moment you sat across from me on the train."

"I've been an idiot."

"No, you haven't. I'm still a Yankee and always will be, but if you can ignore the past, we'll be happy. That's all that ever stood between us."

"But where will we live? I suppose I could live in the woods—"

"That won't be necessary. We'll stay in San Francisco. I can't leave now. I'm helping to build an orphanage and I've got a niece and nephew to raise."

* * * *

Belle had never in her life felt such peace and satisfaction. After all she'd been through, she could hardly believe such happiness could be hers. "That's wonderful," she said. "I've grown to love the children, not only Richard and Beth but Luther and his sisters, too. I hated the thought of leaving them, and now I won't have to."

She thought of Bridger and how she wished he could be here to share this moment. But then... She had a feeling that somehow he was.

Yancy stood back and regarded her with eyes full of love. "It's a beautiful day. Let's take the children and go someplace."

"I think that's a fine idea."

Meet the Author

Shirley Kennedy was born and raised in Fresno, California. She lived in Canada for many years and graduated from the University of Calgary, Alberta, Canada, with a B.S. in computer science.

She has published novels with Ballantine, Signet, and several smaller presses. She writes in several different genres including Regency romance, western romance, and contemporary fiction. She lives in Las Vegas, Nevada, and is an active member of the Romance Writers of America, Las Vegas chapter. Please visit Shirley at www.shirleykennedy.com, or follow her Twitter account @ladyk360, or on Facebook at https://www.facebook.com/shirley.kennedy.52.

River Queen Rose

If you enjoyed *Bay City Belle*, be sure not to miss the first book in Shirley Kennedy's In Old California series!

The ramshackle River Queen Hotel is home to vagabonds, gamblers, and heathens—and now, to new widow Rose Peterson. The rundown Gold Rush establishment is the only thing her late husband, Emmet, left her. Despite its raucous saloon and ladies of the evening, Rose can see the hotel's potential. Her late husband's family claim that sheltered Rose isn't capable of running the Sacramento inn herself. But she is determined to make a new life for herself and her young daughter, even if it means flying in the face of custom and propriety. She feels as if she hasn't a friend in the world.

Except, perhaps, one. Decatur "Deke" Fleming, a tall, lanky Australian who once served as Emmet's farmhand. Pride prevents Deke from revealing his moneyed past; conscience keeps him from confessing his feelings for the still grieving widow. But when Rose is tempted by wealthy civic leader and hotel owner Mason Talbot, Deke may be the only person who can save her—and the one man capable of reviving her bruised and battered heart . . .

Keep reading for a special look!
A Lyrical e-book on sale now.

Chapter 1

In the foothills of the Sierra Nevada, September, 1854

Rose Peterson shivered in her underwear as she stood in the freezing cold creek. She flinched as she splashed cold water on herself. She'd gone days without a bath and gladly endured the shock of it just to get clean. She turned to her sister-in-law who stood in her chemise beside her. "Just one more day. Think of it! One more day and we'll be there."

Drucilla returned her familiar mocking smile. "Just one more day? Thanks for telling me, Rose. I hadn't noticed."

"I'll wager you hadn't." Rose accompanied her words with a scoop of creek water splashed over her sister-in-law's head.

Drucilla splashed her back. "Are you excited about seeing Emmet again?"

"Of course I am." Rose hoped she sounded convincing. Strange, how she didn't feel the least excited, even though she hadn't seen her husband for over two years. She wasn't the only wife who'd been deserted when word of the Gold Rush reached Illinois. Like thousands of others, Emmet rushed to California. Unlike most of the thousands, after finding a little gold, he concluded there were other ways to make money without breaking his back in a freezing cold stream. He bought a hotel in Sacramento and a small farm outside of town. Everyone rejoiced when he finally sent a letter asking his family to join him.

"I'm clean enough," Drucilla announced. "Let's get out of this freezing water."

Rose readily agreed. She was getting goose bumps from the cold. She ran a hand over her thick, golden-bronze hair that hung halfway to her waist.

What a relief to have it clean again. She laughed to herself. Before they left Illinois, she'd taken great pride in her appearance. Perhaps that pride involved a bit of vanity, but when she looked in her mirror, she couldn't help but be pleased at her tall, slim figure, her even-featured face that everyone said was pretty, and her long, thick hair that she loved to wear hanging loose or sometimes swept in a bun atop her head. Those days were long gone. After spending five miserable months in a wagon train with her in-laws, she didn't much care what she looked like, nor did anyone else. Her main interest now was keeping her daughter safe and staying alive.

As they climbed from the water, Drucilla called, "Just think, the next time I take a bath, it will be in a real tub with real hot water."

"I can't even imagine it." Her teeth chattering, Rose quickly pulled her dress over her head. There were lots of things she couldn't imagine. Like sleeping in a real bed. Like eating at a real table.

Like being a wife to Emmet again.

Since they were married, they'd lived with his family, so she'd never had to worry about cooking his meals or washing his clothes. Coralee, his mother, did all that. Thin and wiry, a never-stopping bundle of energy, she treated her daughter-in-law as nothing more than a willing helper. The one area that didn't belong to Coralee was the bedroom. On the long trek west, Rose hardly gave it a thought, but now, with their destination less than a day away, she was remembering those many less-than-thrilling nights when Emmet insisted they "make love." He misspoke. Love had little to do with his near nightly performance: a quick kiss—climb on—a few hard-breathing grunts—final big grunt—roll off, and it was over. How very tiresome. In fact, Emmet and his wooden personality were tiresome. He was a good husband in many ways, but not in the bedroom, not like...

Anthony. Like a sinful pleasure, thoughts of that long-ago night crept uninvited into her head. She quelled them quickly, as she always did, telling herself it never happened, that she could never have behaved in such a wanton, disgraceful manner.

The truth was, she'd enjoyed these last two years when she slept alone and didn't have to deal with Emmet's attentions, but she'd better face the fact that those enjoyable days were nearly over. She recognized her wifely duties and would never dream of complaining. After all, Emmet wasn't a bad man, a bit quick-tempered, perhaps, but in all other ways, he'd been kind to her. He was surely a good provider, and when Lucy came along, he got tears in his eyes when he saw his new daughter for the first time. Indeed, he couldn't have been a better, more loving father. So, of course, she'd be glad to see him again. Not thrilled, maybe, but happy enough, and really, what more could she expect in life than the role Fate had assigned her as a wife and mother?

Or so she kept telling herself.

Sometimes a hunger rose from deep within her for something more in her life. The trouble was, she didn't know what. At the age of twenty-six, she sometimes got the feeling that life was passing her by and what had she accomplished? Lucy, of course. Watching her little girl grow was an ongoing, joyful miracle, but couldn't she have something more?

Well, of course not. After all, she was a woman, so what more could she expect? She should count her blessings and forget such foolishness.

* * * *

The Petersons were part of a train of fifty-five wagons, now parked in a circle far down the western slope of the Sierra Nevada Mountains. Returning to the campsite, Rose sensed the excitement all around her. California! After months of grueling travel, they'd reached the Golden Land. Fortunes would be made. Life would be good in this sun-drenched state that brimmed with opportunities. She searched for Lucy. Of them all, her five-year-old daughter had fared the best on their wearisome journey. She never complained about the monotonous beans-bacon-and-biscuits diet. After a long day on the trail, when the adults moaned about sore muscles and aching feet, Lucy was running around with other children on the train, bright and happy with endless energy.

Rose spotted her daughter playing at the wagon next to her own. As she drew close, she sensed something different. Something, but what? Somehow her little girl with the bright eyes and long, blond curls didn't look the same. Oh, no, her hair! This morning, Rose had swept it back from Lucy's forehead and fastened it into two braids. Now it hung loose, and someone had cut low-hanging bangs so long they nearly touched her brows.

Lucy skipped up to her, blue eyes sparkling. "Mommy, how do you like my hair?"

"Why, I... I..."

"Grandma cut my bangs. She said I'll look my best when I see Daddy again."

The nerve! To conceal her rage, which surely must show on her face, Rose bent low, as if to closer inspect her daughter's new hairstyle. How dare Coralee cut it without even asking! That was a mother's job and nobody else's, not even a doting grandmother's. But too late now. Above all, she mustn't make Lucy feel bad. With an effort, she forced her lips into a smile and raised up. "You look very pretty, sweetheart. Daddy will think so, too."

As Lucy ran off, Rose took a deep breath to compose herself. This sort of thing had happened before, and she shouldn't have been surprised. No use complaining. Emmet always took his parents' side. She'd long since realized she wasn't first in his heart, not like a wife was supposed to be. Even when he sent the letter telling them to come, he'd addressed it to Ben and Coralee, not to her. She and Lucy were a mere mention at the bottom of the list. She admired his fierce loyalty to his family, but there were times when her resentment ran deep, especially the times when she pleaded for a home of their own, and he turned a deaf ear.

But she always tried to count her blessings. Thank goodness she got along well with the Petersons. Their trip west, spending five months cramped in two wagons, could have been a nightmare, but it wasn't. Ben and Coralee were strict but fair. They adored little Lucy, and she adored them. Thirty-year-old Drucilla, her sister-in-law, was the ongoing despair of her parents, but Rose got along with her just fine. Often they rode together, Rose on Star, her chestnut mare, and Drucilla on her beloved buckskin gelding, Arion, whom she'd named after a Greek god. As for Raymond, her strange brother-in-law, what could she say? He certainly wasn't her favorite, not with his silly jokes and childish behavior, but he had a generous heart and not a mean bone in his body.

When Rose led Lucy back to the wagon, they were met by a beaming Coralee who asked, "Doesn't she look darling in bangs?"

Rose forced a smile. "Yes, indeed, she looks adorable." No use complaining. Although Coralee had a heart of gold, she blundered through life with absolutely no conception of how her actions might affect others. At least she adored Lucy, her one and only grandchild. In her own mind, she was only being a good grandmother. The thought would never have occurred to her that she was wrongly invading a mother's territory. That settled it. Rose felt a new sense of purpose as she made up her mind. Ever since they were married, she'd pleaded with Emmet for her own home away from her in-laws. Now she'd demand it. She would not be a submissive daughter-in-law any longer. As soon as they reached Sacramento, she would inform him she wanted a home of her own. High time he cut the apron strings, and he'd better not say no.

* * * *

The next morning, in a high state of excitement, they packed up for the last day of their journey. As usual, Rose's father-in-law took complete charge of everything. A tall, broad-shouldered man with a full head of snow-white hair, Ben had such a domineering nature that as always, they scurried around to do his bidding. They started out in their usual fashion, Ben driving the first wagon, Coralee and Drucilla beside him. Raymond drove the second wagon, Rose and Lucy sharing the seat. As the train wound its way down the ever-more-gentle western slope, Rose gave thanks that tomorrow she wouldn't have to sit beside her brother-in-law all day, listening to his silly conversation and raucous, unnecessary laughter. Raymond might be twenty-eight years old, but he'd yet to find a purpose in life, although to hear him talk, you'd think he was on his way to becoming a millionaire. "Soon's we get there, I'm heading back up the hill," he'd just declared. "I'm going to find me some big gold nuggets and get richer than anyone."

"That's fine, Raymond." She'd long since learned the best way to handle her brother-in-law was to humor him. He always had big plans that went nowhere. He and his brother, Emmet, looked alike, both with a large build, but there the resemblance ended. Whereas Raymond was a fool with no ambition, hard-driving Emmet never had an idle day in his life. He took life far too seriously, but maybe the past two years had loosened him up a bit, at least she hoped so.

Besides all that, Lucy loved her father and could hardly wait to see him again.

By noon the train had left the last of the foothills behind and was rolling along the flat surface of the northern San Joaquin Valley. They began to pass farms where fields of vegetables and cotton lay ready for harvest. Finally they reached the outskirts of Sacramento, and the train stopped for the last time. Rose and her family said goodbye to their fellow travelers. From now on, they'd go their separate ways.

Rose's heart beat faster as they headed through town. Real streets! Real houses with front and back yards! Following Emmet's careful directions, the two wagons came to the edge of town and traveled two miles farther on a country road. They started looking for a small sign on a fence that said Peterson Farm. "There it is," Ben called. "Ahead to the right."

The two wagons turned off the road, down a long driveway that led to a large, two-story farmhouse with a wide front porch that wrapped around three sides. A large barn stood in the yard behind, along with a stable and corral, tank house, and what looked like a large chicken coop. As the two wagons pulled to a stop, Raymond let out a whoop, stood, and waved his hat. "Hey, Emmet! We're here!"

All smiles, everyone climbed from the wagons. Holding Lucy's hand, Rose looked toward the front door. Emmet would be coming out any second now, big smile on his face, delighted they'd finally arrived. "We're going to see Daddy?" Lucy asked.

Rose swept her up in her arms. "Yes, we're home, sweetheart. We won't have to live in a wagon anymore."

They waited. The front door remained closed. "Do you suppose he's not home?" Ben asked. He started up the porch steps. "Maybe he's sleeping."

Coralee followed him. "Emmet would never sleep in the middle of the day."

They had almost reached the front door when they heard someone calling. Two people came around the corner of the house. One was a tall man around fifty with a neat beard who looked like a farmer in his button-down shirt, soft, felt hat, and twill pants held up with suspenders. The other, a small, white-haired lady with a hunched-over walk, spectacles, and a deeply wrinkled face, could well be his mother, or maybe his grandmother. As they approached, the man called, "Are you the Petersons?"

Ben answered with a nod. "This is Emmet Peterson's farm, isn't it?"

Close up, Rose could see the man had a strange look on his face. He was not smiling as he extended his hand to Ben. "Hello, sir, I expect you're Emmet's father. I'm Tom Murphy, his neighbor from next door." He glanced toward his companion. "This is Dulcee Bidwell, my mother." He cast an affectionate glance her way. "She looks fragile, but you don't want to mess with her."

"Yes, I'm Ben Peterson." Ben shook his hand. "Pleased to meet you." Not one to mince words, he asked, "Where is Emmet?"

Tom Murphy's brows drew together in an agonized expression, as if he had something terrible to say and dreaded saying it. What was wrong? Rose got a sick feeling in her stomach, watching the man struggle for words.

Her father-in-law broke the heavy silence. "Out with it, sir. If you have something to say, then say it."

Dulcee Bidwell jabbed her son with an elbow. "Wait, Tom." She nodded toward Lucy and addressed Ben. "I believe I'll take the little girl inside. Do you mind?"

Ben shot an inquiring look at Rose. Sick at heart, she nodded. She was beginning to guess what Murphy was going to say.

They watched in silence as the old lady led Lucy into the house. When they were gone, Murphy gave a decisive nod, as if recognizing he had an unpleasant task to perform and no way out of it. His gaze swept over them, eyes full of sympathy. "I can't tell you how excited Emmet was, waiting for his family to arrive. That's all he talked about. But now? We were all shocked. Such a tragedy. I'm sure sorry to have to tell you this, but we buried him this morning."

* * * *

Afterward, Rose had only a vague memory of those terrible moments after they learned her husband was dead. Drucilla breaking into rare tears. Coralee's piercing scream and near collapse, and Ben and Raymond holding her up. Rose couldn't remember how she acted, other than she stood frozen in shock, staring in stunned disbelief.

Ben was the first to speak. "Tell us what happened."

"There's something you must see." Murphy turned, motioning them to follow. Along with the rest of her stricken family, Rose trailed him around the side of the porch where a row of tall Eucalyptus trees shaded the house. A grave lay under one of the trees. Plainly, it was newly dug with its mound of dirt on top, strewn with fresh bouquets of flowers. Rose drew close. On a small, roughly constructed cross at the head, someone had neatly printed, EMMET PETERSON.

In stunned silence, the family gathered around the grave as the neighbor continued to speak. "A fine man if ever there was one. If we'd known you were coming so soon, we would have waited, but we didn't know, so we held the service this morning. Quite a few came. Neighbors. People from town. Reverend Walters was in charge. You can rest assured, Emmet got as fine a sendoff as his friends could give him."

Ben's face had turned a sickly white. His arm around Coralee, who was quietly sobbing, he asked, "My God, what happened? Far as I know, my son was in good health."

Murphy shook his head. "He didn't get sick, Mr. Peterson. Health had nothing to do with it."

"Was it an accident?"

"No."

"Then...?" Ben could hardly get the words out. "You mean he was murdered?"

"Not exactly. You could say he was and he wasn't."

Through gritted teeth, Ben exploded, "For God's sake! Tell us what happened."

Murphy heaved a regretful sigh. "I wish it had been his health, a stroke maybe, or his heart. Or some kind of accident, but the truth is, Emmet was killed in a duel with a fellow named Mason Talbot. He's a big man in these parts. Owns a brewery as well as the Egyptian Hotel. He keeps a collection of paintings there and fancies himself an art connoisseur. The thing is, I reckon you can't call him a murderer, being as Emmet started the whole thing. He's the one who did the challenging."

Ben's jaw dropped open. "Emmet never held a sword in his hand in his life."

"Oh, it wasn't swords, Mr. Peterson. It was dueling pistols. I don't know as he ever held a gun in his hand either, but a bullet to the head is what killed him."

GOLD RUSH BRIDE

Letitia Tinsley's well-ordered spinster life is thrown into chaos when she learns her beloved brother has mysteriously disappeared from his gold mining claim in California. Determined to discover the truth, Letty sets out on the treacherous journey west. But there's only one thing more perilous than a single lady traveling alone into the rugged frontier—and that is sharing the passage with Garth Morgan. The wealthy bachelor is astoundingly arrogant—and dangerously handsome. Worse, Letty is forced to lean on his strong shoulders, again and again . . .

Humbled by the harrowing expedition, Garth resolves to keep Letty safe—though the courageous beauty is unwilling to give an inch when it comes to trusting him. Still, despite her defiant resistance, he's ready to stand with her as she faces the truth about her missing sibling. And by the time they reach California, Garth is determined to stake his own claim on the lovely Miss Letty—if only she will let him . . .

WAGON TRAIN SISTERS

After the death of her abusive husband, Sarah Gregg is free to join her family along with thousands of others in the nation's westward march for gold. But in the middle of the hard journey, Sarah's younger sister, Florrie, disappears. Devastated by the family's failed attempts to find her missing sister, Sarah now wants only to settle into a quiet, uneventful life when she reaches California . . .

But Jack McCoy, a drifter and one-time gambler riding along their wagon train, sees so much more for Sarah. In the roaring mining town of Gold Creek his attentive persistence points Sarah toward new vistas. Then unexpected news of Florrie arrives—and it's worse than anyone expected. But driven by a new hopefulness, Sarah seeks help from Jack, despite his troubled past. The two have traveled a rough road together, and only their hearts can tell them where they are headed . . .

WAGON TRAIN CINDERELLA

1851, Overland Trail to California. As a baby, Callie was left on the doorstep of an isolated farmhouse in Tennessee. The Whitaker family took her in, but have always considered her more a servant than a daughter. Scorned by her two stepsisters, Callie is forced to work long hours and denied an education. But a new world opens to her when the Whitakers join a wagon train to California—guided by rugged trapper, Luke McGraw . . .

A loner, haunted by a painful past, Luke plans to return to the wilderness once his work is done. But he can't help noticing how poorly Callie is treated—or how unaware she is of her beauty and intelligence. As the two become closer over the long trek west, Callie's confidence grows. And when disaster strikes, Callie emerges as the strong one—and the woman Luke may find the courage to love at last . . .